DANNI ARCHER: THE MAKING OF A MISTRESS

THE AUDITION TAPE

Elizabeth Rebecca Shaw

This book is dedicated to all those who wanted a third book in the series.

CHAPTER ONE

Danni Archer awoke in the morning and stretched out her long lean body; she enjoyed the feeling of her muscles straining slightly as she put effort into her movements. It felt glorious, she thought. She recognized that she was feeling excited about the plans for the day. She was to be videoed having sex with Samantha and then there would be a lesbian foursome with Samantha, Rose and the video recorder, Lydia. She was very intrigued to find out what Lydia was like in bed; Lydia had never had a lesbian encounter before and was curious about it, she was a married woman with two children. Danni had met Lydia just two days previously when she had taken nude and clothed pictures of Danni so that they could be forwarded to prospective sugar daddies for Danni's education. Lydia was a nice looking thirty-something with a nice, plump rack; Danni was beginning to realize that she liked a big set of tits on a female sexual partner.

Danni smiled as she got up out to bed and went into the bathroom to take care of her morning ritual; she paid special attention this morning to making sure her legs were well shaved and silky smooth. She also spent a little bit of time trimming her slightly unruly snatch; she wanted to make sure that she showed up well on the video and for her tryst with the other three women. She contemplated taking time to paint her toenails but decided that it might be distracting so she just used her nailfile to shape them a little and buffed them up to a shine. She hummed the tune of a song she had heard recently as she did this. Danni was a bit surprised that she wasn't more keyed up this morning and thought that maybe the regular sex she was having was actually working to keep her on a calm even keel. As she spent a few minutes pondering this, she realized that she had been able to be more attentive in class and that her schoolwork and marks were reflecting her ability to concentrate more on what she was doing. People always said that if you were sex mad, and Danni had to admit that she probably was, that you couldn't perform well in life. It seemed that the reason she was able to concentrate on her tasks so well was because she was regularly getting her brains fucked out. She knew if she were to tell people that, that they wouldn't believe her. She grinned to herself in the mirror as she thought about this; maybe she should make it a topic of an essay in university. She pictured the looks on the faces of the people who read it and broke out chuckling. She gave her hair a quick brush and checked her face in the mirror before heading down to the kitchen to grab a quick cup of coffee and maybe some toast. She hoped that she could do this before her mother got down to the kitchen so that she could grab her breakfast and get back to her room to finish up her homework.

Luck was with Danni as she had just finished buttering her toast and was heading back up to her room as her mother entered the kitchen. She breezed by her mother, giving her a quick kiss on the cheek and telling her that she had a ton of homework to finish. Danni went up to her room, made herself comfortable on her bed and ate her toast as she cracked open her schoolbooks. She spent the next hour doing her required reading and working out math problems; now all of her mandatory work was complete and she had the rest of the day to do as she wanted. She decided to spend a couple of minutes in contemplation of her future and she was a little astonished to find that she was very pleasantly anticipating the challenge that university would bring; she had thought that she would be dreading it more. She giggled a bit, thinking that a busy sex life certainly put one in an enthusiastic frame of mind. She decided that she would spend the rest of the time she had to wait browsing the internet, following up on whatever caught her fancy and so she did that.

When the time came for her to get ready to leave, she rapidly gathered her stuff, which was easy because she didn't keep too much of it at home, and prepared to go meet Ms. Sturm. She headed out and soon arrived at the Honda. When she got into the car, Ms. Sturm turned and gave her a careful looking over; Ms. Sturm noted that Danni was cheerful and seemed to be in excellent shape, she had worried that yesterday's activities along with the excitement of today might have caused Danni to be restless in the night. Ms. Sturm was pleased to see that she'd been wrong about being concerned. Danni gave her a toothy grin but didn't say anything; Ms. Sturm just grunted a greeting and drove them over to Samantha and Rose's place. As they drove up, Lydia and Rose were busy hauling the equipment inside; Ms. Sturm told Danni to have fun, that they would talk later and to go help the two women with carrying the stuff in. Danni grabbed her belongings and hurried to do as instructed. The three women quickly got all of the stuff inside and Lydia began unpacking what she needed.

Danni noticed that Samantha wasn't waiting for them inside and asked Rose "What happened to Samantha? How come she didn't help?"

Rose gave her a small smirk and replied "Samantha's getting herself ready for the videotaping. She's been fretting about how she looks all morning and is busy shaving her legs and pussy for the second time this morning. She's very concerned about looking fat and hairy for the camera so be very careful about what you say to her. She's liable to throw a fit if you look at her in what she sees as the wrong way. She's not been this antsy in a long time." Danni nodded and thought about it for a few minutes. She was fine, happy to be going on camera but Samantha, whom she

3

thought was a totally controlled person, was busy having a meltdown of the prospect of being on camera. She mused about this for a while and decided that she wasn't going to let things put her off her happy feelings; if Samantha wasn't able to perform then they'd do it another time or Ms. Sturm would arrange another partner for her. She asked Rose for permission to go see Samantha so that she could try to calm her down before the action.

Danni headed down to the bedroom the two women shared. When she walked in the door, she could see Samantha lying curled on the bed; it was obvious that Samantha was unhappy. She perched herself on the edge of the bed and started stroking Samantha's bare shoulder. Samantha turned and was surprised to see it was Danni, she had been expecting Rose. "Oh, Danni" she cried out softly. "I don't know if I can go through with this. I look horrible this morning and I feel so fat."

Danni looked at Samantha's svelte figure and hid a smile; she'd been in a similar situation where she'd felt fat when she knew she wasn't. Oh, hush" she soothed the older woman. "You look fine. Very desirable and totally sexy. But if you feel that you can't go through with it, we won't."

Samantha looked at her with a bit of suspicion and asked "How come you're so calm. You have a lot more riding on this than I do. You should be a bundle of nerves and yet you're so placid. What's your secret?"

Danni just shrugged and continued stroking Samantha's shoulder, before replying "I don't know. I just woke up happy this morning and I'm not going to let anything get me down. If we fuck up the taping, we'll just do it again sometime. I don't think that Ms. Sturm needs it immediately. It's not like she has someone in mind for me yet so it can't have been promised to anyone. Just take it easy and decide if you feel up to doing this today. If you don't I'll understand. Okay, Samantha?" Danni got up off the bed and quietly left the room to give Samantha some space to make her decision.

Danni made her way back to the living room where Rose was helping Lydia in setting up an area where Danni and Samantha could fuck and be easily taped doing so. Rose looked up at her as she entered and asked quietly "How is she? Did you talk her into coming out?"

Danni looked back at Rose and replied "She's still upset. I told her that we would put this off until she felt better about it if she wanted. She's making up her mind about it." Danni then turned to Lydia and said softly "We may not be making a movie today. Sorry to put you through this trouble." Lydia just looked into Danni's eyes, impressed by the concern that she had for her lover, and then shrugged and continued setting up her equipment. She determined that she would have everything ready in case Samantha decided that she was able to perform. She'd have bet heavily that it would have been Danni who had an attack of nerves; she believed that Samantha had nerves of steel and would've been ready for anything. Rose looked back at Danni, a little put out by Samantha's failure; she was aware that this was important for Danni and that Ms. Sturm was putting great stock in how this would work for showcasing Danni. Lydia had come all this way and maybe it would be for nothing. She decided that she'd go try to raise Samantha in a few minutes if she didn't come out on her own.

About a minute later, Samantha appeared at the doorway with a tentative smile on her face; she was wearing a robe and it was open, showing off her body. "Hi, everyone" she greeted them softly. "I've decided that I'll try to go through with this. I know how important it is for Danni and I owe her to make the attempt. I'm sorry if I've put a damper on this." Both Danni and Rose gave her reassuring smiles back, happy that she'd ventured out. Lydia looked Samantha over, checking her out to see if there was anything out of place with her that might show up on camera; she wasn't overly surprised to see that the young woman looked great, she'd dealt with women before and was used to some diva behaviour from some of them.

Lydia turned to Danni and said "You should get your clothes off, honey. Ms. Sturm has told me that she'd like for you and Samantha to be clothed in just garter belts, stockings and heels. So if you both get dressed that way, I'll check you over before we start filming." She turned back to her equipment to start doing the final adjustments. Danni quickly began undressing; she figured that since she'd be fucking someone in front of the other two women, there was no sense in being shy and going into the bedroom to take off her clothes. Rose had chosen the outfits for the two of them; she'd picked a bright red for Samantha to wear and a pale blue for Danni. She fitted the garter belt around Samantha's waist and began tightening it. Samantha looked at her gratefully. Lydia stopped fussing with her video equipment for the moment and came over to look over both Danni and Samantha; she was happy with what they were wearing and how it fit and flattered them both but decided that both of them would look better with a fairly dramatic makeup job. She decided that Samantha would wear a bright, almost florescent, pink eyeshadow that would completely cover her eye socket up to the eyebrow and almost half her temple; she drew a black line with eyebrow pencil along the tops of Samantha's cheeks to highlight them. She lightly rouged Samantha's cheekbones and painted her lips with a scarlet lip gloss, outlining their full shape with a purple lip gloss. Rose looked in wonder at how dramatic this makeup made Samantha's face appear; she was definitely impressed with the way it made Samantha look and vowed to talk to Lydia about how she could replicate it in the future. Since both young women had very few blemishes on their faces or body, Lydia decided to forgo any body makeup for them. She turned her attention to Danni and made her up similarly to Samantha but used a bright blue eye shadow and coral lip gloss. She noticed Rose gawking at the two young women and smiled broadly at her.

"I know it's a bit too dramatic for everyday wear but it looks great on camera. It's fairly hard wearing so it should stand up for a while but they're most likely going to wear most of it off by the time they're finished. Even then, the smears of the makeup all over each other will look good for the camera" Lydia said as she made her way back to make the final adjustments on her equipment. Both Danni and Samantha eyed each other's made up face and grinned; they both liked what they saw on the other. They made their way over to the area where they would be performing. Rose had laid out a small foam mattress and covered it with her favourite black silk sheets; there were also some large multi-coloured pillows for them to use.

Lydia gestured for them to sit down on the mattress and then began explaining what she wanted them to do. "I understand that you, Samantha, will be the more aggressive one and that Danni will be more submissive. I want for both of you to engage in a lot of foreplay. Kissing, pinching and licking are very good. I want you to engage in that for as long as you can stand to; I can edit it down if Ms. Sturm wants me too but I can't really extend it too much without it being obvious, so more is better. I'd like for you to separate somewhat if one or both of you orgasm so that I can get good shots of that. If you forget to do that, I'll do the best I can but it really helps if you remember to do that. I know it can be a bit distracting during the heat of the action and neither of you has performed for the camera before but do your best to allow me good shots. And while trying to remember to do that, do your best to ignore me and the camera; I don't want you looking straight into the camera, focus on your partner. It's what looks the best. If I think we're way off track, I'll call for a halt in proceedings but otherwise I'm just going to let you go. Okay. Do you both understand?" The women both nodded and licked their lips in nervousness, anticipation and lust. Lydia then turned to Rose and said "You can sit there and watch but I need you to be quiet and if I move near you, I'd appreciate it if you moved over behind me and the camera. Okay?" Rose nodded and Lydia addressed the three of them, saying "The camera will pick up any sounds so it works better if you don't state any instructions. It's best if the only sounds are your natural sexual responses." Again everyone nodded their understanding and then Lydia signaled for them to begin.

Danni took Samantha by the hand and led her over to the mattress; both of them knelt and Samantha leaned in to kiss Danni on the lips. Danni darted her tongue out into Samantha's mouth. Samantha pursed her lips and sucked lightly on Danni's tongue for a moment before turning her head and pushing more firmly against Danni's, forcing the surprised younger woman back a bit. Samantha began feeling her lust for Danni overtaking her nervousness of the situation and she grabbed firm hold of Danni's shoulders to hold her in place as she made the kiss one of domination. Danni, as was her nature, submitted wonderfully; she held steady as

Samantha smashed and twisted her mouth against hers. Danni began to moan lightly in arousal which further inflamed Samantha's need to dominate her. As she continued with her rough kissing, Samantha's hands began to caress Danni's jutting breasts. The way that Danni pushed against her hands told Samantha that she was enjoying this. Samantha was mindful that Lydia had told them to take their time so she spent more time than she usually did stroking Danni's pink tipped tits, working Danni's nipples into diamond hard nubs. Danni increased her moaning into Samantha's mouth, obviously enjoying the attention to her breasts greatly. Samantha broke the kiss to flick her tongue at Danni's hardened nipples, eliciting soft gasps of delight from the blonde woman. Danni took the opportunity afforded by the change in action to place her own hands on Samantha's full breasts and ran her palms gently over them feeling her aroused nipples press against the middle of her hands.

By now, neither woman was paying too much attention to where Lydia and her camera were; they were just intent on the pleasure they were giving each other. Samantha pushed Danni back slightly and began rubbing her hardened nipples against Danni's; she gave a low moan of delight at the sensations this created. She moved back to kissing Danni roughly as her hands caressed Danni's wonderfully soft belly; Samantha was mindful to keep her hands above Danni's crotch, even though Danni was moving her body to entice Samantha to her pussy, because she was trying to extend the action. She could tell that Danni was just on the edge of pushing things forward faster but she wanted to provide Lydia with lots of footage and, besides, it was very exciting to know that Danni was so aroused and on edge. Danni gave a long, low moan to let Samantha know that she was in need of some sexual relief; Samantha just backed her mouth away from Danni's and leaned in to whisper in Danni's ear, "Suck it up, Buttercup. Lydia wants lots of preliminary action before we get to the heavy duty stuff. You're not going to come for quite a while yet." Samantha just grinned when Danni gave her an exasperated whine.

Samantha began rough-housing Danni's tits a little harder, rubbing the erect, pink nipples off to the side as she enjoyed the expression of joy, desire and need flit across Danni's face. After a few more minutes of this, she bent down with her mouth and began to rake her teeth across Danni's aroused nipples. Danni gave a startled squeal as Samantha started doing this to her and then she was moaning and bucking as she had a small orgasm; Samantha gave her a feral grin of triumph as she realized that she had made Danni come without even touching her pussy once. Then she recognized that Lydia had asked them not to do that so she stole a quick glance over to where the older woman was filming them with the camera to see if she could ascertain her mood. Lydia just gave her a quick smile as she continued filming Danni's pulsing pussy. Emboldened, Samantha reached down and slipped her forefinger and index finger into Danni's sopping blonde pussy; she gathered some of

Danni's juices and brought her fingers up to Danni's luscious mouth. Danni sucked her own juices off of the fingers without hesitation, groaning with delight. Samantha eagerly kissed Danni on her plump lips as she reached down for a second time. This time the two women shared the delicious taste of Danni's cum.

Then Samantha decided that it was time for Danni to perform so she pulled the young blonde woman's head down so her mouth was on her large, heavy breasts. Danni liked being directed so forcefully and moaned and groaned her appreciation as she applied her mouth to Samantha's engorged nipples. She sucked on the other woman's whole aureole and flicked her tongue hard at the erect nipple, eliciting grunts of pleasure from Samantha. She loved the feeling of the turgid nipple in her hot mouth and worked it over as hard as she could for more than a few minutes. She felt Samantha's breathing speed up and deepen as she enjoyed the attention Danni was paying to her. She really wanted to stroke the older woman's pussy for her, imagining it was extremely squishy and wet from her desire but kept in mind that Lydia wanted them to engage in extended foreplay. It felt wonderfully confining to try to perform under such restrictive instructions and she could feel her own juices dripping down her thighs. She clamped her legs open and closed to try to relieve her arousal.

Both Lydia and Rose could see Samantha's arousal from Danni's extended licking and Danni's reaction as well. Rose muffled a groan as she imagined how wet both of her regular partners must be and how sweet and juicy they would taste. Lydia was quite surprised to find that her nipples were straining against her bra; she liked some nipple play herself but had never reacted too much to watching other women doing it to each other. She could feel her own internal temperature rising and her pussy started to moisten. She was hoping that her camera was picking up how hot the action in front of her was. If it did, this would be an amazing tape and would do Danni extremely well. She tried to push her reactions to the back of her mind as she tried to be as professional as she possibly could. She moved the camera quickly down to show the wet sheen on Danni's lean, muscular thighs to show her excitement but then quickly returned to capture the action. She smiled broadly as she caught both of the young women flexing their hands as they fought the desire to touch one another more. She wondered how long it would be before they succumbed to their craving.

Finally Danni decided that she had to advance matters, she knew that she couldn't keep this up for much longer and was surprised that Samantha hadn't caved in first. She moved her hand up to caress the brunette's waist as she prepared to shift her weight and attention to a new position. She was surprised to feel the other woman trembling under her hand and paused slightly, moving away from Samantha, to look at her concerned that Samantha was upset. She almost laughed out loud as she recognized that Samantha was trembling because she was so intent on trying to keep control over her body because her arousal was so great. Samantha had almost bitten through her own top lip as her teeth grasped it as she fought her own feelings. Her eyes were closed and she was almost whistling air through her nose as she sucked in deep breaths. Danni quickly kissed those contorted lips and rotated her mouth somewhat over them as she pressed the kiss fairly hard.

Samantha lost her battle of control and roughly grabbed hold of Danni's shoulders pushing her over backwards onto the pile of pillows. Danni knew what Samantha was intent on doing and knew that Lydia probably didn't want that yet but found herself powerless to stop the other woman. Danni recognized that she wanted this as much as Samantha did. When she was on her back on the pillows, she grabbed one of the bigger ones to stuff under her hips so she would be more comfortable. Samantha moved over quickly to help her and then pushed Danni's long, lean legs up over her body; Danni grabbed hold of her ankles to support herself for what was to come. Samantha pushed her head firmly through Danni's toned thighs so her face was right above Danni's squishy pussy. Danni was quite aroused as Samantha paused to inhale Danni's scent before applying her long, wet tongue against Danni's small peach-like cunt. Danni felt a shiver of pleasure run down her back and leg muscles as Samantha slowly ran her tongue over her pussy opening, teasing her with her slow strokes. Danni opened her mouth and moaned in pleasure and ecstasy. Samantha increased her intensity and pressure, relishing the moans and groans she was forcing from the aroused blonde. She could feel her already raised level of arousal increase even more and started her own moaning as she buried her face into Danni's sopping pussy. It took less than a minute for her to climax Danni who bucked and thrust her hips as her orgasm overtook her. Danni was now keening loudly in her pleasure as she writhed on the pillows.

A niggling worry overtook Samantha as she watched in bliss as Danni orgasmed and sent juices spurting slightly from her gaping, engorged cunt. It was a very pleasant sight, she thought. Then she recognized what was bothering her and took a quick look over her shoulder to find out where Lydia and her camera were. She was concerned that the older woman would be upset with them for pushing things along too fast. She'd also forgotten to separate from Danni to give the camera a better shot as Danni orgasmed. She could see that Lydia was concentrating quite hard on capturing the action but couldn't tell if she was unhappy or not. She frowned slightly as she realized that Rose wasn't close by watching them. She knew that Rose loved to watch her or Danni orgasm, taking great pleasure in it, so she looked more carefully around the room to find the older redhead. Rose had been wearing a pair of tight, short shorts and there she was now, face down in another pile of pillows with her shorts and panties down around her ankles as she lay face down fingering her plump pussy. Her rather large, round ass was bouncing up and down as her fingers worked herself. Obviously she'd been aroused by their performance,

Samantha thought with a brief feeling of satisfaction. She decided that she needed to ignore the older woman and return to what she was doing with Danni.

Danni could feel her body slowly coming back under her full control after her explosive orgasm with the stew of endorphins still swimming in her brain. She could feel her body languidly responding as she lay there panting from her recent effort. She was quite delighted with herself and Samantha. She expected Samantha to let her up so that she could reciprocate but Samantha held her firmly in place and once more press her face down between her thighs. Danni wiggled her hips a bit to evade Samantha's tongue to suggest that they should change positions but the brunette refused to take the hint. Samantha ran her tongue over Danni's plump pussy as she forced her fingers into Danni's opening quite hard. Danni gasped in shock as the brunette roughly forced her open. Her long nails grazed Danni's sensitive flesh as she pushed her fingers deeply into Danni's cunt. Danni moaned and wriggled as she accommodated those insistent digits; they felt totally wonderful in her wet pussy. Samantha began thrusting them hard in and out as Danni bucked her hips up and down enjoying the feeling of the penetration. Danni could feel the electric spark of another orgasm building in her hips and coursing up into her mind. She wailed her enjoyment as she encouraged Samantha to treat her even rougher. Samantha responded with even more vigour causing Danni to start screaming as she lost control and delivered a second climax. She had to reach down and push Samantha's hand from her so that she could start to regain control over her body. Samantha fought with her, refusing to let Danni push her away. Danni was fighting as hard as she could because she thought that she couldn't survive if Samantha didn't stop. She thought her heart and mind would burst with the pleasure the other woman was causing in her. Then, Danni had a third climax and fainted away from the sensation.

Lydia was concerned when Danni bucked her body and then collapsed bonelessly. She'd gotten great pictures of the action between the two women even though Samantha had forgotten to move aside to give her unfettered access. She really couldn't blame the brunette because she'd been so intent on what she'd been doing to Danni. She knew that her own face was a mask of concentration as she fought to keep her own body under control after the erotic display in front of her. She could hear Rose's muffled moans as she continued to enjoy the feel of her own fingers and gave serious consideration to doing the same thing. She stopped the camera and asked Samantha "Is she okay? Should we do something?"

Samantha looked up at her with a smile, her face a mask of ruined makeup because most of it had been rubbed off against Danni's now bedraggled pussy. She replied "She's fine. She tends to do that when she'd been driven to complete enjoyment of her body. She'll recover in a few minutes with an intense desire to fuck even more." She paused as she stroked Danni's soaking cunt and then said "I hope we didn't ruin what you were trying to do. We did try to take it as slow as we could but the intensity of our desire got the best of us."

"I know. I think that I got some great pictures of the two of you and the intense action between you, so don't be too concerned. I'll review it in a few minutes to see if we might have to try for some further footage." She paused and looked slightly shamed as she said "I have to take care of something first." She put her camera down and moved away. She undid her pants and plunged her right hand down to stroke her aroused pussy. She grunted as she enjoyed the feeling of her fingers pushing her wet aroused flesh open. It only took her a few minutes to relieve her intense pressure. It felt fantastic. She looked over and realized that Samantha had been watching her as she fingered herself. She expected to feel some shame about being watched but found that it actually aroused herself somewhat. She looked over to where Rose now lay recovering from her own actions. The older woman wasn't conscious about anything else in the room but her own recuperating body. When she looked back to where Samantha and Danni were, she could see Danni beginning to stir. She pulled up her clothes and walked slowly over to where Samantha and Danni were. Samantha grinned at her and directed her to where the bathroom was so that she could clean up and wash her hands. As she left, she noticed that Samantha was slowly and gently massaging Danni's back as she lay there still slightly dazed from the intensity of her orgasms.

When she returned, she discovered that Samantha had left Danni to go over to Rose. The two women were kissing deeply and intensely as she entered the room. She ignored them, leaving them to their actions and went over to get her camera so that she could look at the footage she'd shot. She thought Danni was asleep as she lay there and was surprised when Danni asked softly "How did it look?"

"It looked incredibly hot and sexy to my eyes" Lydia replied truthfully. "But I just have to check to see that the camera caught the same thing. If you want to, you can come over and look at it with me."

Danni nodded and said "I will in a few minutes. I just need to get my legs to be a little steadier so that I can stand without falling down." Lydia smiled at her and nodded, feeling some sympathy and a bit of envy for the young girl. She went over and started setting up her equipment so that she could work on the footage. She noted that Rose and Samantha had disappeared and wondered with some surprising jealousy if they had gone off to do more than just kiss. She was quite shocked to discover that she felt annoyed by the fact; she had no claim over either of them and should just feel happy for them. As her hands worked with familiar tasks, she thought about her feelings; she thought that it was simply based on lust because she didn't have the time for it to be love. She wanted to be a part of what these women had, she realized and looked forward to the action set for later in the day. She was still unsure as to how much she would like the actual sexual act with another woman but was beginning to discover that she liked the easy interaction they had with one another. She got the feeling that they had a deeper mental contact with each other since they kind of knew how each other felt. She loved her husband, enjoyed their sex life but knew that she sometimes didn't understand his thoughts at all. She smiled slightly as she thought about the previous night. She'd been fairly uneasy because of what had been planned for this day. She felt fat, dirty and unattractive and he'd insisted on fucking her. She'd tried quite hard to dissuade him before giving in and letting him have his way. After her initial non-participation, he'd gotten her aroused enough to start moving under him. Of course, she thought with some annoyance, he'd gotten off before she was anywhere near her own orgasm. But he'd been sweet and offered to help her climax. She'd assured him that she was fine since she knew she would be involved in sex the next day. So he'd lay there and was asleep within minutes. She felt that her dissatisfaction was her own fault because she knew that her husband would have spent the necessary time to arouse her sufficiently to climax during the penetration if she'd responded well when he'd initiated the sex.

Danni came over, tottering slightly at the beginning but steadying as she approached the table. She was still naked and her makeup was smeared all over her face but Lydia felt a stab of envy as she made her way over. Even all messed up like that, she was beautiful; much better looking than Lydia had ever been. She was surprised to find herself watching Danni's small, firm breasts bob slightly as she walked over. She'd never really been one to look at another woman's breasts too much before, she thought speculatively. Except when she was much younger and was envying some of the other girls their large, heavy breasts, she supposed. She grinned as she saw that Danni had noticed where her attention was focused and arched her back somewhat as she walked over. The girl liked to be looked at and desired, Lydia thought with some understanding. When she made her way up to Danni's face, she saw that the young blonde was grinning toothily back at her, her eyes sparkling with enjoyment. Neither of them said anything as Danni came over and leaned her taut, warm, nude body against her as she looked over her shoulder towards the screen. Lydia was somewhat uncomfortable to have her personal space invaded so easily but then decided that she liked the feeling of the younger woman pressing against her. That was quite unexpected, she thought as she continued to view the footage. It looked marvelous to her eyes and she was pleased as to how desirable it made Danni look.

Danni watched about thirty seconds of the footage and was appalled. "Is that how my face contorts when I cum?" she asked, incredulous. "I look like I'm trying to pass a watermelon. We better shoot this over so that I can improve what I look like."

Lydia turned and looked the young blonde fully in her gorgeous face as she replied with astonishment "You look fantastic. The viewer can tell that you are really enjoying yourself and giving your full effort. You look both vulnerable and strong. I know some women that would love it if they could even fake facial expressions like that. I'm not going to waste my time trying to better something that is already so beautiful and perfect. Look how your bottom lip quivers so wonderfully just before you start screaming your delight." Danni scowled at her for mentioning that and Lydia had to stop herself from laughing out loud. The young blonde was trying to look ferocious but with her ruined makeup she just looked young and ridiculous. Lydia was surprised when Rose and Samantha joined them. She looked carefully at them without trying to make it too obvious; she thought that they would have been gone longer if they had been engaged in sex. They both had cleaned themselves up somewhat and Lydia was feeling very overdressed now that Rose had also removed all of her clothing. She saw that Samantha had brought a damp washcloth and a makeup removal sponge and was busy cleaning off Danni's face. Danni was still trying to watch herself on the screen and was fending the brunette off somewhat without much success.

Danni broke free from Samantha's ministrations long enough to ask Rose in a slightly querulous voice "Don't I just look awful in this video? I think we should reshoot it."

Rose watched for a couple of minutes after Lydia had rewound the tape and showed the footage of Danni climaxing so wonderfully. Then she looked at Danni tenderly and replied "You look absolutely sexy and stunning. I wish that I looked a tenth as good as you do. This video will absolutely get you a sponsor." She looked over at Lydia with a big smile and stated "Look at how her whole face quivers just before she cums. Have you seen anything as beautiful as that in your life?" Lydia grinned and nodded as Danni scowled mightily at both of them.

Danni appealed to Samantha, asking her "You agree with me, don't you, Samantha? I look like a cow in this video. We should reshoot it while we are all here still." She gave the brunette a coy, sexy smile as if she hoped that would help sway Samantha's opinion.

Samantha tinkled a peal of laughter at Danni's obvious attempt and said firmly "Suck it up, buttercup. You look absolutely gorgeous in the video. Just look at how fat my ass looks when I'm going down on you. You have absolutely nothing to complain about." She looked over at Lydia and asked, plaintively "Couldn't you have shot that from a better angle? My fat ass is all over the screen." Rose and Lydia just smirked back at her. Samantha had a very trim, taut rear end and she looked great on the film as well.

They all watched the film for a few minutes as Lydia checked it over to see that she had enough to work with. They were silent as they watched her work but Danni scowled an awful lot at the images on the screen. Finally Rose decided that she'd allowed Lydia enough time to examine the footage. So she stepped in and pressed her large, heavy right breast against the other woman's left shoulder while slipping her right hand into her back pocket, cupping her ass. Lydia jumped with surprise when she did this. She would have expected the move from a man but was shocked to have it done to her by another woman. She glanced over at the other woman who was smiling and raising her eyebrows at her in a sexy, suggestive manner. She could feel Rose's hard, erect nipple boring into her back. She realized that she liked the feeling of it pressing against her. She spared a quick glance towards Samantha and Danni and recognized that they all wanted to get on with the other matter they were here to do. That matter was a four way lesbian dogpile. Lydia could see that they felt they had waited for her long enough for her to examine the footage and were eager to start enjoying the rest of their day. She felt herself get wet again as she thought about what was going to happen. So, she started packing up her equipment and said, softly and huskily "Well, I think that I have lots of good footage to work with and will be able to deliver a wonderful film to Ms. Sturm like I promised. I guess we should start taking care of the other matter we are here for. I'll just pack my stuff up so that it isn't in the way."

Rose nodded and stated "Danni will help you. Samantha and I will go get the snacks and the wine. We'll spend a little time getting you comfortable with us as we eat. We want you to be relaxed before we start fucking you in earnest. You'll enjoy it more that way." The two of them left and Lydia directed Danni with what she wanted her to do. Soon everything was ready to go and Rose and Samantha hadn't returned yet. Danni was standing a little ways away and was ogling her with obvious interest that made Lydia feel a burst of arousal. She returned the favour, enjoying the sight of the pretty, young woman in front of her. She imagined how soft her skin would be and how her face might contort, eyes widening, as she was made to orgasm. She wondered how this gorgeous young woman would taste. She enjoyed the feel and taste of a man's cock in her mouth and wondered if she would feel the same way about a woman. She took a small step towards Danni and the young blonde glided quickly to press herself against her and search out her mouth for a kiss. Lydia enjoyed the feeling of the younger woman's plump lips against her own. Rose and Samantha bustled in with the food and wine just as Danni began forcing her pointed tongue into Lydia's mouth. Lydia backed away in embarrassment but Danni was reluctant to let her leave gracefully, she continued to press up against her seeking to extend the kissing. Lydia had to use her hands on the young woman's shoulders to dissuade her. She looked over at Rose and Samantha, flushed, and was surprised to see that they weren't upset but were watching with some interest.

"You've discovered that Danni can be very enticing and difficult to discourage" Rose stated, a little dryly. "Are the two of you finished putting the equipment away and ready to have some food now?" She paused to watch as they both nodded and then asked "Lydia, are you going to remain clothed or are you going to join the rest of us? I don't want to push you into doing anything that you don't want to do but it seems only fair that we get to see your body the same as you can see ours." She paused once more as she frowned in thought. "Have you chosen a safe word yet? So we know if we cross the bounds of what you consider appropriate with you."

Lydia nodded and replied "Yes I have; it is butterscotch." She started to remove her blouse and Danni joined her in undoing her buttons. She looked up at the blonde in surprise but didn't say anything to prevent her from helping. Danni rubbed her soft palm against the upper part of Lydia's right breast before helping her to take off her blouse. Lydia was quite surprised to register that she liked the boldness of the young woman; feeling her up while supposedly helping her. It created quite erotic feelings in her as she imagined what else the other three women might be doing to her that afternoon. She smiled in invitation after Danni did that and Danni once more pressed against her to kiss her. While they were still locked in the kiss, Danni unhooked and assisted her in removing her bra. Lydia's plump breasts hung there, pressing somewhat against Danni. Danni broke the kiss and moved slightly away; she cupped and weighed Lydia's nice sized tits in her hands, rubbing them and cooing slightly in delight over their feel. Lydia felt her internal temperature rise as she was aroused by the sounds Danni was making. Her husband enjoyed the feel of her plump breasts but he'd never made any sounds like this; it was very erotic, she thought. She decided that since Danni was fondling her, she might as well return the favour. She tweaked Danni's semi-erect pink nipple with her fingers. She hadn't done that to another woman before but had done it to herself often enough to know that it felt good. She kind of expected Danni to be shocked and move back but the younger woman muttered in pleasure and pressed her small tit harder against her hand, inviting her to continue doing what she'd been doing. Lydia looked over to see what Rose and Samantha thought about what they were doing, expecting them to be disapproving but they were watching with rapt attention and faces showing rising desire. When her attention was focused elsewhere, Danni took advantage to tweak her nipple back hard. Lydia gasped in surprise and desire. She felt a thrill of yearning run up through her back muscles, causing her plump breasts to sway somewhat, to Danni's delight. The younger woman grabbed Lydia's swelling nipple firmly and pulled on it with some strength. Lydia moaned as her nipple got stretched, closed her eyes and enjoyed the rough treatment of one of her most sensitive parts. Danni was quite intrigued by Lydia's reaction and wanted to continue exploring it. She pulled hard on the older woman's nipple once more and Lydia moaned quite loudly.

"You're supposed to be undressing her so that we can eat" Rose interrupted firmly. "There is plenty of time for such as that later when we can all enjoy it. Just get her undressed, Danni." Danni glanced over towards Rose and Samantha, gave them a sheepish grin and then let Lydia's nipple go. She reached down to waist level and undid the older woman's pants, unzipped them and started to work them down the other woman's broad hips. She squatted to pull them down her legs, pausing just slightly to look over her legs. Lydia wasn't slim like her and Samantha but was broader like Rose was; Danni noticed that her thighs were somewhat heavy but looked quite nice and inviting. She ran a hand quickly along Lydia's plump thigh, enjoying the soft feel before helping the older woman to step out of her slacks. Lydia stood in front of her in only her soft flats and panties watching to see what Danni might do next.

CHAPTER TWO

Danni knelt down beside Lydia's feet and grinned back up at her with a mischievous grin before darting her head forward towards Lydia's crotch. Lydia was unsure about her intentions and shivered in anticipation. Danni planted a quick kiss on Lydia's panty covered crotch and then reached up to hook her thumbs into those panties. She quickly pulled the blue lace panties down to Lydia's ankles, exposing her trimmed brown bush. Lydia visibly braced herself for Danni to either finger her cunt or kiss it; she wasn't sure which one she desired more. But Danni was mindful of the admonishment that Rose had given her and just tapped Lydia's right ankle so the older woman would lift her foot so Danni could get the panties off of her. Lydia felt a spike of disappointment that delayed her but then she complied and lifted her foot a couple of inches. Danni slipped the small bit of material over her foot and then took the panties off completely when Lydia raised her other foot. Then Danni locked eyes with the older brunette once more just before sucking noisily on the wet crotch of the panties. She widened her eyes so that Lydia would know that she was enjoying the other woman's taste. Lydia gave a small low moan as she felt her arousal spike once more from the blatant display in front of her; she found it quite sexy. "Danni, quit fucking around and bring her over here so that we can all enjoy her" Samantha snapped, slightly irritably. "Do you have to make everything such a production? You'll get lots of time to play with her later." Lydia looked over at Samantha with concern about her burst of anger; she could detect more than a tinge of jealousy in the younger woman's voice. Then she thought that she'd probably feel the same way if she was in such a close relationship with Danni as the other woman was.

"Sorry, it's probably my fault" Lydia apologized, trying to ease the tension somewhat. She could see that Samantha was starting to flush slightly from embarrassment as she recognized that all of the other women detected her jealousy.

"No, it's my fault. I should be more gracious. I know how enticing Danni is and that I have to share her with everyone she chooses to be her sexual partner. I apologize for my temper" Samantha muttered as she looked around the room refusing to meet any of their eyes. Danni hurried over and rubbed her arm in an act of compassion and understanding. Lydia was a bit surprised about how deep the relationship was between the two younger women. Rose also went over and gave

Samantha a hug. Danni initially stepped back to give them room to do that but both of the women pulled her into the hug. Lydia was shocked to realize that she wanted to join in the group hug; she'd never really felt an urge like that before. She remained where she was looking at them with a slight longing. The three women looked over at her and invited her to join them with their eyes; she drew a deep breath to steady herself a bit before going over to hug with them. She felt a happy smile creep onto her face as she pressed against the other nude sexy women. She'd been afraid that this would feel very weird to her and she would have to decline from participating but it really felt pleasant.

They held the hug for a few minutes and then Danni complained "Can we please eat. I'm starving. And we can then get on with the sex." She grinned hopefully at the other three women.

"You're always ready to eat" Samantha chided gently. "It's a constant factor with you. If you weren't getting fucked so much you'd have to take up running to keep off the weight." Danni looked a little hurt until Samantha stuck out her tongue to show that she was just pushing Danni a little. Danni returned the gesture and then squeezed Samantha's large right breast firmly. Samantha grasped Danni's hand in her own and held it in place as she grinned at the younger blonde woman. "You made a mistake now" she stated playfully. "You know I like you fondling my tits and I'm not going to let you go eat until you've satisfied me."

Rose said in mock severity "Well if we can't eat until you're satisfied, Samantha, we're gonna end up starving to death. But if that's what it takes, I'll give Danni some help." She grabbed and firmly squeezed Samantha's other breast causing her to gasp in surprise and delight. Lydia backed away slightly from the trio as they continued their roughhousing but watched them with interest. She was amazed at how comfortable and confident they were with each other. She knew that she would feel that way with her husband but didn't really think that she'd be that way with him and someone else. She'd be too worried about how everyone felt. The three women played with one another for a few minutes until Rose called a halt to proceedings, declaring "We're not being good hosts. Let's go eat and then get our guest into the swing of things. I think we're going a little too fast for her right now." She smiled broadly at Lydia before reaching over to take her hand and lead her over to the food. She offered the other woman a glass of wine and Lydia accepted gratefully. Samantha grimaced, slightly playfully, at Danni and then the two of them went over to join them; Danni joyfully dug into the food and took the edge off her appetite.

The four of them chatted quite easily for about twenty minutes putting Lydia more at ease. She appreciated that they took the effort to help her ease into the situation. She decided that she was about ready to start and beckoned Danni over to her. When Danni stood in front of her bending over to see what she wanted, Lydia planted a wet kiss on the young blonde woman's lips. Danni wasted no time in responding and slipped onto the couch beside her. Samantha and Rose watched them kiss for more than a minute and then moved the coffee table away from the couch so that they would have more room to play. They both knelt beside the kissing couple and began to run their hands over their naked bodies. They made sure that they caressed Danni more than Lydia so she wouldn't feel too pressured. They knew that Danni would like being stroked immensely. Lydia noticed what they were doing and appreciated their consideration. She decided to step matters up somewhat and reached out and stroked Rose's large breasts while still kissing Danni. So Rose began to stroke Lydia more in return; she noticed that Lydia was responding quite well without shying away at all. She gestured with her head to Samantha to bring her attention to that fact. Samantha nodded in understanding and started to stroke Lydia's nearest thigh softly and gently. She was pleased that the older woman opened her legs in response, inviting even more touching. It seemed that Lydia was now ready to play.

Samantha decided to see how far Lydia was now prepared to go; she gently but firmly eased Danni away from Lydia and slid into her place. Although Lydia had enjoyed kissing and petting with Danni, the fact that another woman was now in her place increased her excitement and she eagerly began kissing and stroking Samantha. Danni wasn't upset that Samantha had taken her place; she knew that each of them would get their turn with one another. She used her left hand to alternately stroke Samantha and Lydia as they kissed on the couch while she started stroking Rose's bare back and ass with her right hand. She knew that Rose would appreciate being fondled firmly so she put effort into her actions. Rose was initially surprised but responded to Danni's hard ministrations; she moaned and muttered her appreciation to what the younger woman was doing to her. When Rose began making so much noise, Lydia broke her kiss with Samantha to determine what was going on. She was concerned. Samantha knew that Rose's noises were sexual in nature and wasn't troubled at all so she quickly brought Lydia's face back to hers and resumed the kissing. Lydia realized what was happening and felt her passion grow a bit more; she was surprised that she found another woman's moans to be so arousing. She started being more passionate in her interaction with Samantha who began increasing her own actions. Samantha moved her hand down to Lydia's pussy and started stroking the other woman's erect, sensitive clitoris. Lydia moaned her approval into Samantha's mouth. Danni began to feel a bit left out so she moved in behind Rose, pressing her body against the other woman's padded back and began stroking the older redhead's pussy with both of her hands. Rose opened her legs as wide as she could to accommodate the younger blonde's actions. She started to feel her juices flowing down her thighs as her pussy began to feel like it was plugged into a light socket. She wailed her immense appreciation for what Danni was doing to her and then grunted deeply and loudly as she orgasmed. Lydia felt incredibly moved by hearing Rose's climax and could feel her own control being lost. Just over a minute later, she came as well.

Danni helped Rose to get up onto the couch so that she could comfortably lie on her back as she recovered her composure. Danni pressed her face down between Rose's thighs so that she could gently lick and taste the other woman's pussy, keeping her quite aroused. Rose was making constant noises as Danni sucked on her cunt. Lydia wasn't as vocal but she understood Rose's feelings entirely as Samantha was busy eating her pussy as well. The two older women were ecstatic that the two younger ones were so busy licking their wet, sopping pussies. But soon, both older women were quite satisfied and needed to rest. Lydia was the first to push Samantha's head from between her legs; Samantha let herself be pushed away without too much problem, she understood why Lydia wanted her to leave her alone. Samantha knew that Rose would soon be doing the same thing to Danni so she started getting prepared to continue on screwing with Danni. She put her favourite harness on and hunted down Danni's favourite dildo. She was joyously humming a tune while lubricating the pink plastic cock as she waited for Danni.

Soon Rose decided that she'd had enough; she'd been watching Samantha getting prepared to mount Danni and was willing to keep her occupied until Samantha was ready. But now that Samantha was ready, Rose pushed lightly on Danni's shoulders to signal her desire to stop. Danni quickly obeyed, knowing that Rose would only do that when she was quite tired and needed to rest. Danni was delighted to find that Samantha was prepared for her and wanted to fuck her with the dildo. She loved the feel of a cock or dildo in her cunt and Samantha was cognizant about how hard she liked to be ridden. Samantha helped Danni get down on the rug and into the proper kneeling position so she could support Samantha's weight while the slightly heavier brunette thrust deep and hard into her without enduring rug burns. She lightly fingered Danni's cunt to check on her wetness and decided that she was a bit dry. She quickly put her face down between Danni's slim, toned thighs and licked her pussy lips for a moment to help her lubricate herself. Danni muttered quietly in enjoyment and anticipated joyfully the first hard thrust. Soon Samantha was satisfied and moved behind Danni.

She knew that Danni was looking forward to being penetrated and wanted it to be as hard as Samantha could manage but she wanted the young blonde woman to be a bit more aroused because she'd been made to wait. So she teased Danni by gently pressing the tip of the pink dildo against Danni's slick slit; Danni took the top two inches easily and braced herself to press back once Samantha grabbed her shoulders and started pulling her over the plastic cock. But Samantha didn't do that. Instead she pulled the dildo away from Danni's pussy and lightly ran her fingertips of her left hand over Danni's exposed asshole. Danni moaned in frustration; she knew that

Samantha was just teasing her to get her hotter but she really wanted to feel that plastic prick up inside her. She wiggled her ass to entice Samantha to stick the cock in her but Samantha just slapped her on the ass and pushed her hips back down again. She slowly pushed five inches of the cock into Danni's wet pussy ignoring Danni's encouraging noises to take her harder. Once again, she pulled the dildo back out of Danni's cunt. Danni groaned loudly in frustration knowing that Samantha was deliberately making her wait for fulfillment.

Rose wiggled her body over to where Lydia still lay sprawled watching the two young women; Rose put her arm around the other woman's shoulders and gave her a firm squeeze. Lydia expected Rose to caress her breasts and was prepared for it; it wasn't what she particularly wanted but she was willing to accept it. But Rose surprised her by doing nothing more than just cuddling her. They companionably watched as Samantha continued to tease Danni with the dildo. She inserted the dildo as much as half its length into the blonde's cunt before quickly pulling it out and rubbing the tip along Danni's sensitive slit. Lydia was slightly amused that Danni was now muttering in her frustration and growling slightly. She recognized that Samantha was showing off for her and felt a small concern that the young brunette might push things too far. Rose had decided that Danni had endured enough and said, quite quietly but firmly "Enough Samantha, give her what she needs."

So Samantha grabbed a tight hold of Danni's slim hips and pushed forward with all of her strength. The dildo glided easily up Danni's slick cunt until Samantha's hips banged hard into hers, forcing Danni forward about six inches. Danni grunted in satisfaction as she felt the plastic cock deep up inside her; it felt wonderful and she pushed back hard with her own hips to keep the dildo as deep inside her as she could. Samantha let her enjoy the filled feeling for a moment and then used her hands against Danni's ass to push her forward and off of the dildo as she moved her own hips backwards. She knew that Danni would be reluctant to let the dildo go and would have tightened her strong cervical muscles around it. She wondered what that might feel like if she were a man and the cock on her was real flesh; considering that men liked fucking, it must feel pretty good. She dismissed the thought from her mind and immediately thrust back hard into Danni once the dildo was slightly more than three-quarters out of the blonde cunt. She didn't give Danni much chance to enjoy the penetration but immediately started pulling it back out. Danni almost screamed in frustration because she didn't get the chance to hold the dildo inside her for a while. Samantha let a slightly malicious smile cross her face as she enjoyed Danni's frustration. She knew that the other woman liked it when she was intentionally denied what she wanted. Danni definitely had a submissive's personality and it was something that Samantha wanted to explore more in the future. But she was just going to take advantage of that right now and she continued to bang her hips hard and fast against Danni's as she thrust the dildo deep and hard in her willing cunt. Samantha could feel her body starting to tire from the exhaustive effort she was putting out; she could feel beads of perspiration start to pop out along her legs and under her heavy breasts. Danni was beginning to pant from her own efforts while she continued to moan out her approval of the pace and depth of the penetration. Samantha resisted the urge to look over to see how well Lydia might be enjoying the demonstration in front of her because she was worried that it might interfere with her pace and control. She wanted to make sure that Danni appreciated the fucking as much as she was able to do. She wanted Danni to have an immense, mind-blowing orgasm.

Lydia was watching the action with extreme interest; she felt comfortable being cuddled by Rose, much more so than she'd thought was possible. She found that she liked the feel of the other woman's plump body pressing against her and the slightly floral scent of her fading perfume over the more acrid smell of her perspiration. She was used to a sharper scent that her husband exuded when he cuddled her after having fucked her. She found that she didn't mind the lighter scent at all. She snuggled her body somewhat closer to the other woman feeling her breast pressing against the other woman's large tit. That felt different and quite nice, she decided as she shifted her shoulders to feel it slid on the other woman's skin a bit more. Rose was aware of what Lydia was doing and was content to let the other woman explore her feelings on such matters without pushing matters too much. She remembered how scared she'd felt the first time she'd participated in a group sex session and how worried she'd been that everyone else was better at it than she was. She now knew that most of the other people had similar feelings as she'd had. She could tell from the gasps coming from both Samantha and Danni that they were totally lost in their own feelings as they fucked one another. Samantha was working hard to keep her pace up and she was dripping streams of sweat onto Danni's wet, arched back. Danni was wheezing and groaning as she was pushing back with all her might; she was obviously enjoying both the pace and penetration that was happening. Suddenly Danni stopped, screamed sharply and bucked her hips spasmodically as she came with great intensity.

Samantha smacked her hands down on Danni's shoulders as the blonde woman tried to raise herself up to relieve some of the pressure in her cunt. Samantha forced Danni's chest down onto the rug as she kept pushing the dildo in and out of her. Her pace had decreased because Danni's orgasms made her tighten her muscles and grab hold of the plastic cock, slowing it down. Samantha was aware that a man wouldn't be able to stand the pressure that Danni was now exerting on the dildo inside her. The man also wouldn't be able to remain as stiff as the plastic cock was able to do. But she wanted to drive Danni to an even higher level of arousal. She braced her hands hard on Danni's shoulders as she pushed and pulled the dildo through her tight but slippery cunt. Danni's face was turned to the left as her head was pushed hard against the floor by Samantha's pressure on her shoulders. She was wearing a mask of pain, desire and discomfort as she grunted out in pleasure about what was being done to her. Samantha dug into her reserves and kept it up as Danni writhed and wriggled beneath her. Danni howled intensely once more as she was driven to her second orgasm. Samantha decided that Danni should be forced into a third orgasm so even though she was tiring, she continued to press Danni hard. Her hands dug into Danni's hips as she kept her in position. Danni was just starting to recover from her second orgasm and began to realize that Samantha wasn't going to give her any respite. She recognized that Samantha was showing off for Lydia; she quickly assessed her condition and decided that she couldn't endure a third crashing orgasm. She knew that if she protested, that Samantha would just ignore it as just more foreplay between them but if she used her safe word, Samantha would honour it and stop immediately. She felt that she had to do just that and grunted out "Bananastand."

Samantha stopped immediately and looked down at Danni in horror as Rose came flying off the couch to check on Danni. Lydia watched what was happening in confusion, unsure as to what was going on. Samantha was attempting to pull the buried dildo out of Danni's cunt but Danni muttered "No, no, don't pull it out. Leave it in me." Rose pressed her face down close to Danni's as she checked the young girl out. Danni had tears leaking down her face but Rose was unsure as to whether that was a result of feeling pain or was just a reaction to her efforts. Danni's face was screwed up but again Rose was unsure if that was from pain or not.

"How badly does it hurt?" she asked the young blonde woman gently. "Should we move you to a more comfortable position?"

"I'm not hurt" Danni replied as she grimaced from the intensity of the aftermath of her second orgasm. "I just needed Samantha to stop and thought that was the only way to ensure it. I'll be fine in a few minutes, just let me recuperate for a few minutes." Rose nodded and began to massage Danni's tight neck muscles to help her to relax more; she glared at the recalcitrant Samantha as she soothed Danni. Lydia had stayed out of the way so that they could handle the problem without her getting in the way and began to feel reassured that Danni was going to be okay. Samantha moved her hands up to below Danni's shoulders and carefully put her hands on Danni's tense back muscles and gently but firmly began stroking some of the tension out with her thumbs. She was somewhat pleased, even though she still felt fairly shook by the experience, when Danni began sighing as she started to relax her tight muscles. The two women worked on Danni for a few more minutes. The dildo slid out of Danni's cunt as she relaxed her contracted muscles and Samantha moved her position somewhat so that it wasn't poking into her.

Rose helped Danni down to a comfortable position on her side so that the young woman could regain her strength. She looked over at Samantha and noted her tense, scared face. "I'm sorry. I guess I tried too hard with her. I should've had more control" Samantha said softly.

"Yes, you should have but it doesn't appear to be any harm done" Rose replied, almost as quietly. "But you should be apologizing to her not me." Samantha nodded in agreement and Rose went over to help the brunette to take the strap-on harness off. She'd initially felt like giving Samantha a sharp smack for doing that to Danni but was feeling glad that she had resisted the temptation. It wouldn't have been helpful at all, she thought. When they got the harness removed, Samantha lay down beside Danni, cuddling her and softly reassuring her. Rose felt quite proud of Samantha for taking responsibility for her actions.

She moved back over to where Lydia was sitting, watching the proceedings. "How is she?" Lydia asked with concern.

"She's fine. Samantha was just showing off for you and pushed her much too hard. Danni likes it a bit rough and enjoyed the first two orgasms but didn't think she'd be able to handle the third one that quick and hard. So she used her safe word because she knew that it would stop Samantha immediately. She'll be right as rain in fifteen minutes or so" Rose replied as she kept watch on Lydia to determine what her reaction was going to be. The other woman could easily decide that she no longer wanted to participate in the activities of the day. Rose would be very disappointed if that was her decision.

Lydia nodded as she considered the information. It had been quite scary when she thought that Danni was hurt but knowing that she wasn't calmed her quite a bit. "I was impressed by how fast you and Samantha went to care for her" Lydia said, softly. "You were right there checking on her and comforting her as quick as you could. Even when she stated she wasn't hurt, you guys still took quite a bit of time to console her."

Rose looked at her with her eyes widened in surprise and said slightly coolly "We care for her and her well-being. I imagine your husband would react in the same way for you."

Lydia nodded in agreement but thought that the two women were still to be admired for their actions. She decided that there was no point in extending the conversation. Rose wasn't taking her comments as the compliments that she'd intended them to be. She decided to change topics. "I wouldn't mind riding a dildo for a bit" she suggested, lightly.

Rose looked at her, brightened a bit and then said "Samantha is the most experienced one wearing a dildo. She'll be much gentler on you than she was on Danni." She smiled to reassure the other woman.

Lydia frowned and shook her head as she said "No, I don't think that I would be comfortable with her right now after having seen that incident. I'm sure that she would definitely be gentler but I would be so nervous that it wouldn't work out for us."

Rose now frowned and stated "Danni is quite inexperienced with wearing the harness and dildo and I wouldn't really recommend her for your first time. I know that she's gorgeous and a lot of fun but there are still some things that she doesn't excel at yet." She paused and then continued "Still it is your choice in the matter. She'll be ready in a bit."

Lydia shook her head once more and stated firmly "I wasn't thinking that it should be Danni either." She stopped and looked expectantly at Rose.

"If not Samantha or Danni, then..." Rose said slowly. "Oh, you mean it to be me" she stated with a happy smile. "Are you sure? I'm flattered but I'm not as beautiful or graceful as those two young women are." She patted her broad hips and said "I'm also pretty wide." Lydia didn't mention the fact that her husband was about as wide and she was used to wrapping her legs around him. She just silently smiled at the redhead. Rose nodded and asked "When do you want to do it?"

"I wouldn't mind if we did it soon" Lydia replied. She was feeling fairly horny from watching Danni orgasm. She'd suppressed it when she'd been concerned that the young blonde was hurt but it now reared its head once more. She gave Rose a hopeful half grin and was pleased when the redhead raised her eyebrows and nodded in agreement.

"Let's go pick out the dildo you want to ride and whatever other toys you'd like to try" Rose suggested and held her hand out to Lydia. They went over to the selection of toys and Lydia spent a few minutes fondling them and deciding on which ones she thought she would like. She picked out a seven inch brown dildo that had some girth but not too much as the one she wanted Rose to wear; it reminded her of the shape of her husband's cock and she thought she'd find that most comfortable. She was also intrigued by a pair of nipple clamps and showed them shyly to Rose. Rose immediately smiled, bent down and started to suck and flick Lydia's thick nipples. Lydia groaned a bit in pleasure as Rose got her nipples erect and then put the nipple clamps lightly on the turgid flesh. Lydia eyes widened as she felt an almost electric shock travel from her nipples up to her brain. She gasped at the sensation and Rose grinned and tugged on the nipple clamps gently but firmly. Lydia panted a bit in response as her temperature and blood pressure began to rise. Rose got her leather harness, took Lydia's hand once more and led her back over to the couch.

Rose helped Lydia lie back down on the couch and placed three silk covered pillows under the other woman's lower back and ass to help her get into proper position. Lydia had indicated that she wanted to be taken in the missionary position rather than doing it doggy style like Danni had done. She'd done that position before and wasn't too impressed by it. She preferred lying on her back and wrapping her legs around her partner. Rose was ambivalent about the missionary position but willing to participate in that way if that was Lydia's preference. As Lydia lay back, wiggling her hips to get into a comfortable position, Rose began to pour some lubricant onto her pussy. She started to work the slick oil into Lydia's cunt with her fingers, teasing the other woman somewhat as she did it. Rose was aware that Lydia wouldn't produce as much of her own lubricant as Danni or Samantha did and therefore would need some help to enjoy the penetration to its utmost. Rose needed the same help herself. As she fondled Lydia's cunt, she reached up and tugged lightly on the nipple clamps occasionally, eliciting grunts of pleasure from the brunette. Finally she was satisfied that Lydia was prepared and situated herself above the recumbent woman; she placed the broad head of the dildo at Lydia's entrance and gently began to push it up into her. Lydia gave a small gasping moan at the initial penetration that turned into mutterings of approval as she accepted the dildo deeper inside her. It felt good and because of all of the lubricant she found no problem in accepting it. She gave a sigh of happiness that made Rose pause and look into her eyes. Rose was quite pleased that Lydia was enjoying herself so much.

Rose began to pull the dildo back out of Lydia's cunt after the dildo had sunk in to about half of its length; Lydia gave a murmur of disappointment and tightened down her cunt muscles to slow the exit of the plastic cock. Rose grinned at her as she saw what the other woman was doing. She let Lydia grasp the dildo with her muscles as she paused in her withdrawal. Then she slowly began to push it back up into her slowly giving the other woman time to relax her muscles enough to take and enjoy the penetration once more. Lydia raised her hips slightly to change the angle of the penetration, loving the fact that the redhead was taking her time in fucking her. Her husband generally wanted full penetration of her as soon as he could and she was finding this slower method quite arousing. Rose could quickly see that Lydia liked what she was doing and she maintained the slow and easy penetration of the other woman; she hadn't actually planned to do it so slow but was just giving the other woman a chance to accept the dildo inside of her. She put her hands on Lydia's shoulders to steady herself as she rode her. Lydia grunted in pleasure about being held down as Rose leveraged her thrusts against the other woman.

Rose worked over Lydia for more than five minutes, keeping her pace slow but making sure that Lydia took the full length of the dildo with each thrust. She could hear the breath whistling through Lydia's nose each time she bottomed out. Then she realized that they had an audience and looked over to see Danni and Samantha kneeling beside the couch, watching them with interest. Neither of them intruded on the action but just observed the action. Rose gave them a quick little smile and then focused on her screwing. Lydia began tilting her hips and thrusting against her efforts. Rose figured that she was showing that she was fairly close to her orgasm and therefore she increased the pace slightly to keep her stimulated. Suddenly,

Lydia gave a small wail, grabbed Rose around her shoulders and pulled her tight against her body as she rocked her hips hard against the dildo deep inside her. Lydia panted and cried as she orgasmed, pulling Rose tight against her with her strong legs. Rose was content to just let the other woman dictate what they did; she was just along for the ride.

Danni and Samantha watched Lydia climax with interest; it wasn't as spectacular as quite a number that they had seen but it was intriguing to watch the woman orgasm. They weren't sure how Lydia would react if they started petting her so they held off to let her enjoy herself without any concerns. Once she'd released Rose, they would explore what she might like to do. Samantha signalled that they should go over and get a drink while they were waiting and Danni nodded, thinking that a snack might also be in order. So they moved away. Rose clasped the recovering woman hard against her, enjoying the feel of her breasts pressing against Lydia's warm flesh. She murmured soft, sweet things in Lydia's ear, telling her what a good woman she was.

After a few minutes of being cuddled and of recovering, Lydia loosened her grip on Rose's hips to allow the redhead to move off of her. Rose moved back, pulling the dildo out of Lydia's now flaccid pussy. She straightened up and removed the harness. She'd asked Lydia if she wanted to suck on the dildo after it had been pulled from her like some women liked to do but Lydia had declined the offer. Rose pulled the dildo off of the harness and put it into her own mouth, tonguing the tasty juices from it. No sense in wasting it, she thought. Lydia was still laying there and watching Rose with curiosity. She'd never found her own juices to be too attractive the few times that she'd bothered to taste them and was wondering if maybe that was mostly because she'd only tried them after a man had been in her. She slid a finger into her wet cunt and lifted a small bit to her mouth. She didn't find the taste to be too much better than she'd remembered; she made a slightly sour face in reaction. Rose noticed her expression and just laughed lightly before she went down and cleaned up Lydia's messy cunt. Lydia wriggled and thrashed somewhat as Rose used her tongue to rasp off all of her pussy juices. Lydia found the experience to be extremely pleasant.

Danni and Samantha had drifted back, carrying glasses of wine for the two women. Danni had eaten four desserts while they had been away sipping on their own wine. Samantha had refrained from chiding her, knowing that Danni didn't have a weight problem and used up the calories quite quickly. She thought that teasing Danni about it might start to give her a complex and she didn't want to cause that. She was amazed and somewhat envious about the blonde girl's ability to eat that much. She knew that she was in very good shape and exercised to keep her body well-toned so she could eat fairly well but it would be nice to just ignore the problem altogether like Danni did. They waited and watched as Rose finished cleaning Lydia's cunt. When Rose straightened up, moving away from the wet pussy, Samantha gave her the glass of wine she held. Danni moved up by Lydia's head and instead of letting her get up and take the wine, rested her left hand gently on Lydia's shoulder, indicating to her that she wished the other woman to remain lying there, and used her right hand to tilt the wineglass against Lydia's mouth. Lydia found the gesture to be quite touching and sipped a small bit of the wine before smiling her thanks. She tried to get up but Danni pressed down on her shoulder to hold her in place. Samantha had pushed Rose away from Lydia so that she could get in and take her place. She was now using her tongue to trace along Lydia's still damp slit. Lydia realized that the two younger women had schemed this so that they could also taste her pussy. She felt that she should object but the feel of Samantha's tongue on her sensitive parts was amazing. She decided that she would comply with their wishes and simply enjoy what was being done to her.

After a few minutes, Danni moved down and gently pushed Samantha on her shoulder to signal that she wanted to taste the older woman so Samantha pulled back so the blonde could take her place. She hadn't managed to make Lydia orgasm a second time but Lydia had noisily indicated that she enjoyed the younger brunette's efforts. Samantha had enjoyed her actions as well but was happy that Danni was now eating Lydia's pussy; her tongue and jaw were tired. She enjoyed the taste of her wine when she sipped at it. The wine cut the slightly acrid taste of Lydia's juices quite nicely, she thought as she contemplated the older woman's taste. It was nowhere as sweet as Danni's or even her own but it wasn't too bad, she decided. She hadn't moved away too far when Danni took her place and she now began to stroke Danni's beautiful back as she bent over to her task. Danni paused, turned and gave her a quick grin in appreciation for the attention before returning to her task.

After a few more minutes, Danni stopped and they all moved away to give Lydia some room to recover. They sat down at the small table and chatted easily for nearly ten minutes before Lydia sat up to signify that she'd recovered enough to continue. Danni had spent the time considering having another brownie but she'd decided that she'd had enough sugar for the day and nothing else really appealed. She suspected that she wasn't really hungry but just wanted something to treat herself with; she decided that denying herself the treat would be good for her self-control. But when Lydia sat up they went over to be with her once more. It was evident that Lydia wasn't really in the shape to participate in any sexual activities right away but Rose suggested "Samantha hasn't been made to cum yet today and I think that we should make that happen." She smiled slightly teasingly at the young brunette before switching her gaze towards Lydia. "I was thinking that you might like to see some of those toys you were looking at earlier being put to use on her. She enjoys using most of them and we can help her with some of them. Would you like to see that?"

Lydia raised her eyebrows as she considered the matter; she'd like to see the effect of some of those toys, she thought. She looked over to see what Samantha's feelings on the issue were. Samantha smiled at her showing that she wasn't adverse to the suggestion so Lydia nodded her head in approval.

Rose grabbed Danni's hand and led her over to the toy table and started filling her arms with quite a variety of toys; she hummed happily as she selected toys and piled them in the young blonde woman's arms. She grabbed the remaining toys she wanted and they went back over to where Samantha was now lying on the couch waiting for them. Samantha had convinced Lydia to begin stroking her cunt so she would be prepared and wet enough for them to start using the toys on her. Lydia was enjoying the soft fuzzy feel of another woman's cunt and Samantha was being vocal in her encouragement of the older woman's actions. Both Rose and Danni knew that Samantha was playing up to Lydia; she normally wasn't as vocal as she was currently being. But they didn't begrudge her her actions. They knew that they were all kind of showing off for the new woman, looking to impress her. Danni placed her armful of toys on the couch above Samantha's head and picked out a small vibrator with a knobbed end to it. She quickly moved and knelt by where Lydia was alongside of Samantha's hips. She ran the vibrator along Samantha's damp slit to lubricate it a bit and then began pressing it against Samantha's clitoris to arouse her even more. She tried to make sure that the buzzing toy wasn't interfering with Lydia's enjoyment but tried to make sure that it remained in contact with Samantha's sensitive nub. Samantha loved the feel of the small toy on her clit and was moaning slightly in encouragement. She moved her hips to press against the buzzing toy a bit more. She didn't want to discourage Lydia but the toy was arousing her more than the other woman's stroking had been. She began to massage her own breasts, working her stiffening nipples hard. Rose had sorted out the toys so that she could select any of them easily without having to look too hard at them and now moved up beside Samantha's torso. Rose swatted Samantha's hands away from her own tits lightly and began to rub the aroused nipples. Once they were as full as they could be, Rose attached a heavy set of nipple clips to them. She knew that they were a heavier set than Samantha normally wore; in fact, they were the set that Rose frequently had applied to her own tits. She tightened them down quite tightly causing Samantha to gasp in surprise and then look more closely at the clamps. She realized that Rose had chosen the heavier set and looked at her questioningly. She wondered if Rose was trying to punish her. Rose squeezed Samantha's heavy right breast firmly but in a very friendly manner to let the other woman know that she was just trying to help her impress Lydia more than any thought of punishment. Samantha lay back with an unsure look on her face but didn't voice any protest.

"Don't make her orgasm, Danni" Rose cautioned the young blonde woman. "We only want her wet, horny and wanting more right now. We want her to orgasm with a dildo that is penetrating her." Then Rose turned her attention to Samantha and smiled. She held up an anal plug and said "I think that we should put this beauty up your ass, Samantha. What do you think?"

Samantha looked at the largest of the anal plugs that they had with some horror. She was used to wearing an anal plug but generally it was the smallest of the three that they had that she wore. This large piece of plastic would make her uncomfortable sitting for almost a week; it was one that Rose wore fairly frequently because she loved the sensation of having her asshole stretched out. But Samantha didn't share that love. She tolerated the stretching feeling and it did help her to orgasm more when she had one up inside her but she didn't really love the sensation like Rose did. "No, no" she pleaded. "I'll take the medium one if you insist but I'd rather have the smallest one inside my ass. That one will stretch me out too much." She thought for a moment and said "I won't be able to go dancing with you and Danni on Friday if you force that up my ass." Rose looked at her speculatively; she didn't really expect Samantha to agree to the large anal plug, she was just pressuring the brunette to agree to the medium plug because that was the one she wanted her to endure. She knew that the few times that Samantha had tried the largest plug that she had some discomfort for a number of days. She didn't really want the younger woman to be as sore as that.

But she did want her to be in some pain, so she agreed, saying "Fine. We'll use the medium plug on you." She handed Danni the medium powder blue plug and asked "Danni, would you lubricate it well while I prepare Samantha to take it?" Danni had been playing with the small pink plug wondering what it would feel like up inside her own ass. She contemplated asking Rose to insert it in her once Samantha had the other one up her ass but then decided that doing that might be something that Samantha might really enjoy doing to her. So she pushed that thought away and took the plug from Rose to apply a coating of lubricant. Rose had noticed Danni's curiosity with the pink plug and smiled slightly; they would have to explore that interest at a later date, she thought brightly.

Then she started getting Samantha prepared for the anal insertion. "Would you help me, Lydia?" she asked. She directed Lydia to place pillows under Samantha's ass as she lifted the young woman's legs up over her head, raising up her rear end. Samantha cooperated as much as she could as they positioned her; she was quite happy and excited by what Rose and the other two were going to do to her. Samantha usually liked to be the one that did these sorts of things to others but occasionally enjoyed having the reverse done to her. She knew that she and Rose both enjoyed the role reversal when they did this. She could see Rose's excitement by the sheen on her thighs and her musky scent as the older woman knelt over her head as she guided her into position. She hoped that Danni and Lydia were also aroused as they considered what was going to happen. She turned her head and caught Danni's eye, giving the gorgeous blonde a happy little smile. Danni flushed slightly as Samantha smiled at her, noting that the brunette was happily anticipating the penetration of her ass. She grinned back.

Rose stroked Samantha's clit lightly with her left hand to keep her aroused as she squeezed the tube of KY jelly just over the other woman's asshole. She created a small glob of the gel on Samantha's asshole before she put the tube down and began to work the lubricant up into Samantha. The brunette moaned and muttered as Rose forced her fingers up into her anus. Samantha could feel Rose working and warming her asshole to get her ready for the powder blue plug. It felt quite good and she began to pull lightly on the nipple clamps to increase her arousal. Danni had finished with the butt plug and was waiting for Rose to ask for it; she noticed what Samantha was doing and decided to join in. She reached over and squeezed Samantha's large left breast with her slick hand. Rose heard Samantha's loud gasp and looked down to see what was happening. She was relieved and happy to see that the outburst was just because Danni was fondling Samantha's tit for her. Lydia was watching all of the action with a great degree of interest. She wasn't sure what she should do so she kept out of the way and just observed.

Rose was satisfied that Samantha's asshole was slick enough for her to start taking the anal plug so she reached down and indicated to Danni that she wanted it. Danni handed the plug up to Rose and then started using both her hands on Samantha's tits. She knew that she was distracting Samantha somewhat from what Rose was doing to her and didn't mind that. She thought it would help Samantha to be penetrated more easily if she wasn't paying as much attention to what was happening with her ass. Besides, she thought, slightly evilly, it was fun to play with Samantha's tits. Samantha could feel the electric buildup in her cunt as she approached her orgasm threshold; Danni's fondling of her tits and Rose's fingering of her asshole was working its magic on her. She started panting as she began to anticipate the climax building within her body. Then Rose pressed the anal plug firmly against her asshole and pushed it firmly inside of her. Samantha yelped as her asshole was stretched to accommodate the plastic plug and she groaned hard as it slid up inside her. Rose managed to get the powder blue plug slightly more than halfway inside of Samantha with her initial push. She was satisfied with that result for the moment and left it alone while she used both of her hands to fondle Samantha's clit and pussy lips. She knew that Samantha would soon relax her muscles enough that the remainder of the plug could be forced inside her. There was no sense in trying to force the matter too much she thought, so she might as well have some fun in the meantime.

Samantha grimaced as she got used to the anal plug up inside her; she fought to relax her muscles so she wasn't fighting it. She found the attentions of Danni and Rose really helped distract her from the pressure she felt in her ass. She closed her eyes and appreciated the fondling of the other two women. She was surprised when Danni began sucking and lightly biting the fleshy side of her left tit. She glanced over at the blonde woman who was looking back at her, trying to determine if she should continue her actions or not. Samantha gave her a smile to let her know that she'd enjoyed her actions and wanted her to continue. Rose was keeping watch on how tense Samantha's thighs were contracted. Once those muscles started to loosen, she knew that Samantha would be ready to continue with the insertion. She paused to glance over in Lydia's direction to see how that woman was taking matters. She noted with amused approval that Lydia was busy fondling both her breasts and pussy as she avidly watched what Samantha was enduring. No problem over there, Rose thought with satisfaction. She idly rubbed the inside muscles of Samantha's thighs as she shifted her attention to what Danni might be doing. She watched with interest as Danni placed small love bites on the side of Samantha's large tit. That was something new and different, she thought.

She could now tell that Samantha was relaxing enough that she could push the plug deeper into her and she began to do just that. Samantha let out a breathy grunt as Rose put pressure on the plug. She felt the plug moving deeper inside her and moaned somewhat in pleasure. Now that the initial penetration had happened she could concentrate more on the pleasurable full feeling it created in her ass. She pushed Danni gently away from her so she could concentrate on that one aspect. She knew that the blonde would understand. Danni sat back and watched the play of emotions flicker across Samantha's beautiful but contorted face. She lost herself in imagining what it must feel like and decided that she would suggest it to the others as soon as she was able to do so. She found herself biting her lip in sympathy when Samantha shuddered somewhat as she took in the anal plug. Lydia had moved closer and was amazed as Samantha's legs quivered as Rose forced the plug deeper. She too wondered what it would feel like but was quite undecided about ever finding out. She felt it was something better to imagine than actually find out about.

Rose took one of the vibrators and inserted it about halfway into Samantha's willing cunt before turning it on. She let the chattering tool vibrate against Samantha's tight tunnel, making her mutter with pleasure. After almost a minute she began forcing it deeper and then pulling it back and almost out of Samantha's slick pussy. She knew the pace that the other woman liked because of much practice and easily fell to that pace. She worked the young brunette fairly hard like she generally did and Samantha moaned with enjoyment. Danni had once again moved closer and just caressed Samantha as she enjoyed the work of the vibrator inside of her. Danni didn't want to distract her from her gratification. Rose could feel her forearms start to tighten from the strain being put on them but ignored her own discomfort to make sure that Samantha climaxed. She could tell that the young brunette was getting close because she was beginning to catch and hold her breath.

That was a sure sign that Samantha was feeling the pressure building in her loins. Suddenly Samantha gave an explosive grunt and some liquid seeped from her pussy and down her body as her legs and stomach tensed. Since there was nothing for her to gain purchase against, Samantha didn't move all that much. Rose knew that she would've bucked her body hard if she'd been lying flat on the bed. Samantha was groaning in appreciation as she enjoyed the aftermath of her climax.

But Rose wasn't going to let Samantha off easy so she called for Danni to come and hold the young brunette's legs up while continuing to glide the vibrator down its slick path. Danni was quite eager to do so and Samantha had no problem with the sex being sustained. She was loving the feeling of the buzzing toy sliding in and out of her as her cunt muscles pulsed in the aftermath of her first orgasm. Both Rose and Samantha knew that Samantha was good for a second orgasm usually about five minutes after her first. They had experienced such things many times before. Samantha was a bit surprised that Rose had let Danni tend to her though and wondered briefly about that before such thoughts were driven from her mind by the increasing arousal her body was enduring. Rose had let Danni take over so that she could rest her arm muscles somewhat; she knew that she had the strength to take Samantha through her second orgasm but wouldn't be able to do much more if she didn't rest. She had thoughts of making Samantha endure a third orgasm, somewhat in punishment for pushing Danni too hard and somewhat because of the nice spectacle it would make for Lydia. In order to accomplish that, she needed to rest her arms for a slight while so she let Danni take over for a few minutes. She watched with pleasure and arousal as Danni guided the toy in and out of Samantha who was writhing a bit in pleasure.

Rose took back over before Danni could push Samantha into her second orgasm. Danni was disappointed that Rose wanted to take over but she didn't object; she was quite happy to watch the two of them in action. She moved back to sit on her legs by Samantha's torso so she could watch the brunette's face when she came. She gently stroked Samantha's arm as she lay on the couch, not wanting to distract her from what Rose was doing to her. She just wanted the other woman to know that she was there and observing. Lydia found it touching that Danni was behaving like that. She was surprised that such a romantic action made her quite wet. She knew that actions like that directed towards her made her respond but hadn't realized that she could be so moved by romance not aimed at her. Of course, she might just be responding to watching as Samantha was pushed into a second orgasm.

Rose used her right hand to manipulate the toy in Samantha's cunt as her left arm supported her raised hips; that left her free to use her left hand to touch the other woman's filled, puckered asshole. Samantha enjoyed Rose's fingers tracing along her sensitive flesh; it increased the sensations she was busy undergoing. She bit her upper lip and gave a groan of appreciation as she felt the second orgasm working its way through her lower muscles. She knew that she was going to enjoy the burst of pleasure as it worked its way through her body. She could feel her vaginal muscles contracting and relaxing as she anticipated the climax. Rose was pushing the vibrator deep as she could manage so that Samantha would get the maximum feeling out of it. Samantha gave some grunting gasps and then she screamed as she climaxed once more. She expected Rose to pull the vibrator from her cunt so her muscles could be free to pulse her slit without any blockage but Rose didn't do that. Rose also didn't release her hips so that she could curl up as she climaxed. Samantha felt the need to coil into the foetal position to endure the tremendous sensations screaming through her nerves. She then realized that Rose was teaching and punishing her for what she'd done to Danni earlier.

Danni realized that Rose was disciplining Samantha and was upset about the fact. She knew that her earlier use of her safe word was the cause of this punishment but wasn't happy about it. She didn't like to see anyone suffer. She stood up and gave Rose a small push to get her attention. Rose looked over at her with a questioning look and Danni frowned and shook her head at the older woman. Lydia watched as Rose hesitated; she saw that Danni wasn't impressed by the redhead's actions on her behalf and felt a small spark of respect for Danni's compassion. She was slightly shocked to see Rose release Samantha, pulling the vibrator from the brunette as she slumped down. Danni gently but firmly pushed Rose aside so that she could squirm onto the couch beside the still writhing woman and began to plant soft kisses on her as she stroked the brunette's soft skin. Rose stood there watching the two young women for a moment before giving Danni a reassuring and appreciative pat on the back. Rose drew a deep breath to stabilize her feelings; she knew that she'd gone too far, the same thing that she charged Samantha with doing, and that Danni with her compassion had stopped her from causing further problems. She knew that deep down she would be quite thankful to the young blonde for interfering but she still felt just a small bit of pique about her actions. She moved over to where Lydia was observing with feelings of confusion clouding her mind.

Lydia recognized that Rose was conflicted and patted the area of the couch beside her, indicating that Rose should sit there. When the other woman did so, she pulled her into a comforting hug without saying anything. She soon felt the tension leave the redhead's body and loosened her hold. Rose chose to remain in fairly close contact as they both watched Samantha recover as Danni whispered endearments and comfort to her. Rose drew a deep breath before turning to look into Lydia's face. "Thank you" she said softly and humbly.

"Don't mention it. It was my pleasure" Lydia replied as softly. "Danni will never dominate, will she?" Lydia asked as she watched the young blonde help Samantha into a more comfortable position.

Rose observed the two women for about a moment before replying "No, Danni will always be a submissive." She fastened her eyes on the other woman's and stated firmly "But that is to her credit. She has a wonderful capacity for love. I wish I could copy her but I don't have her sweet nature." Lydia nodded and the two women watched in silence for more than five minutes. Then Rose shook her body and straightened out her body as she moved slightly away from Lydia so that she could talk more easily with her. "Are you interested in sampling some pussy?" Rose asked as she looked into the brunette's eyes. "I would suggest that Danni has the sweetest cunt and is the easiest to climax. She would be your best choice."

Lydia considered the matter for a few minutes and Rose let her have her time to decide. Finally she said "I appreciate the offer but I think that I will have to pass for today. You all have given me much to think about and I need some time to determine what my feelings are. Right now I am quite conflicted. I love my husband and like the feeling of a man's cock in my cunt and mouth but I can see the pleasure and love that you all have for each other. I am a bit jealous about that." She paused to give Rose a slightly tenuous smile as she waited to see what Rose's reaction would be. Rose just nodded and smiled in understanding.

So Lydia gathered her clothes and dressed; she began to pack up her equipment to prepare to load it and leave. Rose got her clothing on so that she could assist her. It was Lydia's intention to make her departure without disturbing Samantha and Danni. She felt it might be better to leave without having to explain that she didn't want to continue with their actions on that day; she thought that even though they appeared quite tired at the moment that they'd feel somewhat slighted by her parting and she was slightly chicken about facing that disappointment. When she'd taken her first batch of items out to the car, Danni was waiting for her to return to the house. The young blonde woman hugged Lydia tightly and said "I hope that you were intrigued by us and will consider returning. But if you feel that you would prefer to continue your life as it presently is, we will understand. Be happy in whatever you choose to do." Lydia nodded silently as she felt a catch in her throat and her eyes started to tear. She believed that Danni meant exactly what she'd said and appreciated the sentiment. She got the rest of her equipment and took it out as Danni watched her and waved.

Ms. Sturm came for Danni about a half hour later and the young blonde happily got into her car. Before they left, Ms. Sturm turned Danni's face towards her and looked at her countenance, especially examining her bright blue eyes; she thought that Danni looked relaxed and happy but wanted to make sure of it. "How are you feeling?"

"Oh, I'm feeling quite well. Somewhat tired from all the activity but loose and happy. It was a pretty good day. I'm not too sure that Lydia got completely into it though. Only time will tell."

Ms. Sturm nodded. She'd had a brief chat on the phone with Lydia, who'd called her once she'd left to set up a meeting in two days to deliver the video. She'd told Ms. Sturm that she thought that the video would be exactly what Ms. Sturm wanted. She hadn't mentioned how she felt about the day and Ms. Sturm hadn't pressed her. "How did the video shoot go?"

"Oh, I guess it went well" Danni replied as began to frown. "Lydia, Rose and Samantha seemed to like it when we reviewed it but I felt that it made me look like a sappy girl who'd never had an orgasm before. I wanted to reshoot the thing since we were already all there but the others told me that it was fine." She looked earnestly at Ms. Sturm and said "When you look at it, you'll see what I mean. You can get them to reshoot it if you agree with me." Then she pouted her lips slightly and said "I also think that maybe we should get Theodore to fuck me for the camera as well. I don't think that too many men are going to appreciate me as much just seeing me with Samantha."

Ms. Sturm eyed Danni speculatively, marvelling at the young woman's innocence; she knew that men would be extremely turned on by watching two beautiful young women fucking each other and Samantha and Danni certainly qualified as beautiful. She decided that it wasn't worth while discussing the matter with the young blonde and just started the car and drove her home.

CHAPTER THREE

After school the next day, Danni hurried up to the blue car where Ms. Sturm was waiting for her. It was a warm, sticky spring afternoon and Danni was wearing a rather modest light dress. She'd been fairly surprised during the day to notice that, although the dress wasn't overly tight and covered her legs down to just above her knees so she conformed to the school dress code, that a number of boys had paused to watch her as she walked by them. She'd liked their hungry looks as they observed her as she strode by and she'd begun to put more of a wiggle into her walk even though she hadn't been wearing high heels. Shortly after starting to do that, she was startled to see some of the girls in the rich, beautiful clique that had previously ignored her existence totally begin to glare daggers at her. She was surprised that their expressions of hatred and jealousy made her feel quite aroused. She also detected that some of her friends had shot her worried glances as she enjoyed the attention of those rivals. She didn't bother to explain her actions to them. So now she was feeling in the need of some release, having spent the whole day building her excitement.

Ms. Sturm looked her over carefully as she threw herself into the passenger seat of the car; she could determine that Danni was hot and bothered and wondered briefly what had brought it on. She'd thought that the girl would still be feeling the effects of the fairly strenuous day before but here she was, practically begging for a good fucking. She decided that it wasn't important what had put her in such a mood and that she wouldn't bother to speak with her about it. Instead, she decided that she would distract Danni a bit by talking with her about her school work as they drove over to meet with Evelyn and Mary. "I've had reports that you are doing very well in school. You aren't able to achieve the top marks but you are consistently in the top five or so. Your teachers feel that you are finally applying yourself to your full potential."

Danni stuck her lip out in a bit of a pout as she thought about the matter. She wasn't able to beat out the three people who were consistently the top mark getters in all subjects but she knew that she was doing what she could to achieve the best marks she could. Now that she wasn't as horny all of the time and worried about sex, she felt that she could make her mind concern itself more with her school work. It still wouldn't be enough to get her too many scholarships but that was why she was embarked on the path that she was. Her marks would get her into the university course that she wanted at whatever university she wanted to go to but wouldn't help her to pay for that privilege. So, she would need someone to pay her way and the best thing she had to offer for that was her young body and sexuality. The fact that she totally enjoyed being used in a sexual manner was just icing on the cake as far as things went. She gave Ms. Sturm a smile, coy little smile and stated "I'm trying to do the best that I can. I know that I am not quite as smart as some of my classmates but that doesn't mean that I can't make them sweat their marks sometimes." She paused for a moment to think and then continued "I'm not going to qualify for any real scholarships so I really do need your help in securing someone willing to pay my way. I want to thank you again for assisting me."

Ms. Sturm nodded and replied "As long as you are working at keeping your marks up, I am willing to help you. I know that you probably can't achieve the top marks but if you are trying, you can get marks high enough to qualify for what you want. That is really all that matters at this point. I can get you funding for your desires but you need to keep your marks at the level required. I can't help you there." She gave the young blonde a small grin and stated "But you have been doing well and I am quite proud to do my part in helping you where I can." She started the car and they drove to Evelyn and Mary's place in silence, each of them somewhat lost in their own thoughts.

Danni pranced up to the door and was starting to knock on it when Mary opened the door to admit her. Danni realized that Mary had been watching for her and wondered with a small flash of shame if she'd seen her walk exuberantly up to the door. Mary flashed Danni a crooked, sly grin to indicate that she had indeed seen the uninhibited display of happiness. Danni decided to ignore her slight feelings of shame and moved up quickly to give the older blonde woman a deep, intense kiss; using her tongue to probe the other woman's willing, warm mouth. Mary was initially startled by the determined display but soon warmed up to the task and returned the affection with interest. Evelyn had approached while they were kissing and had remained back, watching them with happiness. She liked the fact that Mary got to have some sexual action with someone as beautiful and willing as Danni was; she knew that their relationship was strong enough to handle the fact that Mary could find enjoyment in being with someone who wasn't as fat as she was. She knew they had a real emotional attachment that was worth more than the physical enjoyment that they might experience with other people. Besides, she loved the feel of Danni's body against her as well. So she waited patiently for them to satisfy their desires.

When Mary finally broke the kiss and fending off Danni's grappling hands so she could catch her breath and calm her speeding heart somewhat, she gasped "Wheh!

What's gotten into you, girl? You're as excited as I've ever seen you. What have you been doing?"

Danni grinned at her. She had been hesitant about talking about what she'd felt with Ms. Sturm because although she respected the other woman, she didn't feel that she would understand Danni's feelings on the matter. She thought that Mary might better comprehend and she felt that she would appreciate the older woman's thoughts on the matter. So she replied "I noticed the boys in school looking at me with lust so I decided to play up to them somewhat." She paused for a moment and then continued "I then discovered some rich bitches that have ignored me ever since I started in school with them watching me jealously." She paused again and looked down towards the floor before confessing "It really turned me on to know that they saw me as a rival and hated me. Is that wrong?" She wanted Mary to support her but was afraid that the older woman would castigate her.

Mary looked intensely at Danni, seeing how the young woman wanted to be reassured and replied "Well, it's not the best reaction you could have but it is a very human one." She broke out into a smile and continued "I know that I felt the same way when it first happened to me. It gives you a small feeling of power to know that men desire you and women dislike you." Then she frowned and said "But you can't let that consume you or you'll become very shallow. You're a beautiful, young, sexy, incredibly desirable girl, Danni and you need to learn to handle that with poise or you'll be eaten up by this cruel world." She saw that Danni was looking quite crestfallen and gave the young blonde an affectionate pat on her arm while saying softly "But you can enjoy it for today." Danni nodded and smiled in appreciation before moving to kiss the older blonde once again. Evelyn had watched the exchange without interfering and she respected what Mary had told Danni. She moved back into the living room without letting them know she'd been there so they could calm themselves before they joined her. Mary was aware that Evelyn was there and was now leaving; she valued that the other woman was willing to give her and Danni room to discuss important matters without inserting herself into them. It was one of the things that she loved about the heavy woman.

Danni got her feelings back under control while she lightly kissed and hugged with Mary. She was still feeling the need for release though and she soon began to almost tug Mary into the living room so they could join Evelyn and get started. Mary understood Danni's urgency but knew that delaying their fulfillment wouldn't hurt the young woman so she avoided Danni's attempt to grapple her arm and draw her into the living room. She enjoyed the slightly frustrated look that Danni gave her and broke out into a chuckle. When she laughed, Danni gave her a scowl as she recognized that Mary was teasing her so she gave her head a haughty toss and marched into the living room to join Evelyn. Mary realized that she'd given her game away and hurried after her so that she could enjoy the fun of watching Danni disrobe. It crossed her mind that Danni might be peeved enough with her to undress without her there and she would miss the display of that beautiful flesh. She had to admit to herself that she liked watching the young blonde woman undress and dress; she found it to be terribly erotic to watch the material glide across her soft, silky skin.

Danni had strode across to plant herself in front of the startled Evelyn and was already unhooking her dress, when Mary hurriedly took her place beside the other woman. Evelyn spared Mary a puzzled glance which the blonde woman ignored as she grinned at the somewhat angry Danni. Danni recognized that she was acting in a fairly childish way. In a way, she found the teasing of Mary to be quite arousing; she knew intellectually that the teasing was just another way that Mary expressed her love so she willed herself to calm down. She drew a deep, soothing breath and started to move slower as she unveiled her body to the two women. Mary could see that Danni had regained her composure and gave her a broader grin as she darted her eyes along the exposed skin. Danni unveiled her sexy bra briefly before lifting her dress back up to cover her restrained breasts. Then she held the light dress in place against her chest as she reached behind her and unhooked the bra with her right hand. She maneuvered to remove the bra from her body, pulling it off of her body without letting the women see her naked tits. She felt it was a sexy move and was pleased that the two women seemed to find it so as well. She then gave them a couple of quick flashes of her bare breasts one at a time while sporting a sexy, teasing smile. Mary pursed her lips and gave her a couple of wolf whistles at her action. Danni was surprised by the reaction but found herself warming to it. Then she pulled the dress down to her waist and began wiggling it slowly down over her hips. It wasn't as tight to her as she was making it out to be but she knew that her audience would appreciate the shaking of her ass. She took her time in getting the dress down her legs before stepping out of the clothing. She was only wearing her panties and heels now and both of the women could clearly see the damp crotch of the fabric that was covering her wet pussy.

Evelyn gave a low moan and Mary said, with a catch in her voice because of desire, "Why don't you come over here Danni so that we can remove your panties for you? You look like you're ready for some action, alright." Danni gave a fleeting thought to teasing her back but her desire for some action was too great. She eagerly moved forward to stand before the two older women. Mary moved off the couch to kneel before Danni and ran her tongue along the damp, fragrant patch on Danni's panties. She inhaled the musky perfume that Danni was exuding with incredible pleasure as she lightly began to stroke the younger woman's inner thighs. Danni gave a groan-sigh in anticipation of what Mary would do to her and used her hands to grab her breasts and pull on her own nipples to help excite her more. Mary caught the whiff of fresh juices from Danni's cunt and looked up to see what the girl was doing to arouse herself more. Danni found the vision of a woman kneeling with her face at her crotch, looking up at her, to be quite enticing and she felt the need to open her legs somewhat more to relieve her tension.

Mary giggled in happiness as she recognized how aroused Danni was. She slipped her right hand up through the leg of Danni's pink panties and quite roughly inserted three of her fingers into the young blonde woman's slick, wet cunt. Danni gasped as she felt the hard insertion but moaned in enjoyment, pushing her hips towards the thrust of Mary's fingers to be penetrated deeper and harder. Mary considered the situation. Danni was ready to explode, she thought, and it would be a shame to just waste it on her fingers. So she commanded "Evelyn, lay on your back so that Danni can straddle your face. She's as hot and bothered as I've ever felt her to be and you're gonna want to taste that sweet cum. I'll strip off her panties and then we can both play with her until she orgasms." Danni screwed up her pretty face and tried to hold in her climax as they did just that. She was having trouble containing it and could feel her inner thighs dampening with her cunt juices. She silently begged the other two women to hurry with what they were doing so that she could release herself.

Evelyn was barely down on her back before Mary pulled the soaking panties down Danni's toned legs. Danni didn't bother to step out of the panties but once they were down around her ankles and out of her immediate way, straddled Evelyn and pressed her wet pussy against her willing mouth. Mary laughed quite uproariously at the sight before freeing Danni's legs from her panties. As she was doing that, Danni climaxed onto Evelyn's face, giving her quite a coating of her juices. Evelyn loved the sensation of the hot cum on her face and the feel of Danni's soft velvety inner lips against her tongue. Danni whined in her need of a second release and while Evelyn used her mouth on Danni's cunt, Mary slid her fingers along the curve of Danni's left ass cheek to fondle the lower part of her cunt. Danni loved the attention of the two women and tried to press herself against both of their parts touching her. Mary had to fight off the giggles that threatened to overwhelm her and interfere with her stroking as Danni writhed her hips around in her attempt to get the maximum of touching from the two women. She looks like she's trying to do the hula, Mary thought hilariously. She recognized that Danni was just trying to achieve relief and tried to contain herself enough so that she could help provide it.

Evelyn positioned Danni into a more bent over position and started to suck on the young blonde's clitoris; she occasionally used her teeth to rake the sensitive organ causing Danni to hiss and moan. She understood that Danni liked the rough treatment and to ignore her barely muttered protests. Danni's noises just increased her own arousal as she imagined the same thing being done to her. Mary took the opportunity to once more penetrate Danni's blonde cunt with her fingers. Danni lowered herself down more onto Evelyn's well-padded body as she tried to improve the angle to let Mary finger her with more ease. She wanted the fingers inside her and stretching her out. Mary gradually worked Danni open enough to take all four of her fingers as the girl shifted and moaned as she relished the feeling of the digits inside her. Mary dipped her thumb into Danni's cunt juices and then used it to circle the young woman's asshole. Danni drew in a deep breath and stiffened her spine as she felt the caress on her rosebud. She was unsure of what Mary intended to do to her. She quickly cocked her head so that she could look at the other woman over her shoulder. Mary just gave her an enigmatic smile and was quite pleased to see Danni's body shiver a bit as she tried to calm her excited heart somewhat. Mary understood what sort of sensations she was creating in Danni and relished the feeling of power that it gave her. She knew that Danni liked the rush of uncertainty and fear that her action had caused to flood Danni's mind. She liked the same sort of thing and understood how erotic it could be. She wasn't going to penetrate Danni's asshole just yet but she wanted the younger blonde thinking that she might. There would be time at a later date to introduce Danni to the pleasures her asshole could bring her, she thought.

Evelyn had paused her own actions when Danni reacted but once she determined what had caused Danni's movements, she resumed what she was doing. It only took the two older women a few more minutes to force a second orgasm from the totally excited younger woman. Danni screamed three times at the top of her lungs as she climaxed. She tried as hard as she could to clamp Evelyn's face between her thighs and force her flowing cunt over the woman's mouth. But, even though Danni had strong thigh muscles, her cunt juices made it too slippery to gain purchase. Evelyn for her part, wrapped her arms around Danni's slim hips to pull the blonde's pulsing cunt against her warm mouth. Mary pulled back so as not to interfere with the two of them, letting them enjoy their pleasures. She paused for a few moments to watch them as they both slumped down and sought to recover their composure. She then decided to go to get a bowl of warm water and a half dozen washcloths so that she could clean them up.

When she came back, Evelyn was caressing Danni softly and was telling her what a good girl she was. Her face was covered and sticky with Danni's juices and Mary used a damp washcloth to begin cleaning it off. After a while, she let Evelyn take care of it while she used another damp washcloth to clean up Danni's crotch. She was somewhat amazed that Danni displayed that she had to energy to shift her hips around to allow the older woman more access to her sensitive areas. She gave some sighs of enjoyment as she did that and Mary was slightly tempted to give her a smack to try to force her to cease her wriggling but she really couldn't blame the young blonde from enjoying the touching. So she grinned at the happy but slightly dazed young woman and told her naughtily "Enjoy your rest right now, sweetheart. I'm going to fuck your brains out again as soon as you've recovered them. I'm gonna make you beg me to get my dildo out of you so that you can relax. I'm gonna make you whine and wriggle as my big, fat dildo reams your tight, little cunt." Danni was looking at her with increasing interest as Mary described what she was going to do to her. Mary was fully aware what effect talking hard and dirty would do to the young blonde and wasn't overly surprised when Danni started fondling her own tits again. She lightly smacked the young woman's hands away, stating "You're not allowed to provide yourself with any pleasure. You have to wait until one of us does that for you."

Danni looked at her with surprise and then burst out in happy laughter. "Then you better start fucking me and giving me some pleasure" she purred as she stretched to let Mary clean her up some more.

"I want you to be clean so that I can get you dirty again" Mary stated. "Why would I want to fuck a dirty, little girl?" she asked with a smile.

"Because this dirty, little girl wants to suck the knob off your dildo" Danni stated before groaning as Mary stuffed a washcloth up inside her pussy. Man, that felt quite intense and wonderful, she thought as she pushed her hips up at the other woman. Mary placed a hand on her soft belly and pushed her back down on the couch. Danni oofed a bit in surprise but didn't otherwise resist.

"I may get a bar of soap and wash the dirty, little girl's mouth out with it if she doesn't behave herself and let me get some of her nasty, sticky cum off of her pleasing, beautiful body. So lay there and let me wipe you down" Mary almost hissed.

"But you're just gonna get me all covered in cum and dirty again" Danni said in a mock whine. "Why don't you just impale me now and get me started?" She gave the older blonde a grin and stuck out her tongue impudently.

"God, what you two think of as sexy talk" Evelyn said with mock impatience as she joined them. "Twelve year old girls could do a better job of it" she complained. Both Mary and Danni turned towards her and stuck out their tongues before bursting into fits of giggles. Evelyn just smiled and began undoing Mary's clothes. Mary was a little surprised and gave her a questioning look. "How are you going to fuck the dirty, little girl if you're not naked?" Evelyn asked as she pulled off Mary's blouse. Mary grinned at her and started helping to remove her clothes. Danni watched the pair of them, unsure as to whether or not to join them; she figured that they were doing quite well without her help and just lay there to enjoy the strip show.

Soon Mary was nude and smiling down at Danni; she got up and went over to where they'd laid out the toys in preparation for Danni's visit to get her leather harness and Danni's favourite dildo. Danni had mentioned that she no longer had to pack her preferred toys with her over to Rose and Samantha's place because those two had gone out and bought similar ones for Danni. Mary fastened the pink dildo to her harness and began to lube it up as she walked over to where the young blonde woman lay waiting; Mary enjoyed the feeling of the long plastic cock bobbing in front of her crotch as she strode over. She grinned at Danni as she came over and climbed on top of Danni in preparation of penetrating her. "I should make you suck on this cock before I shove it into you" Mary stated, trying to get a nasty tone in her voice. "You should be forced to feel it all the way down your throat before you feel it all the way up your cunt. What do you think of that?"

Danni looked up at her in mock horror and replied "Oh, no. I don't think I'd like that at all. I'm a good, little girl." Danni waggled her eyebrows to contradict her words and suggest to Mary that she might indeed enjoy that if Mary wanted to do it to her. She licked her lips very suggestively.

Mary sighed in mock exasperation and stated "No, I have no time for that. I'm gonna ram this cock up your pussy right now and make you ride it vigorously. I'm gonna enjoy your screams of delight as it parts you entirely as I shove it in and out of you." Danni gave her a shiver as she anticipated the feeling of what Mary was proposing; she was totally looking forward to it. Danni raised her hips slightly to allow Mary better access to place the tip of the cock against her wet slit. Mary pushed the head of the dildo inside of Danni's cunt and then grabbed the slimmer woman's hips and pushed with her hips until Danni absorbed the full length of the plastic toy. Danni groaned loudly in pleasure as the dildo slid up into her until Mary's hips banged against her. She panted in her pleasure of feeling completely filled by the toy. Then she slowly rocked her hips to allow the toy to move in and out of her a bit as she lubricated it with her juices as her vaginal muscles stretched around it. Mary just held her in place as she became accustomed to the pink dildo inside of her; she was prepared to let Danni have the required time to loosen up enough that she could push and pull the dildo through the blonde's cunt. After a moment, Danni indicated that she was ready and Mary started to thrust and pull the dildo with her hips. Danni screwed up her face and moaned her appreciation as to what was being done to her.

Mary found Danni's noises to be intoxicating and she worked hard to ensure that the young blonde woman continue to emit them. She shifted her body so that the dildo changed the course that it penetrated Danni's cunt to give her maximum feeling of the plastic toy. She adjusted her pace so that Danni couldn't anticipate the thrusts even though the younger woman tried to time them and meet them with her own movements. This meant that she sometimes banged her hips quite hard against Danni's; rather than be upset by this, Danni growled her happiness at the rough treatment. Mary pushed down hard with her hands on Danni's shoulders to keep her pinned down as the younger woman bucked and writhed under her. She could feel herself getting tired but wanted to make sure that Danni orgasmed as hard as she could make her. The two women didn't waste their breath on speaking but just panted to inhale as much air as possible so that they could continue their actions.

Evelyn found the sexual action in front of her to be tremendously stimulating and arousing. She just sat back and watched the two of them go at it.

Danni started an almost constant whine as she felt her orgasm build deep inside her hips. The length and girth of the dildo inside her was wonderful in creating enough friction inside her slick cunt to push her physical sensations high enough that her body reacted in the normal manner. She was also aroused by the fact that it was Mary that was doing this to her. She found that the other woman stimulated an erotic sensation in her and her mind was flooding with endorphins because of that. Danni grunted and tried as hard as she could to arch her back against the heavier woman on top of her; she wanted to push her hips up against Mary so that she could take as deep a penetration as she could. She could feel the electric feeling overtake her as her cunt began to climax. She screamed in a feeling of victory as she felt fireworks consume her mind and she lost herself in her orgasm. Mary recognized that Danni was off in her own world even though her body was still arched against her. She held on to the younger woman as she moved around in throes of ecstasy, attempting with some difficulty to maintain her position. She knew that Danni would relax in a moment or so and that she would have to guide her back down into a comfortable position. She also realized that trying to push Danni into a fourth orgasm wouldn't work very well because of the intensity of the one she'd just experienced. It would be akin to beating a dead horse, Mary thought, a little snidely because she felt a stab of jealousy that Danni was able to experience such joy. She pushed her envy from her mind as best she could and just tried to feel pleasure in her part of making Danni enjoy her orgasm. Even though she was expecting it, she was surprised when Danni just relaxed her body and let herself fall back onto the couch. She adjusted the dazed girl's body so that she wouldn't recover with any cramps or soreness due to lying on some part of her body. She had the spiteful thought that Danni would probably have the feeling of some friction burns from the dildo and nastily enjoyed that for a moment before dismissing it from her mind.

Evelyn got off the couch and came up to her to stoke her back lightly while she was looking down at the dazed Danni and said "We should leave her alone for a while to recover. Do you want me to eat your pussy while we wait?"

Mary gave a sigh, stretched her shoulders slightly to remove a kink, and replied "No, I am fine for the moment. Just a bit tired. This young girl really takes it out of me sometimes. She's so strong and demanding."

Evelyn frowned and asked "Do you regret being with her, then?"

Mary turned to face her, letting a grin grace her face, and replied "Not on your life. She makes me feel the most alive that I have ever felt." She paused for a moment while she searched Evelyn's face before continuing "I love you and I cherish our fucking but for pure physical enjoyment, Danni is the best I've ever had. Does that bother you?"

Evelyn gave her back a giant grin and replied "No. I have to agree with you that Danni is the best. I love what you do to me, too, but I really enjoy being with Danni as well." She looked down on the now dozing girl and said slyly "We're both nothing but a pair of old perves, aren't we?"

Mary smiled at her and said "Let's go have some coffee and cookies. You should probably prepare a bunch of warm cookies for her. You know she's going to wake up starving." They moved off to the kitchen where Evelyn got the coffee and cookies going while Mary phoned Ms. Sturm to come pick up Danni in a short while. Ms. Sturm had told them not to keep Danni too long because she had schoolwork to do but had also told them to work her over hard so that she'd be satisfied. Mary felt that they had done exactly that and was feeling pleased with herself. She reflected that Danni would soon be too busy to accommodate them and that they would really miss her. But the best distraction for that, she thought, a little smugly, was to make sure that they used Danni as hard as she could stand while they had her.

After fifteen minutes, Mary went in and woke Danni, bringing her into the kitchen where Evelyn plied her with warm cookies and coffee. Danni had been in a fairly deep sleep but had woken totally clear-eyed and energetic. Mary felt a stab of envy that the young woman could recover so well; she remembered a time where she could almost do that but nowadays, she took a fair amount of time to get oriented when she'd been sleeping. Danni was surprised that they had already contacted Ms. Sturm; she'd wanted to do something for them, like they had done for her. They assured her that they had truly enjoyed themselves already and that she didn't need to reciprocate. Mary mentioned her schoolwork and Danni sobered and said that she did need some time to work on it. There was less than six weeks left in her school year and she needed to start preparing for finals as well as finishing projects. Danni knew that the two older women were showing her how much they cared for her and she was deeply touched by their actions. Ms. Sturm arrived a few minutes later and collected her, taking her home.

CHAPTER FOUR

The next afternoon Danni made her way back to Ms. Sturm's car; today she was more circumspect in her approach since her mind was concentrating on the fact that she had a math test coming up at the end of the week. She liked math but felt that it did not like her; she needed to work quite hard at it to keep her marks up. She had spent the previous night reviewing the material and still felt that she didn't have a good grasp on what she was supposed to know. She slid onto the passenger seat without doing anything more than nodding hello to Ms. Sturm. Ms. Sturm noted the difference in Danni from the day before and felt some concern; she decided that she needed to know what was bothering the girl so that she could help her with it. "What's eating at you, Danni?" she asked quietly. "Is there something that I can do to help you? Do you want to cancel your afternoon with Theodore?"

Danni sighed and slumped back into the seat as she replied "It's nothing that you can help me with. I'm just having problems understanding the math that we are doing right now. I can't seem to get a handle on it and I worry about the test I have at the end of the week." She paused for a moment and said "I think that visiting Theodore will help me take my mind off it for a while so that may help me. I'll make sure that I keep our session short though so that I can get back to studying." She gave Ms. Sturm a fairly tentative smile.

Ms. Sturm nodded and started driving. While they were on their way, she told Danni "I got the chance this morning to look at the video that Lydia made of you and Samantha."

Danni interrupted "Don't you think that we need to do something else? I know that Lydia worked hard on it but I don't think that it shows me in too good of a light. Maybe we can get Theodore to fuck me instead?"

Ms. Sturm didn't say anything for a moment but just concentrated on her driving. She was thinking about what Danni had said; she disagreed totally with the young blonde woman. She thought that Danni looked absolutely fabulous in the video with Samantha and she knew that men would find her irresistible. The way her face went slack and her eyes rolled when she was at the height of her orgasm was fantastically sexy and arousing. It also didn't hurt that Lydia had caught Samantha's smirk of triumph as she made Danni orgasm. Plus, Samantha looked gorgeous on camera as well. She had made plans to send the video out to many people for them to consider sponsoring Danni. She considered her options in handling the young blonde and her seeming insecurity about the video. She decided that being blunt was probably the best way to handle it. "Danni" she said with a sigh. "Neither you nor Samantha would ever look bad on film. The camera seems to love you. Your orgasm is one of the most arousing things that I have ever seen. Lydia and the people who have already seen it agree with me. Men are going to love the fact that you're getting off with another beautiful woman and will imagine being with the both of you. I know that Samantha isn't interested in being in a threesome with you and a man but they won't even think about that. Just being with you will be enough to set their hearts racing as they think about it. And women will want to be with the pair of you but if it is just you, they will still appreciate it. I want you to accept that while you don't think that the video shows you at your best, the rest of us see your vulnerability and sexiness in your actions and it turns us on. I suspect that I will have a lot of requests for copies of it even if the person has no ability to help you out." She looked over at Danni quickly as she continued "Would that bother you? If a lot of people wanted to see you orgasm, even though they aren't ever going to be your sponsor?"

Danni looked slightly stricken at Ms. Sturm. She was mortified that Ms. Sturm didn't agree that the video needed to be redone. Then she began to recognize that Ms. Sturm was telling her that it was incredibly sexy and that she should be proud of it. She puzzled about how other people could like it so much when she hated it. She didn't say anything as she thought about it. Ms. Sturm could tell that Danni was contemplating what she'd said so she didn't push the girl to answer her question. She hoped that Danni would come to the realization that she looked wonderful in the video and that they should distribute it to whoever may want it.

Danni hadn't made any decision by the time that they reached Theodore's place and Ms. Sturm felt that it was something that she should take her time about. So she said "Think about it and let me know. Tell Theodore that he has you for only an hour so he better work fast." Danni frowned at her about the time limit but didn't protest. She knew that Ms. Sturm wanted her to pay attention to her schoolwork and if she was worried about her math test, then she should be spending more time on it. Telling Theodore that Ms. Sturm set the time limit would make her blameless in his eyes and she was grateful about that. As Danni got out of the car, Ms. Sturm pondered her problem; an idea formed in her mind and she set off to start it in motion.

Danni was happy that Theodore greeted her warmly at the door, inviting her in and wrapping her up with a big, sloppy kiss. She could feel her body warming in his grasp as she started to whistle air through her nostrils as she suddenly felt a need for more oxygen. She let him keep her trapped for a couple of minutes before she decided that she needed to tell him about their time limit. She broke her mouth away from his and avoided him as he tried to engage her once more. She moved her hands up between them and gently but firmly pushed him away from her somewhat. "Ms. Sturm says that she's going to be back in an hour to pick me up and I have to be ready. So she says that you better get started fucking me right away. You know how she is. If you're in the middle of climaxing when she comes back, she'll storm in here and pull you off of me without hesitation." Danni almost giggled when Theodore gave her a stricken look; he'd expected to have some time with her and looked forward to warming her up to enjoy her at her best. Now, he'd have to cut down on what he had planned. He thought quickly that if he fucked her immediately without worrying if she climaxed, he could recover enough to enjoy her a second time before Ms. Sturm returned. He would use some toys while he was recovering to give her an orgasm. It wasn't the best option in his opinion but he felt that they could both endure that.

"Okay, I'm not happy about it but if that is how things have to be, we'll live with it" he told her. "I don't want Ms. Sturm mad at me because she'll be cruel enough to not let me have you at all and I certainly don't want that to happen. Having a short time with you is much better than no time at all." He grabbed her hand and hauled her down to his bedroom; Danni didn't mind being pulled along and tried to keep up with him. "We better get started" he told her. He began helping her to remove her clothing as quickly as possible. Of course, once she had her top and bra off, he delayed a bit to fondle her breasts, causing her nipples to perk up as she undid her skirt. She gave him a small glare as his hands got in the way of her actions of trying to get out of her skirt. She wasn't too surprised when he ignored her look to continue to squeeze her tits. She had to admit that it felt quite nice, though. She decided that instead of folding the skirt like she had intended to do, that she would just let it fall to the floor. Once they were done, she could take care of it. She hooked her thumbs into her panties to start them down her legs and wiggled her hips to let them slither to the floor. Of course, her movement in her hips also made her tits wobble and bounce and Theodore loved the feeling and sight of that.

She had to say, a little dryly "We only have a short time. Are you going to waste it by feeling up my tits or are you going to fuck me?"

Theodore gave her a slightly sheepish grin and said "I'm gonna fuck you but I really do enjoy your tits so when I'm recovering from my orgasm, I'm gonna come back to them." Danni grinned back at him to indicate that she was certainly fine with that as Theodore speedily removed his clothes. Danni tried to help him but she was actually slowing down proceedings by getting in his way. He gently placed her hands on her tits to indicate that she would do better by feeling herself up. She didn't take offense to his actions but grinned excitedly at him. He also stopped her from kneeling to take his cock in her mouth, which she did feel a bit peevish about, and indicated that she should just arrange herself on the bed. She gave him a small look of disappointment but did as he asked. He quickly sat beside her and used his right hand to massage her cunt to get her lubricating; he used his left hand to tweak her nipples. Danni began to give him some sexy, breathy moans that made his cock stand up and he bent in to kiss her mouth. She assumed that he was trying to shut her up and stopped with her noises. He broke the kiss long enough to whisper "No, keep going. I fucking love hearing you moan." He had trouble reinitiating the kiss because she started to giggle before she got herself under control; she did moan deep in her throat as they kissed and he could tell that he needed to be inside her immediately.

He pushed her down into position on her back and raised up her legs so her ankles were higher than her shoulders. She spread her legs open so that he could climb on top of her; she was beginning to get tremendously excited. He situated himself so that his cock was at the entrance to her pussy. He knew that she wasn't wet or lubricated enough to take him with extreme ease but he couldn't wait for that to happen. He understood that she'd feel some pain from his penetration and that he'd also experience some discomfort due to friction but he just couldn't delay long enough to get her fully ready. He made a silent promise to make it up to her and forced his erect cock into her. She grunted as he pushed his cock inside her and he groaned from his own pain. He was now partially inside her and he started to use his weight to penetrate her even more. Her vaginal muscles yielded to his pressure slowly and he now had his cock almost totally inside of her cunt. She was grunting and murmuring as he pierced her tight pussy and he found that it drove him wild. He pulled his body backwards so that his cock was now sliding back out of her body. Her pussy didn't seem to want to release his cock and he felt a fantastic pressure on his prick. He couldn't stand the pain any more so he reversed himself and pushed back down inside of her. He grunted from relief.

He worked her over slowly making his thrusts deeper and longer inside her as she started to lubricate the pair of them with her cunt juices. After a few minutes, he was moving fairly well in and out of her pussy. He was in bliss as he felt his balls begin to swell in preparation to orgasm into her. He looked down at her and noticed that she was steadily looking up at him. He could tell that she wasn't anywhere near the point where she would climax and he felt a small shiver of shame about that. But there was nothing that he could do to prevent his own climax at this point so he just selfishly enjoyed himself as he spurted his hot cum into her. He groaned with relief and let his body slump down onto her. She whined slightly as he made her take his full weight but he was beyond caring for the moment. He could barely feel her trying to move him into a more comfortable position for her as she lay beneath him.

Once Danni had him lying on her without feeling like he was crushing her, she ran her hand down in between her thighs to start caressing herself so that she could enjoy a climax. She didn't really expect that much help from Theodore for the moment because he seemed to be too much out of it. She got her fingers worked into her cunt so that they were pressuring a sensitive area and moved them in and out. After about five minutes, with her breathing increasing in pace as her arousal grew, Theodore put out his arms and levered himself off of her. She squeaked a bit in surprise when he first moved because she was so intent on her own feelings. He gave her a small grin and moved over to select a toy from the nearby table before returning. He held a multi-coloured, bulbous dildo which he inserted into her lubricated cunt. Danni grunted as he pushed each slightly larger section into her; she was enjoying the feeling that it was creating in her mind. He was well aware of what she liked and made sure that he put enough pressure on her to keep her highly aroused. Then he took a firm hold of the handle on the end and rapidly pulled the toy out of her tight, slick cunt. Danni yowled as the toy speedily left her and Theodore shoved it back into her before she could catch her breath. She screamed at this treatment but he was aware that it wasn't noises of pain that she was emitting but were noises of pleasure. Danni wriggled her hips around somewhat so that the angle of the toy and the places where it contacted her were to her satisfaction. Theodore gave her a brief period of time before he once more pulled the toy out of her cunt. They spent almost ten minutes doing this before Danni felt the electric beginnings of her orgasm. She screwed up her face and moaned her condition at Theodore; he knew that she wanted to be treated even rougher so that she'd cum harder. He complied with earnest, enjoying the sounds that she was making as her body took over from her mind.

Danni arched her back, pushing her hips up as high as she could manage, and screamed out her triumph as she pushed the toy out of her along with a fairly copious amount of cum. Theodore immediately let the toy fall to the couch as he grabbed the cheeks of her ass with his hands and buried his face in her pulsing cunt. He used his mouth to suck in her turgid clitoris and raked his teeth along it. Danni emitted a series of grunts approving of his actions. She used her hands to try to force his face deeper into her. Both of them were enjoying what was happening immensely. He worked her over for a few more minutes but wasn't able to push her into a second orgasm. She was more than satisfied with his efforts though. As she lost her arousal, she began to slump down and he felt the weight of her in his arms; he was aware that he could hold her up in position if he wanted to but knew that she was indicating that she wanted to be released. Therefore, he eased her down onto the couch and crawled back up onto her to kiss her slack, pleased face.

Theodore amused himself by using his fingers to tweak her nipples, enjoying how she moaned and muttered as he pulled on her sensitive nubs. He figured that he had a few minutes to wait before she recovered enough for him to fuck her once more. He could already feel his cock starting to twitch as his arousal level increased;

it would be a few minutes before he felt well enough to use it on the beautiful blonde again. After a couple of minutes, he could tell that Danni was beginning to recuperate because she tried to swat his hands away from torturing her tits. If he felt that she was being serious about the matter, he would have quit bothering her immediately but since she was only making half-hearted swats at him, he continued to tweak her nipples.

"Stop it" she moaned as she tried to twist her body underneath him. "Leave me alone. I'll bite you if you're not careful."

He paused to look at her face to see if she was serious. She frowned at him because he ceased in torturing her tits. He grinned, knowing that she wanted him to continue, and pulled hard on her right nipple. She screamed in apparent pain but pushed her breast harder against his hand. He squeezed the soft flesh as hard as he could and she moaned in enjoyment.

They continued with their play for a few more minutes with Danni writhing and pressing against him with her soft body. Soon he realized that he was getting quick stiff once more; he paused to assess his condition and decided that he could perform once more for Danni. Danni had noticed that he paused to evaluate his condition and she waited for just thirty seconds before she slipped her hand down to check for herself. Theodore was a bit shocked when Danni grabbed hold of his burgeoning erection and gave it a firm, but friendly, stroking. "Whoa, girl. Take it easy or I'm gonna cum all over your belly rather than deep in your cunt. And we both want me to orgasm in your pussy." He grabbed her hand and wrestled it away from his cock. Danni fought him but was happy to let him force her hand back up. She wanted him inside her again if he was feeling up to it.

"Well, big boy" she purred. "If you want to fuck me again, I want my pussy cleaned by your tongue. When I'm nice and clean, you can get me dirty again." She gave him her sexiest look. He laughed and she felt hurt.

He noticed her look of hurt and he apologized "Oh, Danni. I love you and you're tremendous fun to fuck. But you have to work on your dirty talk and sexy looks. It's not as easy as it seems and sometimes can seem ridiculous. We'll give you some practice during our time together but not today. Today, I'm gonna lick your pussy like you suggested and then fuck it as hard as I am able." He was pleased that she perked up somewhat and then plunged his face down to her crotch to begin slurping at her sticky cunt. He made sure that she was quite clean and could feel his cock was as erect as it could be.

So he maneuvered her down onto her back once more and got on top of her. He pushed his stiff cock up into her entrance and stopped to enjoy the feel of her soft flesh around its tip. She gave him a small glare and mouthed fuck me at him; she wanted him up inside her where she would achieve her greatest enjoyment. But he was content to hold his position for the moment while appreciating what he was about to do. Danni showed her impatience by bucking her hips up and forcing him deeper into her wet cunt. She was slick enough this time that he glided along her tight pussy with ease. He decided that since she had spoiled his pleasure somewhat that he might as well proceed. He didn't really feel any unhappiness with her; he knew that she had needs as well and he would do his best to fulfill them. Danni let him push her down onto the couch with his thrust. She made sure to wrap her legs around his back so that she could keep them out of his way and also steady him as he rode her. She ran her hands down his back, considering raking it with her nails; she decided that he might not enjoy that and she really didn't want to distract him from what he was doing to her. She did run them lower to cup the cheeks of his ass briefly though. She concentrated on timing his thrusts into her so that she could match them. She liked when she could do that and knew that Theodore also enjoyed that response from her. It really made her feel a part of the action rather than just a doll to be fucked. She'd heard that some women just lay there without moving too much and couldn't believe that they would do that. She'd also heard that some men liked that in their women. She knew that she would never be happy with a man like that; she liked to move and perform.

However, she was quite content to let Theodore take control of fucking her on this occasion and she watched his face as he thrust his cock into her. She could see the strain and happiness flash across his face as he worked her over. She contemplated grabbing his face as it came near hers and giving him a kiss of appreciation but thought that it might put him off his stroke and she didn't want him to stop. She moaned encouragement at him, knowing that he liked for her to make noise and then grinned as she thought that she really couldn't help herself. She felt the need to make sounds as his hard cock slid in and out of her cunt.

Theodore concentrated on keeping control of himself as he rode Danni as vigorously as he could manage. He heard her moaning, grunting and whining slightly below him and felt his attraction for her grow. He knew that she made most of the noises because she needed to but also recognized that she was aware that he liked her to be vocal during sex. He appreciated her vocal effort as well as the physical feeling as her body met his during his thrusts. She was a fantastic sexual partner and really pushed all of his buttons; he thought that she felt the same about him and that really helped with his mental arousal as well. He could feel his body tiring and felt that he was soon going to lose control and that would lead to his orgasm. He didn't think that Danni was tiring at all. He was quite amazed at her control and endurance. He screwed up his face and started to pant and moan at his effort to hold in his release so that he could continue riding her. He was aware that he couldn't last long in this condition. Danni sensed that Theodore was on the ragged edge before his orgasm and felt a small stab of disappointment. She knew that Theodore was lasting longer than he had earlier and was doing good compared to most men but she wanted the fucking to last forever. It felt so wonderful, she thought. But all good things come to an end, she mused, as she felt him orgasm into her; she wrapped her long legs tightly around him to keep him from removing himself from her. Theodore grunted slightly as Danni squeezed him in the tight, strong vice of her legs.

They lay entwined for a few minutes without speaking. Theodore fought to regain his breath and his composure although he wasn't as dazed as he had been for his first orgasm with her. Danni hadn't orgasmed but she'd loved the feelings he'd created in her by his efforts. She wasn't physically tired but recognized that Theodore was and had put forth more effort than her so she was content to rest and hold him to her. She did give some consideration to seeing how he might respond if she was to finger his asshole. She almost laughed out loud as she imagined his expression as she forced her finger into him. Theodore saw the fleeting grin cross Danni's pretty face and wondered what the mischievous little minx was thinking. He thought that it might be a good idea to get off of her before she did something to him that he might regret. He placed his hand down on her thigh to let her know that he wanted her to release him as he lifted his body. Danni glowered at him briefly before relenting and letting him go. She'd been enjoying their contact.

"We've got about ten minutes or so before Ms. Sturm will be here to collect you" he told her. "I know that you won't want to keep her waiting so I figure I should give you five minutes to get your clothes on to go with her. But we can spend five minutes cuddling if you want to." He looked at her expectantly. She thought about the suggestion for a few seconds to determine if that was what he really wanted to do; she got the feeling that he was going to enjoy simply holding her for a brief while. She nodded her agreement and was surprised when he immediately began to walk away. He looked back and called over his shoulder "I'll be back in a jiff. Remain there." So she lay back on the couch, decided that she needed a pillow under her head and reached up to pull one over to her.

Theodore was back in less than thirty seconds carrying a damp washcloth. He sat down beside her slim body on the couch and carefully but thoroughly began to clean her up. Danni lay there appreciating the feel of the fuzzy washcloth rubbing firmly against her soft skin; she especially liked the feel of it on her more sensitive areas like her breasts and groin areas. Theodore felt quite a bit of pleasure in watching how Danni enjoyed the simple domestic task of him cleaning her body off. He recognized that the young blonde woman appreciated the consideration that he showed her and he knew that he was definitely of the opinion that she deserved it and more. He found an awful lot to like in the young woman and thought that any sane person would. She was lively but extremely sweet in her personality. He hoped that she would never find herself involved with anyone who may cause her to change that lovely attitude.

He finished wiping her down and squirmed in beside her on the couch, pushing her towards the edge. Danni was concerned that he was going to push her off of the couch but he lifted her onto him as he worked his way under her. She realized that he was just positioning them so that they could cuddle without her having to bear his heavier weight. She squirmed around to assist him and rotated onto her side so that they could be face to face. He grinned at her and asked "Are you comfortable enough?"

"Yes, this is quite nice" she replied as she smiled back. "Thank you for cleaning me up. It was great too."

"Well, since I was the one who got you dirty, I figured I should take the time to clean you up." He gave her an even saucier grin and stated "I really liked doing it for you as well. You've got an amazing body." She frowned a bit, feeling somewhat slighted by that complement. She was more than just a beautiful body, she thought. Theodore realized his mistake at once and hastened to assure her "You're a wonderful, intelligent young woman with a fantastic personality as well." He looked her straight in the eyes as he stated "I don't usually spend a lot of time cuddling but I'm really enjoying this time with you. You know that, don't you?" Danni thought about it for a moment and then nodded her understanding and acceptance.

He sighed slightly and asked "You said that the test that you were concerned about and that Ms. Sturm wants you to study hard for was on Friday, didn't you?" Danni nodded carefully in agreement but didn't say anything. He continued "I was hoping that Thursday I could invite some men and we could see how well you might like taking a gangbang. I guess that will be out right now though. I'll talk with Ms. Sturm about it to see if we will have to change it. I guess we can do it next week if we can't do it Thursday." He examined her face and asked "You would still like to do that, wouldn't you?"

Danni had been thinking about how good a gangbang sounded. She knew that Theodore was assuming that she didn't have any experience in that direction and that he was totally mistaken. She'd been taken by multiple men twice before and had enjoyed it thoroughly. She gave some consideration to telling him that but decided that she didn't particularly need for him to know. She thought it might be better if he thought that he was the one who introduced her to things like that rather than having him know that she was gaining a lot of sexual knowledge from quite a set of sources. She licked her lips and said softly "I think that I would like that. But I really do need to pass that test and I am having trouble understanding this section of math. I need to spend whatever time I can trying to learn it." She looked quite miserable and he gently kissed her mouth.

"You do what you have to do, little minx. We have lots of time yet to explore things together." He paused and looked over at the clock. "Well, it looks like you only have four minutes to get dressed for Ms. Sturm." He got off of her and helped her to her feet.

Danni was happy but slightly pensive as she approached the car. She stopped in confusion as she determined that there were two people in the car. She frowned and concentrated on that fact for the moment wondering what Ms. Sturm might be up to; surely she wouldn't be introducing Danni to a client considering what she'd just been doing with Theodore. Well, she thought doggedly, there is only one way to find out. She walked up and opened the rear door for the small car and got in. The two women occupying the seats in the front turned so that they could look at her. The woman in the passenger seat was brown haired and eyed, somewhat plump and short and probably around thirty, in Danni's opinion. She was eyeing Danni as much as Danni was doing to her. Ms. Sturm was aware of this but content to let it go on for a moment. Then she broke the silence, stating "Danni, this is Anna Thelmont. Anna, Danni Archer." She paused to let them acknowledge their introductions.

Danni didn't address Anna but instead looked over to Ms. Sturm and asked "So why is Anna here?" She tried to do it in a calm, controlled manner but was surprised when she kind of squeaked the question out. She was more perturbed than she thought, she reflected.

Ms. Sturm gave her a firm smile and replied "She is here to help you with math. Anna is a math teacher."

"Not in my school" Danni squeaked out, cursing how she sounded. She noticed Anna smiling at her in an obviously, superior way and was further annoyed.

"No, Anna is not a math teacher in your school" Ms. Sturm confirmed in a supercilious tone. "She is a teacher at the private school for girls, Landry's School for Young Ladies. She was a woman who was in the top math classes at university who decided that she wanted to teach. Landry's was able to offer her the best salary so she ended up there. She should be able to tutor you with your math so that you can do well on your test." Anna still didn't say anything but kept looking Danni over.

"My mother will be expecting me to be at home" Danni protested.

"She will be going home with you and tutoring you there" Ms. Sturm informed her.

"How will I explain her?" Danni questioned.

Ms. Sturm recognized the question that was bothering Danni, how could she explain a tutor to her mother. "Samantha helped you to arrange her when you spoke to her about your concerns" Ms. Sturm replied.

"Mom will interrogate her about Samantha if we do that" Danni said.

Ms. Sturm frowned and thought for a moment before saying "Then you'll tell her that a parent of a child that you and Samantha teach dancing recommended Anna when Samantha put the question to them. Anna won't know who Samantha is so she can't be questioned about her. Your mother will simply have to accept her as your tutor."

Danni scowled as she considered the plan; it might work, she determined as she contemplated it thoroughly. She recognized what Ms. Sturm was doing for her but wished that she had chosen to talk to her about it before she did it. She thought that Ms. Sturm had some concern for her beyond being simply a commodity and that this was proof of that but it bothered her for some reason. "I guess that will work" she conceded grudgingly.

Anna broadened her grin and stated "I'm sure I can help you, Danni. Math can be fun if you look at it the right way." She didn't even flinch when Danni just scowled at her. She hated math and this woman wasn't going to convince her otherwise. Ms. Sturm just flashed a small smile and turned to drive them off to Danni's house. Anna kept herself turned so that she could watch and smile at Danni during the trip. Danni slowly felt herself losing her anger and beginning to warm to the woman. By the time they had arrived, Danni had decided to try as hard as she could to fulfill the trust that Ms. Sturm and Anna had in her to accomplish what they wanted from her.

Ms. Sturm let them off a half block from Danni's house to avoid her family noticing her. They got out and walked up to the door. Danni guided Anna into the house, pleased to note that the woman was wearing jeans and looking like an ordinary teacher and not anything else. Danni's mother came up to greet Danni and looked in surprise at the woman with her. She waited for Danni to explain with raised eyebrows.

Danni looked downwards and muttered "Mother, this is Anna. She's a math teacher here to tutor me so that I can pass my test on Friday. One of the parents in our dance class recommended her to Samantha when I requested help. We're just going to go study. Can we use the kitchen table for that?"

Danni's mother smiled welcome to Anna and they quickly shook hands and exchanged greetings. "You may use the table" she confirmed with a smile. She was pleased that Danni was applying herself so diligently to her schoolwork. "Have you eaten yet? We had hamburgers so there are a couple left over and I could make you some fries to go with them if you want."

"That sounds wonderful, Mrs. Archer" Anna replied with a brilliant smile. "We'll just get started while you prepare that, if you don't mind." Danni's mother smiled back and nodded her agreement. Danni started slightly as she realized she should lead Anna into the kitchen but recovered and did that. She opened up her books and started to explain what they were currently covering in math. She tried to explain her problem with what she'd been shown but wasn't really able to get the idea across to Anna. The woman covered the same information as Danni's math teacher because that was usually the way that students understood the work but it was obvious that

Danni wasn't able to integrate it in her mind. Danni's mother brought over the plates of food and the two of them spent a few minutes eating the hamburgers while Anna considered the problem. Danni smothered a grin as she realized that her mother had spent some time creating an attractive salad for them; she was sure that it wasn't just leftovers. It showed to her, that her mother wanted to display her approval of what she was doing and she felt the love that it implied.

After they had finished their food and thanked Danni's mother, Anna showed Danni a different way of looking at the math problems. Danni was amazed that she now started to feel some understanding about how to tackle the math problems. She demonstrated what she grasped and Anna encouraged her to continue and improved on her technique. Danni began to gain confidence in her knowledge of the subject as she worked through the questions. By the time they were done for the night, Danni knew that she would be able to do well on her test. She thanked Anna for helping her. Anna phoned her husband to come pick her up. Danni wondered why she hadn't called Ms. Sturm.

When her husband texted that he was waiting outside, Anna asked Danni to walk out with her. Danni wondered about that but complied. Anna took Danni up to her husband and introduced her. "Danni, this is my husband George." Then she stood there calmly as George looked rather hungrily at Danni as his eyes explored her body. Danni then understood part of the payment she would have to provide for her tutoring. She returned his looks and determined that he wasn't too bad looking and might just be fun in bed.

"I take it that I will be required to have sex with George as part of your payment" she said coolly to Anna without bothering to look over at her.

"Ms. Sturm felt that you would have no problem with that" Anna stated, slightly worried. "Do you? I also want to be a part of the action. I've only had a couple of lesbian experiences and want to be a part of a threesome with my husband and another woman. Is that going to be a problem for you?"

Danni looked over at her and smiled. "No, that shouldn't be too much of a problem. When is this supposed to happen?" She wondered what other conditions Anna had placed on her help.

"Ms. Sturm said that it couldn't be until after you've finished all of your tests. If you need any help in understanding anything else in math before your final test, contact me and I will show you how to solve the issue" Anna replied. She then looked towards the house to check to see that no one was observing them and determining that no one was, moved in and kissed Danni firmly on the lips. She shooed George back into the car, got in herself and they drove off. Danni stood there bemused for a moment watching them leave before going in to get ready to sleep.

CHAPTER FIVE

Danni walked towards the car in a pensive mood; her mind was occupied by her thoughts and she greeted Ms. Sturm in a slightly offhand manner. Ms. Sturm looked at her in worry; Anna had assured her that Danni was confident and prepared for her math test later in the week but it didn't seem like that to her. "What's on your mind, Danni?" she asked with concern.

"Oh, nothing much really. I just heard something that made me think about my future and everything. I'm not too sure how I feel about things right now and I'm just kinda muddled up. I don't know how I should feel regarding my choices" Danni replied with tears starting to glisten in her eyes.

Ms. Sturm looked at her with alarm; this was not how Danni usually was and definitely wasn't how she expected to find her. "Are you regretting your choices then, Danni?" she asked as she prepared herself to hear the answer.

After a few minutes of thought, Danni answered "No, not really, I guess. I wonder if I should be though and that kinda worries me." She met Ms. Sturm's eyes and said "I know that you have put a lot of work into me and I am terribly grateful for what you have done for me. I don't want to disappoint you." Ms. Sturm made a waving motion with her hand to dismiss the importance of what she'd been doing for Danni but Danni still felt a great obligation to her. "I'm not sure what you've had to pay Anna for her help. It's just one more thing that I owe you for." She turned away to let a few tears leak down her face.

Ms. Sturm grabbed a firm hold on Danni's chin and forced her head around so that she could meet her eyes. "Do not worry about what I promised Anna. I really didn't offer her any more than I would have if she'd been seeking a favour and I didn't need for her to help you. The main payment to her is to be yours. I got the impression that she talked about it with you. Is that what is worrying you? Being with her and her husband? I didn't think that it would be a problem for you but if it is, I will make alternate arrangements."

"No, no" Danni protested. "I am fine with that. I'll likely enjoy myself as I always seem to do. It's just everything." Danni pulled her chin out of Ms. Sturm's hand and looked out the window.

Ms. Sturm looked at her, mystified. She was aware that teenage girls could be fairly moody but Danni usually wasn't. She thought that she needed to know what set this mood off so that she could do something about it. "What is bothering you, Danni? I want to help you but I need to know why you're so despondent suddenly. Did someone say something that upset you? Did I do something to upset you? Talk with me, Danni."

Danni sighed and said "A girl I know, Julie, told us that she is pregnant and won't be able to continue on with her education. She's gonna have to marry the boy who screwed her, even though it was only once when she was drunk at a party. Her and his families are insisting on it. She'd hoped to become a lawyer and is now literally screwed. She doesn't love the boy and thinks that she doesn't even really like him but now she has to be married to him. She's very upset about it. I was just thinking about what would happen to me if I end up in similar circumstances and it depressed me."

Ms. Sturm looked angry and asked "What is Julie's last name?"

Danni gulped and replied "Julie Starmont. You're not angry at me, are you? I don't want you unhappy with me. I'll try to do my best for you." She was dismayed to see that Ms. Sturm was so angry that she could hear her breath whistling through her nose as she clenched her jaw tight.

Ms. Sturm softened her gaze as she replied "No, Danni, I'm not upset with you. It's just that some people insist that other people have to meet an unfair moral challenge and I don't agree with it." She looked intent at Danni and said "You know that if you end up pregnant and don't want to bear the child, that you have a choice in the matter, don't you?"

Danni gulped again, thinking about the matter of abortion and whether she would feel right about going through with that, before nodding and squeaking out "I know that, Ms. Sturm. But I'm not sure if I would feel right with myself if I did something like that." She then began to tear up again as she continued "But Julie doesn't even have that choice. Her family would never allow it and she needs them to support her. She doesn't want to end up being poor and unwanted."

"She doesn't have to be" Ms. Sturm assured Danni. "I will arrange to talk to her. If she doesn't want to have an abortion, I can arrange things so that she can go to school, bear the child and give it up for adoption to a good home. I'll make sure that she is taken care of so she doesn't have to marry a boy she doesn't like."

"Why would you do something like that for her? You don't even know her." Danni frowned and then asked "Do you?"

Ms. Sturm smiled and replied "No, I don't know her, Danni. But part of what I do, with some of the women that I am involved with, is to help young women out of situations that they may get themselves into. That is what I have promised Anna. She has a couple of girls that need some assistance and I will help them. You don't need to know what they have involved themselves in so I am not going to tell you. Just be cognizant that I can and will help Julie out. I am not doing it for you. I am doing it for her. I don't want you getting yourself into trouble just because I may be able to help you. You are taking birth control, aren't you?"

Danni nodded vigorously and replied in a steadier voice "Of course, I am. Mother insisted on me knowing about it and getting a prescription a couple of years ago. She would be most upset to find me in a situation like Julie." She paused as she thought and continued "She would be the first one to help me decide what to do though and would support me no matter what."

Ms. Sturm nodded and said "She certainly would. But obviously Julie doesn't have that support and I will ensure that she gets it. Do you want to go home so that you can think about your future? We can talk about it in a few days. If you don't want to continue how we have been, I can accept that and will make arrangements for something else." She looked steadily at Danni as she thought.

Danni spent a few minutes contemplating things and said "Damn it, I'm not going to let what happened to Julie make me question myself. I don't believe that I am going to turn out like that. Not that it is entirely her fault. I want what we discussed and think that you will help me achieve it. I like sex. And I like most of the people that you have introduced me to." She gave a brief grin and said "We both know the one exception." Ms. Sturm nodded without saying anything. "I want to continue and I want to go to Mary and Evelyn's place" Danni said firmly.

"Okay now that that is settled, we have a few more things to discuss" Ms. Sturm said firmly. "Anna said that you were feeling confident about your math test. Theodore has been pestering me about getting you gangbanged tomorrow. Do I put him off? And why does he seem to think that this will be a new adventure for you? Haven't you told him about your other exploits?"

Danni gave a sly little grin to Ms. Sturm and replied "Anna is right. I am feeling much more confident about the math test. I think I can handle going over to Theodore's tomorrow to get gangbanged. I didn't tell him about other matters because I didn't think he needed to know about them." She looked quite steadily into Ms. Sturm's eyes.

Ms. Sturm grunted and said "I agree that Theodore doesn't have to know everything that happens to you and neither does Samantha for that matter. But you better not keep anything from me. I want to know what happens to you and what you are thinking. I need to know in order to help you. Do you agree?"

Danni just nodded meekly while keeping a steady gaze on Ms. Sturm's face. Ms. Sturm was satisfied that Danni understood and would keep her informed so she started the car and they drove to Evelyn and Mary's place. Danni trotted up to the door where Mary quickly opened it and greeted her.

Danni broke the warm, wonderful kiss with Mary after a moment and suggested breathlessly "We should probably go so I can also greet Evelyn." Mary nodded, a bit reluctantly, and put her arm around Danni's slim waist so she could walk her into the living room. Danni was a bit shocked when Mary cupped the cheek of her ass and then gave her a firm pinch as she guided her in. She bumped her hip against Mary to show her that she enjoyed the treatment and Mary quickly pinched her again. Evelyn watched the pair of them playing and she felt a surge of happiness for the three of them.

She smiled at Danni as they approached, opened her arms for Danni to slide into, and said, teasingly "Finally, you deign to allow me to enjoy your presence. I was wondering if the two of you got lost. It's such a long way from the front door to here." Danni just flashed a smile and slipped in beside the heavy woman while Mary stuck her tongue out at her partner.

"Mary and I were just showing each other how much we'd missed one another" Danni said loyally. She kissed Evelyn with similar enthusiasm for more than a moment before saying "Surely you can't blame us for that." She gave Evelyn an impudent grin. Evelyn just harrumphed and screwed up her face to wrinkle her nose at the young blonde showing some disagreement which caused Danni to smile even more.

Mary moved over and started to disrobe Danni who twisted her body so that she had easier access. Soon Danni was totally nude. Mary had fondled her a great deal as she worked the clothes off of her and she was feeling fairly aroused. Her pink nipples stood firmly erect and she lightly stroked them. Evelyn noticed what she was doing and pushed her hand away so that she could take over. Evelyn pulled harder on Danni's sensitive flesh and made the younger woman gasp in pleasure. Mary had ran her hand down the curve of Danni's ass to stroke the lower part of Danni's dampening slit. Danni closed her eyes as she enjoyed the feeling of the two older women's hands on her more intimate parts; she was content to let them stroke her for more than a few minutes.

Mary could tell that Danni was ready for more because her cunt was becoming quite juicy and she placed her hand in the middle of the younger woman's back to push her down onto the couch. Danni tried to kneel on the couch but Mary grabbed the soft flesh of her inner thigh to prevent her. Danni huffed in surprise at this move but soon understood that Mary wanted her to bend over but remain standing. Mary turned Danni slightly as she sat down on the edge of the couch and placed her face against Danni's silky rear end. Mary speared Danni's wet cunt with her tongue, wiggling it inside the younger woman, making her groan in delight. Danni wiggled her hips slightly to encourage Mary to continue with what she was doing to her. She then realized that Evelyn had continued to fondle her breasts, pulling firmly on her nipples. She felt a great deal of arousal by their actions and started holding her breath as her body responded. The three of them continued their actions for a few minutes as they all enjoyed what was happening. Danni could feel the beginnings of an orgasm forming inside her and started to whine as her need increased.

Mary recognized the sounds that Danni was making and thought about continuing with her tonguing until Danni was able to achieve her climax. She decided that she would probably get tired before making Danni orgasm so she moved away from Danni. Danni felt Mary stop with what she was doing and wailed a bit in frustration; she wanted the other woman to push her into climax and now she was leaving. Mary just smiled and gave her a sharp smack on her ass as she got up. Danni turned and gave her a look of desperation. Mary moved over to the table of toys and selected a short, thick vibrator. She brought the toy over and began to to run it around the entrance to Danni's sopping pussy. She enjoyed Danni's gasps and moans as she enjoyed the feeling of the plastic on her flesh. Mary spent a moment or so, making sure that Danni's juices coated the thick toy before she pushed it up into the young blonde's willing cunt. Danni moaned as she was penetrated, relishing the feeling of her cunt lips spreading over the vibrator. She tried to push her hips down to absorb the toy deeper inside her but Mary gave her another smack on the ass and pulled the vibrator away from her. Danni was astonished by the treatment and grunted in disapproval, she wanted that toy inside her and was surprised that Mary was denying her it. Mary was feeling a great deal of satisfaction from teasing the younger blonde. She knew that Danni wanted to orgasm but that she would experience a much more intense one if she was denied it for as long as possible. She also recognized that Danni actually loved being teased and denied even though she gave voice to many protests as it was occurring. She felt a thrill of superiority as she deprived Danni of her desire; she knew that she would be as frustrated as the younger blonde if someone was doing the same thing to her and she felt her own arousal level rise at the thought.

Danni had straightened up somewhat as Mary pulled the vibrator away so Mary once again pushed her back into position. Danni growled at her and she giggled before giving her a smack on the ass once more. Danni felt a small surge of enjoyment as she was hit and wiggled her ass a bit. Mary ignored her invitation and once more guided the toy into Danni's cunt, letting her have only a third of the short length. She knew that Danni wanted the full length inside her but wasn't prepared to let her have her wish right then. She turned the vibrator on to its lowest setting and it just barely buzzed. Danni moaned as she felt her body begin to lose its arousal level. Mary delighted in the younger woman's distress for a moment or two and then started to ramp up her actions.

Danni groaned happily as she felt Mary increase the pressure on her. Mary pushed her down so that she was now lying on the couch with her ass raised up to give Mary access to her cunt. Evelyn felt Danni being pushed against her and moved backwards to give the girl more room. She knew that Mary would be working Danni over vigorously to give her an intense orgasm so she stopped fondling Danni and shifted over so that she could pay some attention to Mary's larger breasts. Mary was surprised when Evelyn moved over and squeezed her tits but she enjoyed the attention. She pushed the vibrator hard up inside of Danni so that the young blonde was encompassing the full length of the toy and turned it up to its highest setting. Danni gave a pleased yelp as the toy buzzed noisily inside of her. She could feel the pressure building in her as she leaked out juices. Mary left the toy inside of her and used her fingers to flick Danni's swollen clitoris as hard as she could. Danni moaned loudly and shifted her hips so that Mary had better access to her sensitive clit. Mary fondled and pulled on the sensitive bit of flesh as Danni writhed and groaned. Mary could see by the intensity of Danni's expression that she was close to climaxing and gave some thought to shutting off the vibrator to make Danni wait even longer for her relief. She decided that doing that would be too cruel to the younger woman so she just gently began to massage the lower part of Danni's cunt lips. Danni was initially confused by the gentler treatment but then found it to be caring and compassionate; it increased her erotic level. Danni grunted hard as she started to climax. Her vaginal muscles clamped hard around the vibrator; she loved the feeling of it deep in her as she climaxed. She keened in pleasure as she let her body do what it was made to do.

Mary grinned as Danni made her noises of pleasure and looked over at Evelyn to question if she wanted to clean Danni's pussy up. Evelyn nodded that she was interested so Mary tried to pull the vibrator out of Danni. She was slightly shocked when Danni clamped her cunt around it and refused to give it up but grinned in pleasure at the younger woman's actions. She turned the vibrator off and worked three of her fingers in around it. Danni moaned as she felt her pussy entrance being stretched even more; it felt incredible. Mary took firm hold of the toy and pulled it out. There was a small audible pop as Danni's slick cunt gave it up. Danni moaned in distress that turned to pleasure as Evelyn's nimble tongue replaced the toy. She shifted herself so that Evelyn had more room to work on her.

Evelyn energetically tongued her as Mary went off to get wine for all of them and cookies for Danni. She also got a small plastic basin of warm water and four washcloths for cleanup of the pair of them. While she was in the bathroom, she carefully washed off the vibrator before taking it back to the toy table. When she was done these tasks, she returned to find Evelyn finishing up. She dampened a washcloth and wiped down Evelyn's face gently. Evelyn was a bit surprised that Mary chose to clean her up first rather than Danni and felt a surge of love for her partner. She grinned her appreciation to Mary who nodded in return and mouthed 'I love you' to her. Danni watched their affectionate display with warmth; she was very happy with the love they showed in one another. Mary looked over to where Danni was now leaning back and watching them. She quickly shot out a hand and tweaked one of the young blonde's nipples eliciting a shriek that turned into laughter from the younger woman. The two of them grinned at one another and

Evelyn knew that her tender moment was over and that Mary would be occupied with Danni. She regretted it slightly but dismissed it from her mind. She took another washcloth and started to clean Danni up. Danni gave her a dazzling smile as she moved around to let Evelyn get at all parts of her body. Mary caressed Danni's breasts as Evelyn did this.

When Evelyn was done, Danni was feeling quite fine and sat up. She hugged both women and they sat there drinking their wine and chatting. Danni gobbled down the ten cookies that Mary had brought out for her. Danni wanted to do something sexual so she quickly began stroking both women to get them in the mood as well. Both of them smiled at Danni's enthusiasm even though they hadn't fully recovered enough to get too aroused. They were once again impressed by Danni's fast recovery. Evelyn decided that she needed more time before doing anything further so she encouraged Danni to play more with Mary. Mary just grinned at this, she knew that Danni could arouse her quite easily even if she was somewhat tired from their actions because she found her so enticing. Mary stroked the back of Danni's head, feeling her soft, silky hair as Danni used her mouth on the older woman's nipples. Danni ran her tongue and teeth over the sensitive flesh for almost five minutes making Mary's nipples glisten with her saliva. Mary could feel how hard they were and was making moaning sounds every time Danni applied any pressure to them. She was surprized at how wet she was without Danni even touching her cunt. Danni pushed Mary down onto her back and moved so her mouth was now one her wet pussy. She could smell Mary's musky scent and inhaled it deeply. Mary watched as Danni positioned herself. "You don't have to do this, Danni" she said softly thinking that Danni was only eating her out because she felt she needed to reciprocate.

Danni frowned and stated "I know I don't have to do this. I want to do this. Both you and Evelyn are always making me orgasm and I want to try to do the same to you. If I am to be a good sex partner, I should do what I can to please whomever I am with. I know that I'm not as good at this as the two of you are but I think that I will get better with practice." She looked at Mary and asked "Or are you reluctant to be my guinea pig?"

Mary laughed fairly loudly and replied "No, Danni, I'm not reluctant to be your guinea pig. My cunt is always wet for you and if you want to practice your cunnilingus, I'm prepared to lie on my back so that you can put your tongue up my pussy. I hope that you will at least allow me to direct you somewhat without feeling too affronted about it."

Danni grinned and said "I know that you will only be trying to teach me so feel free to tell me what to do." She ran her tongue over Mary's wrinkled inner lips that peeped out of her cunt. They felt quite velvety to her tongue. Mary shivered at the soft feel of Danni's tongue and shifted her hips; she gave a groan of appreciation.

"That felt nice, Danni, but you need to work me harder and faster to get me more aroused" Mary instructed. "Stroke my clit while you're licking me. That will help me build my orgasm." Danni quickly returned to her task, attempting to do exactly what Mary had told her to do. They proceeded for nearly ten minutes. Mary enjoyed what Danni was doing but she wasn't able to generate the orgasm in Mary and Mary could see that the younger woman was now faltering. She stroked Danni's head lightly and pushed gently at it. "That was fine, Danni, but it doesn't seem that I am going to orgasm right now." Danni sat up in frustration. Evelyn had been watching and now she moved Danni out of the way and replaced her. Mary hadn't really expected that but lay back compliantly for her partner. She knew that Evelyn would be able to make her climax in short order because she knew exactly what would work on her. Danni aroused her mind but Evelyn knew exactly what parts of her body to touch. Danni felt some disappointment in herself as she watched as Evelyn quickly got Mary to start breathing hard. She knew that the two older women knew each other better than she did but she decided that she would try to get as much practice as she could. She swallowed her feelings and moved so she could caress Mary as Evelyn made her climax. Both older women welcomed her with smiles.

When the action was over Evelyn moved away and gestured and pushed Danni into position so that the younger woman could cuddle with Mary while she recovered from her climax. Evelyn had done it hundreds of times with Mary and knew that she would appreciate it more if Danni were to do it. Danni felt somewhat honoured that Evelyn would let her do that and she snuggled in against the other woman with enthusiasm. She made low cooing sounds in her throat as she hugged and stroked the other woman. Mary smiled happily at her in a slight daze. Danni decided the other woman was recuperated enough but still somewhat stunned so that she would be compliant in answering some questions for her. "What exactly is Ms. Sturm? Does she truly help people who need assistance?"

"You know who Ms. Sturm is, Danni" the older blonde told her unhelpfully. "And she helped us to find each other." Danni glowered slightly at her.

Evelyn hadn't been far away enough not to overhear, which Danni had hoped was the case, and she came over and asked Danni "What are you trying to find out about Ms. Sturm, Danni?" Danni sighed and relayed the story of Julie. She was pleased to see that further understanding slowly crept back into Mary's eyes as she talked. "Danni, Ms. Sturm will do as she told you she would" Evelyn stated as she comfortingly stroked Danni's bare back. "She has many friends who help her. She will help any woman in need and it sounds like your friend needs help." Danni didn't bother to correct the older woman and tell her that Julie wasn't a friend, just someone she was acquainted with; it didn't really matter.

"I know what she is doing for me and I appreciate all she has done for me" Danni stated. "But Julie doesn't really have anything to offer her for her help like I do.

Will she really make sure she is alright? Has she helped either of you?" She was surprised to see the two women share a look before glancing back to her. "What?" she demanded.

Mary sighed and said "Ms. Sturm has helped Evelyn and I, also Samantha and Rose and a few others you have come in contact with. I was in a bad marriage with a man who was beating me. I was terribly confused by his actions and my own feelings of sexuality. Ms. Sturm not only got me away from the man but she helped me to recognize that I liked women more than men. I'm terribly grateful to her for that." She gave Danni a look to show her that she was sharing one of her most intimate secrets and Danni felt honoured to hear it. She hugged the other woman to show her that she appreciated the tale and understood the effort it took to tell it.

Evelyn made to tell her own story but Danni stopped her, saying quietly "I appreciate that you want me to know your story but I don't need to hear it right now. If you feel that you would feel better by telling me it, I will listen attentively, but if you don't feel that need, please save it for a later time between us." She gave the older woman a look of compassion and honesty. Evelyn nodded and paused to think for a moment. Then she indicated that she would save her tale for another time while Danni held Mary who was softly crying because of what she'd relayed to Danni. Danni was conflicted. She felt closer to Mary, knowing her past somewhat and understanding some of her problems, but understood that it dismayed the other woman that she knew of some of her secrets. She felt some horror that the older woman had undergone such difficulties but knew that it had made her a stronger woman. She was pleased that Mary told her that Ms. Sturm had been involved with helping her. Danni tried to sort out her feelings. The two older women also were sorting out their feelings. The three of them sat there quietly for more than five minutes as they composed themselves.

They went into the kitchen where they drank some coffee and Evelyn persuaded Danni to consume another half dozen cookies. They chatted about inconsequential things for the forty minutes they waited for Ms. Sturm to arrive to take Danni home. No one felt like doing too much since all of them felt rather drained emotionally.

Ms. Sturm could tell that Danni wasn't feeling as chipper as she usually did when she finished up with Mary and Evelyn. She wondered if she should try to force Danni to talk about it but decided that she would leave things alone for a couple of days. If Danni hadn't snapped back to her usual self, she would force the issue then. She had some information to impart to Danni and some decisions to make about the next few days so she would discuss those matters with her. "I have started things in motion to help Julie" she stated firmly. "She will be taken care of. Theodore wants you to join him and three men so that you can get gangbanged tomorrow. I need to let him know as soon as possible. Are you feeling up to doing that?" She looked expectantly at the young blonde.

Danni grabbed her upper lip in her teeth and pursed her mouth as she considered the matter. She decided that she would enjoy herself doing that so she said "Yes. I am feeling up to doing that. I think it would do me good. I am quite confident that Anna has taught me what I need to know to pass my test and the physical activity will relax me and put me in a good frame of mind to write the test." She looked over to Ms. Sturm and asked "Do you think it's a good idea?"

Ms. Sturm looked at Danni steadily for a moment and then replied "I think that you know your body and moods better than I do. I trust your judgement in this matter. If you think you are up to it, I think you should go ahead and do it. However, I think that you should take Saturday off and spend the time with your family. You are going to see them less and less over the rest of your life and you should enjoy it while you are able. They are good people."

Danni nodded a little somberly but said "I will do as you suggest." She thought about teasing a little and asking what she should do if she got horny but decided not to try to lighten the mood that way. "But I can still go out with Samantha and Mary Friday night?"

Ms. Sturm nodded and stated "Yes, especially if you feel you've done well on your test. You can enjoy yourself as much as you can. Another matter we have to discuss is that I am going to take you away from Evelyn and Mary on Wednesday afternoons in two weeks. They will have you only on Monday and Friday up until you graduate."

"Why?" Danni asked, feeling quite perturbed. "I like being with them and I think that they are helping me discover myself."

Ms. Sturm frowned at her, unhappy with her display of discontent and said quietly but firmly "You have outgrown them, Danni. You are ready for more and they know it. You also owe some other people and may not have too much opportunity to reward them before you graduate. Things are going to change for you once you graduate."

"Who am I going to spend my time with, then?" Danni asked despondently.

"You will be spending that time with Samantha and Rose" Ms. Sturm stated. "They have been a more significant part of your growth than I thought they would be and you need to reward them for that help. It's going to be harder to do later so you will do it now. Are you going to fight me on this issue?"

Danni was surprised that it would be Samantha and Rose and her happiness about it outweighed her dismay. "No" she replied quietly and seriously. "If that is who it is going to be, I won't put up any argument. I know that they have helped and I enjoy being with them. Do I have to tell Evelyn and Mary or will you?"

"We have discussed the matter and they are aware that it is coming. Do we need to talk about anything else before I take you home?" Danni shook her head negatively so Ms. Sturm drove her home.

When Danni entered the house, her mother was watching a comedy with Kate and Molly. Danni sat on the edge of the couch and waited for a commercial so she didn't disturb them. Her mother noticed Danni waiting to talk and as soon as the commercial started, she muted the television and asked "Did you want something, Danni?"

"I was just wondering if anything was planned for Saturday night" Danni said.

"No, there's nothing planned. Gina was hinting that she would like to go to the movies with a couple of her friends but that was it. Did you have anything in mind?" Charlene Archer asked her daughter with a small smile.

"I was thinking of staying home and maybe playing some board games with all of you. I may not get too much more chance to do that" Danni replied.

Her mother nodded and said "That sounds good. Let's plan that." Danni nodded and went up to her room.

CHAPTER SIX

The next afternoon, Danni was once more headed towards Ms. Sturm's blue car; she was feeling quite happy, having had a good day in class and was looking forward to what she was going to be involved with. Danni slung her backpack into the car and followed it in, landing with a small thump. Ms. Sturm noted Danni's exuberance and approved of her happy mood; obviously the down mood from the prior day was forgotten. Ms. Sturm looked Danni over as she sat there and grinned back at her. "Are you looking forward to being with Theodore and his friends today?"

"You betcha" Danni cooed. "I'm hoping to get fucked silly."

Ms. Sturm eyed Danni coolly and said, slightly snidely "That may not take too much to do." She smiled to take the sting out of her words and Danni just shook out her hair without replying. Ms. Sturm flashed another smile at the young woman and said "I'm glad you've recovered your good mood. Let's get going. I'm sure that the men are looking forward to meeting with you as well." She started the car and drove over to Theodore's place. She bid Danni a good time and drove off.

Danni walked up to the door; she'd left her backpack in the car and had worn one of her shorter skirts to school. She'd been quite pleased to notice most of the boys in school looking at her legs all day. She'd even noted that a couple of her male teachers had given her a once over. She'd been somewhat surprised to catch a few girls and one of her female teachers also examining her legs. So she knew that she looked fairly good and that boosted her confidence. When Theodore answered the door, she hesitated about jumping into his arms as she usually did, since there were other people in the apartment. Theodore solved matters by reaching out and pulling her into his arms. She kissed him eagerly, rotating and grinding her mouth all over his. Theodore reached down to cup the cheeks of her ass and pull her hips into his so she could feel how hard his cock already was. Danni wriggled her hips so that she could enjoy the feeling of his erect cock grinding against her hips. By the increase in Theodore's breathing, he also enjoyed her maneuvers. They amused themselves like that for a few minutes until the three men waiting for them decided that they had to interrupt. They came out to see what was keeping Theodore and Danni. They were eager to see the girl that they would be fucking. Theodore had described her as beautiful and eager to be fucked.

Danni noticed the men over Theodore's shoulder and pushed herself lightly away from him; she wanted the men to look at her because she was excited to discover their impression of her. She was ecstatic to see that they were all looking her over with expressions of desire. She smiled and posed for them so that they could observe her beauty. Theodore let them alone for a couple of moments before he grabbed Danni's hand and led her into the living room. The four men had rearranged the living room so that there was an area where they could fuck Danni while the rest of them watched the action. Theodore was aware that Danni had no aversions to being watched. He was surprised that two of the men had expressed some apprehensions about performing in front of everyone though. He'd told them that they had the choice of fucking Danni here or not at all. He wasn't about to let them be alone with her. The men had all agreed.

The men rushed in behind them and found seats around the open area that Theodore had led Danni to; he began to undress her. She stood there grinning happily at him as he undid her silk blouse. He made sure that he took his time because he wanted to build up the tension in the men watching. Danni, however, also wanted action and she was trying to assist him in getting her clothes off; he had to smack her hands away a couple of times before she desisted. She frowned and moaned her need at him. He heard a couple of muffled but excited gasps from the three men watching when she made her sounds of desire. He decided that he had to stop the slow, erotic stripping that he'd planned to do and just helped her get out of the rest of her clothing quickly. It didn't take more than a minute to get her completely nude. He rotated her around so that all the men could get their first view of her naked body. Then he displayed her willingness by stroking her right nipple, pulling on the nipple hard enough to lift the bulk of her breast from her body. Danni made a face but muttered a sound of appreciation of his treatment of her. The men made sounds of approval once more.

"Danni, we've decided that you'll give me a blowjob first so that the men can watch you perform. Then they will all get their chances to fuck you. I'm hoping that when they're done, I'll have recovered enough to fuck you myself. You may stop the action any time that you need rest and if you can't finish, that will be fine. We will accept that." He smiled at her and asked "Do you have any problems with that?"

Danni looked eagerly around at the seated men before returning her gaze to his face. "No, that sounds fine. Do you want me to start right away or can I go over to introduce myself to the rest of the men?"

Theodore thought briefly. He knew that if he let Danni go over to let the men caress her that she would be further excited by their appreciation but he thought that he might have real problems getting her away from them again to start the action. Ms. Sturm had warned him that she had to finish matters within two hours because she would need to rest up before her math test. Theodore decided that he wasn't going to risk wasting time on preliminaries so he replied "I know that you and the men would love some time to get to know each other but we are on a bit of a time limit so let's just get started."

Danni scowled her disappointment but obediently dropped to her knees in front of him. She reached out and began to open up the front of his pants. Theodore pulled his shirt off over his head as she pulled his jeans and underwear down. His cock was standing erect and bobbed slightly as he pulled his clothes over his ankles. He had to fend off Danni's eager hands as he did this and almost tripped. He shook his head at her and she just stuck her tongue impudently out at him. The watching men murmured in approval. They appreciated her eagerness. Theodore moved towards her so that she could stroke his cock. She only spent a moment just using her hands before she took the tip of his prick into her warm, wet mouth. When she gobbled up the first few inches of his stiff cock, he screwed up his face and groaned in enjoyment of the feeling of her mouth on him. She tried to move her face closer and let his prick slide down her throat but he carefully pushed on her forehead to keep her from doing that. He knew that he wouldn't last too long if she spent too much time with his cock fully in her eager mouth. He kind of wanted to demonstrate his ability to last to the other men so he wanted to make her draw the blowjob out. Danni wasn't in the mood to wait; she wanted to feel his cock deep in her throat and feel the warm gush of his cum as soon as she could. They played a game of cat and mouse for a few minutes before Theodore succumbed and let her have her way. She swallowed the full length of his prick to the point that she started gagging on his cock before moving him back out into her mouth. She could taste the acridness of his precum. She'd been fondling his rather large balls while she sucked on his cock and could tell that he was ready to unload into her mouth. She quickly made a decision. She stabbed her finger into the base off his prick causing him to grunt in pain. It had the desired effect of making his cock deflate slightly once more and she ran her tongue over the velvety head to get him stiffen again. She heard the men mutter about her treatment of Theodore's prick and her continued actions. She wasn't sure if they were upset or impressed by her actions but decided that she really didn't care. She wanted the biggest load possible from Theodore's cock. She was pretty sure that he hadn't wanted her to do that to him because he wanted to be able to fuck her later but she decided that he would have to recover the best that he could. She used her warm mouth on his cock to get him back to the point of climax once more. Theodore had his hands on her shoulders and was pulling her tighter towards him as he sensed that he was going to orgasm. She let him do that as she continued to bob her head up and down on his stiff prick.

Theodore pulled hard on her shoulders, bringing her head up close to his crotch as he orgasmed. Danni choked on his sudden spurt down her throat but quickly got control over herself and licked his shaft. About fifteen seconds later, he had a second smaller eruption that Danni speedily swallowed. She pushed back against his hold of her head so that she could get some breath without his prick obstructing her throat as much. She took a couple of deep breaths and then returned to sucking and cleaning his deflating cock. After a minute, she let his now limp cock slip from her mouth. Theodore had been voicing his appreciation of her sucking and the fact that she continued to massage his balls with her hands. Now that she let him go, he sighed in exhaustion and pleasure. He took a quick look around at the men watching and noticed with exhilaration that they were all watching with envy and lust. He enjoyed the attention of them for a moment before he moved away from Danni. He staggered slightly before her regained full control of his leg muscles. He thought once more about how wonderful it was to have the young blonde as a sex partner. He beckoned for the first man to come up so that he could take his turn with Danni.

Since they had drawn for the order that they were going to be the partner for Danni earlier, the man who won first place now came up to introduce himself. "Hi, Danni. My name is Joe. I get to be first with you" he told her as he helped her up to her feet. He had removed his clothes while she was finishing with Theodore so he was now naked. He pulled her hard to his naked chest, smashing her tits against himself. He enjoyed the hard pressure of her nipples as he rubbed her against him. Danni hadn't expected him to do that and was busy trying to regain her breath even though she too liked the feeling of what he was doing. She hadn't fully regained her breathing when he smashed his mouth down on hers, darting his large tongue down into her mouth. This surprised her too because a lot of men wouldn't have done that since her mouth had most recently been wrapped around Theodore's prick. She felt herself liking the rough treatment and the fact that he wasn't put off by what she had just finished doing. She used her own tongue to trace along his as best she could. He murmured sounds of appreciation at her actions. After more than two minutes, he released her, putting her back down onto her feet. She hadn't even realized that he'd lifted her entirely off the ground until her feet touched down once more. Her mind was whirling as she loved what he was doing with her.

Joe knew that he was expected to move quickly with her so that all of them had the chance to enjoy her. He would have loved to take more time exploring her soft, gorgeous body but couldn't take the time. He hoped that he might get the chance sometime in the future to do that but for now he just pushed her shoulders down so that he could put her into position to fuck. Danni resisted slightly but then accepted his guidance. She frowned as she realized that she was being put down onto her hands and knees. She would prefer to be face to face with the man fucking her, especially since it was their first time, but that wasn't his intention. She knew that she would be able to perform better if she could adjust her actions based on what expressions he made. Not being able to see his reactions meant that the speed and intensity of the fucking would all be in his hands. She wasn't sure that she liked that but decided not to protest the matter. She hoped that Theodore had chosen these men well and she wouldn't have to protest about anything they intended to do to her. She prepared for him to start as he knelt down behind her and pressed her shoulders down to the floor with his cock pressing against her pussy.

He checked to see how wet her cunt was with his fingers; she gasped somewhat at how roughly he pushed his fingers up into her. He was satisfied that she was lubricated enough to take his cock easily; she'd been quite aroused by giving Theodore his blowjob. He took firm hold of her waist just above her hipbones and grasped her tightly as he pulled her hips backwards as he pressed his own hips forward so that her slick cunt rode over his cock. She grunted a bit as he rode up her but she didn't feel too much discomfort; just a wonderful stretched and filled sensation. He held her firmly against her hips, somewhat surprised that she'd been able to take his full length inside her the first thrust. He'd found that most women required a bit more work before they could take his full length. And she was quite wonderfully tight and warm surrounding him. She wasn't loose at all. He was shocked when she wiggled her hips, seeming to want to see if he could get any more in her. He grinned and ran his thumbs over the base of her spine. Danni straightened her body somewhat as he caressed her lower spine. She hadn't been expecting that. Joe laughed at her reaction and pushed hard on her lower shoulders, pressing her body against the blanket on the floor as he pulled his body back so his cock slid out of her. When he was almost completely out of her pussy he slammed his body back hard and fast against her. She gasped and moaned as his stomach made firm contact with her round ass. She once again wiggled her hips under him, trying to entice more from him. He grinned appreciatively, knowing that she was showing him that she liked what he was doing to her.

He gave her a few hard, fast thrusts without letting her react too much, enjoying the feel of her slick pussy along the length of his cock. Then he paused deep inside her as he assessed her reaction. Danni moaned and groaned, wiggling her ass as she indicated that she wanted more of what he'd just done to her. Joe paused as he considered how he wanted to proceed with her. She was proving to be much more active than most women that he'd fucked in this manner. Most women just contented themselves with kneeling there without doing too much to help him penetrate them. Danni was pressing her hips as tightly to him as she could manage and he liked the feeling of it and was aroused by her enthusiasm for being fucked hard. He knew that he wouldn't survive too much more of that before he orgasmed so he decided to set a slower, more deliberate pace. On his third thrust, she met him by rocking her hips back and using her arms to help her push. He oofed in surprise as her soft flesh contacted his hard stomach muscles. He adjusted his hands on her waist to give her more freedom to continue that. He enjoyed the firm contact with her. They continued on for a couple of minutes until he realized that he was in danger of blowing his load into her cunt. He tried to get her to ease down in her actions but she wanted to feel his cum explode inside her and wouldn't ease up on him. He contemplated smacking her soft ass to disrupt her but decided that he might as well just finish with her. She was going to be fucked by more people and they wouldn't want him using all of her time up. So he kept up the pace and less than a minute later, spurted his cum deep inside her slick cunt. When she felt his hot load inside her, Danni moaned in pleasure and pressed her hips as tight against him as she could. She ended up pushing him backwards a few inches in her enthusiasm but he didn't mind it. Her enveloping pussy felt wonderful against his shrinking cock.

But he realized that there were other men waiting to be with her and he couldn't disappoint them. So he said softly "Thank you very much, little one. I enjoyed that immensely and would like to fuck you again when I can spend more time with you. But Kyle and Link want their turn with you. I need to let them have their chance." He separated himself from her and gave her a grin. Danni was a bit miffed that he'd called her little one. She wasn't small. Sure, he had four or five inches on her and weighed more than half again as much as she did but that didn't mean that he had the right to call her little one. She regarded him with a blank stare while he smiled at her until she decided to forgive him. She just gave him a nod without bothering to smile at him.

Meanwhile Kyle came over to take his turn; he guided her down onto her back and lifted her legs up so that they were now above her head. Danni liked the positioning and relaxed so that he could adjust her to his preference. He was already erect and ready from watching her being fucked by Joe so he entered her without any foreplay. She was ready to fuck so that didn't matter. He slid his cock into her and she was a bit astonished to discover that he was longer than both Theodore and Joe. In fact, if she could judge properly, he must be almost two inches longer than they were. Of course, he didn't have their pleasant girth but his cock was thick enough. She could feel him deeper inside her than the others and tried to decide if she liked it or not. She wasn't sure. All she knew for sure was that he felt different up inside her. Kyle grinned at her as he slowly moved his long prick in and out of her. He was happy that she could accommodate his full length. A lot of women couldn't take his cock completely but Danni could. He took his time letting her feel him deep up inside her pussy. He didn't bother wasting his breath and effort talking with her but just maintained a stroke that wouldn't force him into orgasm too soon. He wanted to thrust up into her magnificent cunt for as long as he could. Danni paid attention to his rhythm and then tried to match it like she had with Joe. Kyle barked out "No" so she ceased. She didn't like being a nonparticipant but decided that she would allow it on this occasion.

She lay there while he pumped hard against her until he groaned "Now." She was startled but quickly figured out that he wanted her to start performing. She flexed her thigh muscles so that she could push against his body when he was as deep in her as he could go. Kyle groaned at her sudden resistance and began to pant with his exertion. He sped up and the two of them banged their crotches together with a loud clapping noise. Danni liked this new rhythm and put effort into it. She knew that Kyle wouldn't be able to last too long and just over a minute later, he climaxed. She wrapped her arms around his back and clutched him to her as he slumped onto her, feeling totally spent. She started to kiss him and he turned his face towards her so that she could do it more easily even though he didn't really kiss her back. She figured that he was too tired to respond properly. After a few minutes, he felt extremely heavy on her and she had to shift position to move him around so she didn't cramp up. He recognized that she needed him to get off of her so he raised himself up enough that she could crawl from under him. Then he slumped back down. Danni sat beside him for a moment, looking at him and smiling somewhat. She felt a burst of pride for outlasting him.

Link came over and pulled her to her feet. She looked at where Kyle remained sprawled on the blanket and wondered what Link intended on doing about it. Link ignored the tired man; he'd had no intention of fucking Danni down on the blanket anyways. He wanted to experience her in a different manner. "Hi, Danni. My name is Adam but all my friends call me the Missing Link, therefore I usually go by Link. I think you can guess why." Danni smiled and looked the man over. He was shorter than she was by a couple of inches and was heavily muscled. His shoulders were wide and strong and his arms bulged. He was also covered with the most hair that she'd ever seen on a man. He looked somewhat like a slightly shaved ape. That was why his friends called him the Missing Link, she thought. She wondered if he was going to get the others to help him move Kyle, when he walked right up to her and placed his hands on the backs of her thighs, bringing her up against him. She frowned as she tried to puzzle out his intentions. He lifted her up off the ground and she naturally put her legs around him. He was wider than any other man she'd had to put her legs around and she felt a small strain in her inner thigh muscles. It wasn't enough to make her feel too uncomfortable but it was a different feeling. She was surprised to realize that she was having some quite different experiences and it pleased her. She locked her legs around him, feeling quite secure in his strong arms. She liked the feel of his stiff cock pressing into her inner thigh as she continued to wonder what he intended to do. He carried her over towards the wall. She looked at him, bewildered, even as she enjoyed the rubbing of his cock against her as they moved. He placed her back to the wall and let go of her with one hand. She remained pressed against the wall as he used his hand to adjust his cock so that he was entering her. He put his hand back into place and pressed his strong body into her. She grunted slightly as his thick cock opened her pussy up, stretching it quite nicely. She realized that although he was shorter than the other men he was also quite a bit thicker. She smiled at him as she took him up into herself and he grinned back at her. She ran her hands down his hairy back and was amazed that she liked the feeling under her hands. Most of the men that she'd been with had some hair on their backs and especially their chest and she'd found it acceptable. But his back was so covered with hair that it reminded her of stroking a cat or dog. She liked the soft feel and murmured in his ear that she liked it. He smiled at her in response and began grinding her against the wall. He drove most of the breath from her lungs as he pressed her hard against the unyielding surface. She loved the feel of the hard wall against her back and his hard body against the front of her. She appreciated the feeling of his strength as he held her up and thrust up into her. After three or four strong thrusts by him, she tightened her legs so she held him up inside her as he pushed as deep in her as he could manage. She looked at his face to determine his reaction. He smiled and nodded, indicating to her that he enjoyed what she was doing so they continued on that way. He carefully controlled their pace, ensuring that he remained excited and hard enough to keep penetrating her but not fast enough that he triggered his need for climax. He knew that he could maintain this pace for quite a time and was prepared to do that. He could smell her sweat and other aromas from her, including the scent transferred to her by the other men. He didn't find it unpleasant but actually rather intoxicating. Her perfume had faded to be barely noticeable. Danni was slightly perturbed when she realized that he was smelling her, she felt unclean and therefore undesirable, but was quite pleased when it appeared that he was enjoying it rather than being turned off by it. She decided to return the favour. She smelled his sharp masculine scent over her own and tried to determine if she liked it. It didn't turn her off but it also didn't do too much for her. She rested her chin on his right shoulder as he held her there and thrust up against her. She loved his slow steady pace as well as the hard feeling of what was happening to her body. She closed her eyes and relished what was occurring. After five more minutes, he said to her "I need to speed things up. I'm going to lose my ability to maintain my erection if I don't cum soon. I'd love to keep fucking you this way since you seem to like it but I'm afraid that I can't." Danni moved her head back so that he could see her face and nodded her agreement silently. Link began to speed up his pace and she could no longer time his action so she just let him pound his body against hers. She felt the strain on her hip muscles as he ground hard against her crotch but it wasn't too bad.

He gave a low grunt/moan and spewed his warm cum up inside her. He shot such a great load into her that she felt some of it immediately start to leak out of her and down her thigh. It felt interesting she thought as she wriggled her hips against him slightly causing even more to drip out of her cunt. She liked that he still had the strength to hold her up even though his orgasm had tired him. He looked her in the eyes to try to determine her mood and she gave him a bright, happy smile. His face brightened and he showed some relief about her reaction. He made to move her away from the the wall but she quickly shook her head to stop him. So he held her up there for a few minutes.

She began to worry that she was tiring him too much and asked softly "Do you need to let me down?"

"No, I could hold you here for an hour or so. You're so light. But I think I should let you down because the other guys probably want to spend some more time with you" he replied. "I'm just going to carry you over to the blanket." She nodded and he did so. Her legs were slightly unsteady when he put her down but she felt fine.

Theodore came over and it was obvious that he'd recovered and was ready to fuck her; his prick was erect. He'd seen the wobble in her legs and asked with concern "I was hoping to fuck you but we can put it off if you need a rest. Do you?"

"No" she replied shaking her head. "I'll be fine. What did you have in mind?"

"I thought that I would lie on my back and let you mount me" he replied. "That way you can set whatever pace you want. Let's see if we can get you to orgasm. I think the guys would like to see that."

Danni frowned, wondering why the guys would be interested in seeing her climax. She could understand that they would like to see her getting fucked but what would it matter to them about her pleasure. But she said "Fine, let's do that."

Theodore got down on his back and Danni had to stifle a giggle because his erect prick definitely stood at attention, ready for her to mount. She knelt beside him and then quickly straddled him, letting his cock press against the opening of her slit. He reached up and steadied her as she did that and was now holding onto her waist, just above the swell of her hips. She leaned over slightly, feeling her breasts lift away from her body and smiled at him. He smiled back and she shuffled forward slightly while pushing her body down onto his cock. She closed her eyes and moaned just a little as she felt his hardness glide up into her; she was very slick because of her own and the other men's juices up inside her. She managed to get his full length in her without having to make too much effort. She wiggled her hips to enjoy his cock filling her and wished just slightly that he was just a bit longer. But she would have to work with what she had, she decided, and began to lift herself up a few inches before pushing her body back down onto him. She started slowly so that they could both build their desire. Theodore ran his hands over her lower body, caressing her and supporting her as she moved up and down. Then once she'd established the rhythm that she wanted, he started lifting his hips up to meet hers. Hey, she though a little startled, that was her move. She gave him a grin of appreciation and he openly chuckled at her. She did note that he wasn't able to lift himself as much as she could though.

"Just slightly faster, please, Danni" he said softly to her. "I'm in danger of losing my stiffness, I'm afraid." She complied and rode him faster. He grunted his gratitude before closing his eyes and enjoying the feel of her warm, wet cunt sliding up and down his cock. She rode him that way for over five minutes as she built up the pressure inside her. He gritted his teeth so that he could keep from exploding inside her. When she felt the point that she was going to orgasm she sped up to trigger her orgasm. Theodore got pushed past his control and spewed his cum up into her. The feel of his warm cum up in her pussy pushed her past her own control and she climaxed. It wasn't a bone-shaking, mind-blowing orgasm but it was very pleasurable. When she regained the control of her body after the momentary lapse, she looked down and noticed with some dismay and total amusement, that she'd pushed his cum as well as the other men's and her own juices out onto his belly and crotch. They were both soaking, sticky messes but he got the worst of it because he was below her. She checked to see if he was angry about that but was pleased to see that he had only pleasure and exhaustion on his face, not disgust. He even brought his hand up to dip into the mess and use it to to paint a symbol on her sweaty stomach. She didn't recognize what he'd painted on her and decided that she would ask about it later, not now.

"That was great, Danni. Really wonderful" he gasped as he fought to regain his breath and composure. She could feel his cock shrinking inside her and in about a moment, it slid out of her and more liquid spilled from her pussy. She gave him a slightly haughty, naughty look and then ground her hips against his lower belly smearing more of the combined juices onto him. He grinned at her and waved his finger at her, admonishing her. She just let him feel her weight on him.

Both of them were lost in their thoughts and were startled when Joe came over with some wet washcloths and dry towels for them. He'd noticed how wet their screwing had ended up and assumed that they would want to clean up a bit before trying to move around. He placed his hands on Danni's breasts, capturing her erect nipples between his fingers, squeezing them as he eased her over off of Theodore. Danni gave him a small glare for taking advantage of her and copping a feel but he just gave her a little grin. He figured that she would forgive him and couldn't resist. Once he had her off to the side, he took a washcloth and wiped down her crotch area. He wasn't trying to get her super clean, just clean enough that she wouldn't smear the combined juices onto anything in the living room. Once he'd gotten the worst of it off, he rubbed her down with the dry towel. She found his attention to her body quite pleasurable and pressed into his hands as he did that. She gave small growls of enjoyment.

Then he gave her a small look of regret as he let her have control of the towel and bent down to clean up Theodore. She gave him a confused look as he applied himself to the job. Most men would have let Theodore take care of himself while they applied their attention to her, she thought. She looked over towards Kyle and Link; she noticed that Kyle looked away from her but Link put out his arms to her. He was seated so she went over and sat in his lap as he closed his strong arms around her. He nodded over to the small table beside him where a plate with two thick sandwiches and five deserts sat. "Theodore said that you would want these once you were done. We've all bet him that there is no way you would be able to eat all that food." He grinned at her.

She reached over and took up one of the thick sandwiches; it was corn beef and tasted delicious. She spoke around her full mouth and stated "You're gonna lose." She gave him a messy smile and he grinned happily back at her. She looked over and was somewhat surprised to see that Joe was still wiping down Theodore. She'd assumed that he would have left Theodore to his own devices by now. Suddenly she was struck by the thought that the two of them had some sort of sexual connection. She was surprised and amused by how aroused that made her feel. The thought of possibly being in a threesome with those two made her horny. She squirmed in Link's lap to try to relieve her stress a bit. He slid his hands down onto her hips to prevent her from throwing herself off of him. She liked the feel of his hard, strong hands on her soft skin. Then he decided that he was being too forward with her and removed them. She groaned in disappointment and wiggled her hips harder. He put his arms protectively around her but didn't allow himself to touch her. She quickly stuffed the remainder of her sandwich in her mouth and used her hands to bring his back down onto her bare thighs. He frowned at her as he puzzled out what she wanted.

Then he smiled as he figured out what she wanted. He massaged her thighs with his hands and she groaned in pleasure. She reached over to grab the ham sandwich and began to chew it slower as she enjoyed his strong massage of her muscles. She pressed the upper part of her nude body against his bare one to let him feel the hardness of her nipples. He enjoyed her reaction even though he tried to make sure that he wasn't hurting her in any way. Danni could tell that he wasn't using his full strength and she thought about asking him to do so. She thought that it would interfere with what they were doing so she decided that she should wait until a later date. Then she realized that she was already planning a future date with Link and thought about that for a moment. It was something she decided that she liked, she thought. She wanted him to fondle her roughly and to fuck her as hard as he could. She could feel her pussy dampening as she thought about it.

Joe had finished cleaning up Theodore and helped him to his feet. Theodore looked over at her squirming in Link's lap and smiled at her. "I see that Link gave you the food. These guys bet me that you couldn't eat all of that food" he called over to her.

"I know, Link told me" she replied back to him. "I told him that they were going to lose." She pushed the remainder of the second sandwich into her mouth. The three men gaped somewhat at her and she just smiled back at them. Theodore just laughed loudly and went over to find a chair near her and Link so that they could chat. Link stopped fondling her, expecting her to get up and go over to him. Danni just whined and wiggled her ass, indicating that she wanted him to return to what he'd been doing. He gave her a quick smile and eagerly did just that.

Joe, Link and Theodore sat chatting with her as she consumed her sweets. She gave them a huge smile as she popped the last of her gooey brownie in her mouth, having consumed all that was on the plate and winning the bet for Theodore. The other men paid their five dollars to Theodore; Danni was a bit miffed that it was for such little money. Surely if men bet on her, they should be risking more than just coffee money, she thought. Theodore just laughed at her disgruntled look. Kyle decided that he had to leave a few minutes later and Theodore looked at the clock, determining that Danni had to go have a shower if she wanted to be ready for Ms. Sturm. So Danni headed down to the bathroom as Kyle left. Joe and Link both offered to join her to wash her back for her but Theodore put the kibosh on that, knowing that would delay Danni getting ready. Danni quickly but carefully washed her body down. She could see that she was going to have some real bruises from the men's rough treatment of her but she didn't regret it in the least.

When she went back out into the living room, the three remaining men had put their clothes back on and her clothes were neatly folded on a chair waiting for her. She slipped into them while they watched her, smiling with pleasure. When she was done she made her way towards the door. The three men all picked her up in rib-cracking hugs, kissing her wetly on the mouth, to say goodbye to her. She loved their attention.

She walked outside and saw that Ms. Sturm was parked, waiting for her; it looked like she'd been there a while. Danni checked her watch and saw that she was only a minute or so late. She approached the car and got in, looking at Ms. Sturm to see if she was angry with her. Ms. Sturm just looked her over, noting her relaxed, good mood. "Been waiting long?" Danni asked softly and carefully.

"A few minutes" Ms. Sturm confirmed. She wasn't upset and was just speaking to inform Danni of the information she requested. "You look nice and satisfied" Ms. Sturm said with a quick smile. "A good night's rest and then you should be ready to ace your math test, I think." Danni nodded and they drove back to her house.

CHAPTER SEVEN

Danni wrote her math test the next morning. She discovered that she was relaxed and confident and that allowed her to handle all of the problems with ease. She was sure that she was going to receive a very good mark when she left the class. There was a brief period of time before her next class so she joined the group of her friends to chat. "Did you hear what happened to Julie?" Tina asked with worry pinching her face.

Oh no, Danni thought with sinking feelings, did Julie decide that she could no longer face her problems and hurt herself before Ms. Sturm and her friends could approach her and offer her help. She let her dismay fill her face as she replied "No. What happened?"

"She's disappeared" Tina replied as she took a deep breath to steady her shaken feelings. "Her family doesn't know where she might be and they're very worried about her. They think she might do herself a mischief and they want her back home. You don't know where she might be, do you?"

"No, I certainly don't" Danni replied, relieved by the news. Apparently Ms. Sturm and her friends didn't waste any time when they decided to help people. Or at least she hoped that was the case. She'd find out from Ms. Sturm later that afternoon. She noticed that one of the boys in their class had approached and was now standing in front of her looking nervous but excited. "Did you need something, Bobby?" she asked him, confusion flitting across her pretty face.

He kind of hemmed and stuttered a bit before he managed to ask her "I was wondering if anyone had asked you out to the prom yet?"

Danni shook her head as she thought about the matter. "No, I haven't even really thought about it" she confessed. "But no one's asked me yet." She gave him a small smile as she wondered why he was asking her that.

He straightened up and garnered all of his courage. "Well, I'm asking you to go to the prom with me" he stated.

"Oh" she said, looking quite bewildered. She really hadn't thought too much about the affair and had just assumed that she might ask Theodore to take her. She liked the idea of an older man taking her to the dance and having her friends see him. She wasn't very sure that he would agree though. She looked Bobby over carefully. He wasn't too bad looking but not really someone she saw herself being with. She became aware of some angry murmuring and fake coughing from her group of friends. They were standing behind Bobby and she could see them shaking their heads at her. She frowned as she tried to figure out what they were signalling to her. She glanced over to Tina, who was the closest to her since they'd been talking and was shocked to see an angry look on her face. She was glaring daggers at Danni. Danni knew she hadn't done anything to deserve that from her and tried to determine what was going on. "I don't know, Bobby" she said gently. "I really need some time to think about it, I think. Can I get back to you?" She tried to smile at him but failed.

Tina reached out and grabbed Bobby by the arm. He was looking very crestfallen by Danni's non-answer. "I'd love to go to the prom with you, Bobby" Tina cooed.

Bobby turned and looked at her, frowning a bit in thought. Tina was a pretty girl, he thought, not on Danni's level but still very nice. Danni was rapidly becoming the most popular girl in class and if he could bag her, the other guys would be very jealous of him. But it looked like she wasn't going to accept so maybe he would be better to accept Tina's offer before someone else decided to ask her. Bobby glanced back to Danni, his face showing regret, but he replied "That would be great, Tina." He tried a smile and found that he was fairly pleased with the result.

"Why don't we go talk about it" Tina said as she led Bobby away by his arm.

Danni went over to the rest of her friends feeling bewildered. "What's going on? What were you trying to tell me there?"

Jeanette laughed and said "Oh, Danni, just because you're so busy doing things without us that doesn't mean that we aren't also doing things. Bobby is supposed to go to the dance with Tina. We've decided that is best. You almost ruined the whole thing when he asked you instead." The bell rang for the next class before Danni could ask what the hell was going on; she didn't understand the explanation at all.

After the next class, Danni hurried back to where her friends were gathered so she could get a more complete clarification of what her friends had been doing. "What do you mean that you've decided? Have you chosen someone that I'm supposed to go to the Prom with?" she demanded of Jeanette.

Jeanette laughed and replied "Of course we have. You've been growing in popularity with the boys over the last month so we had to make some changes for you. But we've decided that you get to go with Ronald. You'll look good together." She smiled brightly at Danni.

Danni frowned uncertainly and asked "But I thought that Ronald was going out with Charisse, they've been together more than two years. When did they break up?" Charisse was the head cheerleader. A pretty, tall blonde with a well-padded body and she was rumoured to be quite sexually active. Why would Ronald want to give her up, Danni wondered.

"Well, Susan's brother says that he's become very interested in you lately and he's quite willing to give Charisse up. Apparently he told her that on Monday night. She's been taking it a bit hard." Danni looked over to where the cheerleaders usually gathered and noticed that they were all consoling Charisse.

"Just because he's broken up with Charisse, how can you know that he's interested in me?" Danni asked reasonably.

"As I said, Susan's brother says that it is so" Jeanette explained. "He gives us all of the boy's secrets in return for regular blowjobs." Danni looked at her astounded. This was the first that she'd ever heard of this. She'd known that her friends fairly regularly knew what the boys were discussing but had never asked how they knew.

"Who gives him the blowjobs?" she asked curious.

"Oh, usually Tina, which is why she gets Bobby. But occasionally one of the rest of us. He has quite a nice cock" Jeanette replied. She looked intently at Danni and asked "Did you want to give him a try?" She didn't really think that Danni would go for the suggestion because she was somewhat of a prude.

Danni shook her head angrily; she wasn't interested in Susan's brother. "No, I'll pass, if you don't mind" she said, cementing her reputation. She really didn't want Ronald either. He was good looking but she didn't know what he was really like. The fact that he dumped Charisse so readily really brought him down in her opinion. She didn't want boys. She was screwing men who weren't just out to make a score for themselves. They weren't interested in her just because she was becoming the most popular; they wanted her because she interested them. Danni decided that she had to think matters over fully before she committed to them. She got her books for the next class and headed to it. She kind of avoided her friends for the rest of the day as she thought about her feelings about them and the prom.

She hadn't made up her mind about anything as she made her way to where Ms. Sturm was waiting to take her to Evelyn and Mary's place. She made sure she wasn't distracted enough not to keep a weather eye out to see if any of her friends were following and spying on her. But when she got into the car, Ms. Sturm looked her over and stated "You seem a bit thoughtful, Danni. Didn't you do as well on your math test as you though you would?"

"No, I think I aced the test" Danni replied truthfully. "But something else has me occupied. I need to think a while on it." She'd thought about trying to discuss the matter with Ms. Sturm but wasn't confident that it was something she could help her decide. She determined that she would talk with the other woman if she was still in a quandary on Sunday night. "I heard that Julie is missing" she stated as she tried to steer the conversation in another direction.

Ms. Sturm made a noise of disbelief as she looked Danni over carefully. She was sure that something else was on Danni's mind but decided that she would let the young woman have her privacy on it for now. "Yes, we moved Julie to another city for her protection. She was very grateful to hear from us and accept our help. I think she will be alright and will make the decision she needs to make regarding her baby. We will provide her with whatever assistance she needs, no matter what, of course." She looked a bit more intently at Danni and asked "Would you like to write her a note?"

Danni was surprised but grateful at the offer. "Is she allowed to know that I am involved with her situation, even though it was in a very minor way?" she asked.

"Of course she can. If she chooses to do so, she can write you back" Ms. Sturm replied. "You can't let anyone know about who helped her that might report that information to her family but I trust you to assess that. We won't tell even you where she is though, for her protection. I'm sure you understand that." Danni nodded in acceptance of the terms and Ms. Sturm started the car and drove over to Evelyn and Mary's place. Danni didn't say anything more as she contemplated matters in her mind.

Mary opened the door and ushered Danni in as she took her backpack of schoolbooks. She gave the younger woman a quick but thorough kiss on the lips. Then they went into the living room where Evelyn was seated waiting for them. Danni went over and sat by the heavyset woman and hugged and kissed her. Evelyn enjoyed the young blonde's enthusiastic welcome. Mary came over and sandwiched Danni between her and Evelyn. Danni expressed her appreciation as Mary fondled her tits. "I thought that you could get down on your back and allow Evelyn to eat you out. I'll sit on your face and play with your tits while she does that. You can decide how much licking you want to do on my pussy. Would you like that?" Mary asked as she tugged on Danni's erect nipples, having worked Danni's top and bra off.

Danni replied "That sounds wonderful. Let's do that to start and then we can see what else we want to do after that." Mary had been somewhat concerned that Danni might be too sore to do too much because of what she'd been doing with Theodore and his friends the day before. Ms. Sturm had informed them about it because she felt they needed to know in case Danni was feeling any after effects. The three women removed their remaining clothing and positioned themselves. Evelyn started teasing Danni's sensitive inner lips with her tongue, tracing along the wrinkly flesh. Danni moaned her enjoyment of the action. Mary had brought some nipple clamps over in case she wanted to use them. She quickly examined Danni's nipples to see if she was bruised or sore. She didn't see any evidence that Danni had suffered any abuse and would be able to handle having her nipples played with hard. She grabbed one of the clamps and fastened it to Danni's right nipple. Danni hadn't really been paying attention to what Mary was up to but had been kissing and licking the older woman's fragrant cunt. She felt the cold metal and the tightening of the clamp on her nipple and moved herself so that she could look at what was happening. Mary almost laughed out loud as Danni shifted so that she was now looking up at her from between her thighs.

"Do you want me to stop?" she asked in a teasing voice. Danni paused briefly as she thought about it and then shook her head negatively before returning to her task. Mary tugged on the clamp to ensure it was firmly in place eliciting a moan of pain and pleasure from Danni. She quickly fastened the other clamp to Danni's other nipple. These clamps had a chain running between them and Mary tugged the chain sharply upwards lifting Danni's breasts up off her chest. Danni gave a squeal of pain but Mary had already let her tits fall back again. She wasn't looking to cause the younger blonde constant pain, just small bursts of it to excite her. She knew that Danni liked rough treatment from her sexual partners; she often felt the same way. Danni loved what was being done to her by the two women and she tried to show it by eagerly licking Mary's damp cunt. The three of them continued this way for nearly ten minutes with Mary punishing Danni's nipples on an irregular schedule. Danni found herself keening as the pressure built up in her pussy. She was almost ready to blow. Evelyn was well aware of her signs and was increasing her pace to push her over the edge. Mary pulled up on the chain and held it upwards for more than thirty seconds. Danni screamed in pain and then wonder as she climaxed. Mary relaxed the chain back down as Danni writhed and groaned as she ground her crotch intently into Evelyn's face. Evelyn looked up, her face covered in Danni's juices and caught Mary's eyes; she grinned in intense pleasure and Mary smiled broadly back at her. Danni huffed her breath in and out as she tried to keep her composure and Mary enjoyed the sweet bob of her tits. She grabbed each tit in her hand and freed the nipple from its restriction. Danni grunted in pleasure as the clamp was removed from her. Mary continued to massage Danni's nipples to ensure the blood flow back into them. Danni muttered her appreciation. Mary looked at the younger woman, catching her eyes, and then gave each of her breasts a small, sharp smack with her hand. Danni's eyes flew open in surprise but she voiced her approval. Mary just smiled at her and then pointedly ignored her. She knew that would cause Danni to want more and intended to keep the younger woman in want. Danni could tell that Mary was teasing her and she could feel her frustration rise; she wanted Mary to continue and now that she wasn't, she could feel her arousal increase. Deep down in her mind, she was aware that she absolutely loved being teased; it really increased her horniness. Since she was still down between Mary's thighs, she contemplated giving the soft flesh a bite but instead she traced a circle with her tongue, making Mary shiver a bit in pleasure.

By then, Evelyn was finished and she sat up, regarding the two of them in their play. The other two women finally noticed she'd stopped and looked at her with matching guilty looks. She just smiled at them; she wasn't jealous and actually liked watching them in action. But she said "If you are both finished, maybe we can cuddle for a while and all enjoy each other." She moved away long enough to grab the plate of cookies for Danni before returning. The two women had separated and were waiting for her to return. She handed the plate to Mary and lay down on the couch. Danni quickly squirmed across her body and wriggled her body down between Evelyn and the back of the couch. Evelyn really liked the feel of her soft, warm flesh pressing against her as she did that. Mary handed Danni the plate of cookies and then placed her own body on Evelyn, right beside Danni. She put her arms around the pair of them. Danni grinned and began munching on the cookies.

Then she let some concern flood her sweaty face as she thought about her friends and the Prom. Mary had been watching her face and asked carefully, stroking the younger woman's chin "Is something troubling you, dear? Would you like to talk about it? I'm not sure if we can help but we'd like to try. Is it about your friend Julie?" She continued to gently stroke Danni's face to let her know their concern for her.

"No, Julie's been moved to another town. Ms. Sturm assures me that she will be well taken care of there. She even says I can write her a note and I'm gonna do that. I'm not concerned about her." She flashed a small smile and then sighed. "But my friends surprised me today and I'm not sure I know what I want to do about it." She laid out the situation and her own feelings about it to them. "Do you have any advice for me? I don't think that Ronald is treating Charisse well and I'm not really sure that I want anything to do with him because of that." She shrugged her shoulders and stated "I guess he's handsome enough but is that really sufficient to go out with him?" She looked expectantly at both of them.

"Maybe Ronald finds you more attractive than Charisse?" Mary ventured cautiously. She didn't feel that she knew enough about the situation to give Danni good advice so she thought that she would ask some more questions about the situation.

Danni scowled as she considered the question and then replied "No, Charisse is at least as pretty as I am. She is the captain of the cheerleading squad. That can't be the reason Ronald would want to drop her for me."

"Perhaps, she isn't as pleasant as you are?" Evelyn asked.

"No, Charisse isn't snobby like some of the cheerleaders are. She's always volunteering to help anyone who is disadvantaged as well. She organized a bottle drive to help the homeless shelter as well. I can't say that I am better than her in that way either" Danni replied.

"Could Ronald have heard how sexually active you've become?" Mary asked softly, aware that she could upset the younger woman.

Danni wasn't upset as she considered the matter. She really didn't see how that could have happened and was sure that if Ronald knew that about her, that it would be all over the school. She hadn't gotten the impression that anyone at school knew of her extracurricular activities. "I think that would have gotten back to me is some way" she replied. "Besides, I have it on pretty good authority that Charisse has been letting Ronald have his way with her however he wants to do. I don't think that Ronald would be expecting me to be that compliant right away. Everyone at school tends to think that I'm still a virgin."

"Then because you're supposed to still be a virgin?" Evelyn ventured.

Danni frowned, screwing up her pretty face and said slowly "I don't know. Do boys really care about that? Wouldn't it be better to screw someone that knew how and knew that she liked it?" She glanced at each of their faces.

"Some men like virgins" Evelyn replied. "Although I'm not sure that a young boy would put it at the top of his priorities."

Mary had been giving the situation some thought and she asked Danni "Does it really matter why? Do you want to go to the Prom with Ronald or not? You can justify your feelings once you've established what they are."

Danni thought briefly and then replied "I'm not interested in Ronald in any way. I can't imagine enjoying the Prom with him. Especially if it hurts Charisse. She's not my friend nor is she my enemy." She paused a moment and then continued "I thought about asking Theodore but that might cause too many questions and get back to my mother." She looked expectantly at the pair of them.

"Are there some boys that wouldn't usually go to the Prom with a girl that you think are good people?" Evelyn asked slowly. Danni nodded, frowning from thought. "Perhaps, rather than waiting for Ronald to approach you, you should go up to one of them and ask him to take you." Danni looked at her questioningly, slightly bewildered. Evelyn explained "You don't really care which boy might take you. You're not gonna date him or fuck him, are you?" Danni slowly shook her head in a negative fashion. "No, you've got grown men who are going to do that for you. So give a deserving boy some confidence and a story to tell his friends by letting him take you to the Prom. What have you got to lose?" Danni thought about it and decided that she liked the suggestion.

"I'll think about it" she replied with a kiss for Evelyn. "I'll probably do just that."

"Are you feeling tired or are you up for some more action?" Mary asked with some anticipation. She hoped that Danni might still want to do more.

Danni looked over at her and smiled; she recognized that Mary still desired to do more with her. "I think I can handle some more. What did you have in mind?"

"I thought that I could put on a strap-on and you could sit in my lap and ride it" Mary replied. They both looked over to Evelyn to see if she wanted to participate.

"I'll just watch" Evelyn told them as she grinned. She felt quite happy about doing just that. Mary grabbed Danni by the hand and took her over to the toys. She selected a longer, fatter dildo with a huge bulbous tip rather than Danni's favourite and showed it to the younger woman. Danni looked a little apprehensive about her choice thinking it might just split her in two. Then she decided that since she had nothing sexual planned for the next day that she could recover easily if she found it challenging. Of course, if it hurt too much, she'd make Mary change for her favourite. She nodded her acceptance of Mary's choice. Mary grabbed some lubricant and took Danni back over to the couch. She was quite pleased that Danni had accepted her selection; she thought the younger blonde would enjoy the feel of it up inside her but had been unsure how sore she might still be from the men.

She attached the harness to herself with Evelyn's help and then began lubricating the dildo thoroughly. Evelyn beckoned Danni over, took some lubricant from Mary and started to rub the liquid up into Danni's cunt. Danni liked the feel of the older woman's strong fingers working her open and pushing the lubricant up into her slit. She held her pussy lips open to give Evelyn complete access into her. Mary sat down on the couch and beckoned Danni to come over and mount her dildo. Danni straddled her and lined the dildo up into her. She pushed down firmly until she had nearly two thirds of the dildo up inside her. Then she began to feel some restriction. She looked into Mary's eyes and smiled. She wriggled her hips so that she slid just over an inch further onto the plastic cock. She raised her body up so that the dildo pulled out of her. She was careful not to go too high and lose it completely out of her cunt. She pushed quickly and firmly back down onto the toy as Mary steadied her so she could concentrate on that instead of her balance. She took even more of the dildo up inside her and she paused to enjoy its feeling deep within her. Mary caressed her body and then reached up and tweaked her nipples. Danni grinned happily at her and raised herself once more. She started to move her body so that the dildo slid in and out of her, increasing her pace as she got more spread and lubricated by the action. It seemed like Mary's hands were all over her, she thought, as she closed her eyes to enjoy her sensations. Her breathing deepened as she expended more effort and she began to groan in her pleasure. It became evident that she wasn't going to push her body into climax but that didn't mean that she didn't enjoy what was happening to it. She could feel sweat dripping down her neck and along her breasts before dripping onto Mary. She began to slow down and brought her body to rest on Mary with the dildo as fully inside her as she could get.

Mary grinned up at her as she sighed her contentment. "Feels good, doesn't it?" Mary asked.

"Uh-huh" Danni moaned. Mary just wrapped her arms around Danni to give her a hard hug. After twenty seconds, Evelyn came and sat beside them, wrapping her arms around the pair of them. They remained there for over five minutes before Evelyn told Danni that she needed to get ready for her date that night. Danni showed regret on her face when she disengaged from them and then headed down to shower.

She completed her shower and was drying herself off as she headed back to the living room with the towel. She knew that Mary would have chosen a couple of outfits for her to pick from and would be waiting to watch her dress. She carried her towel over her shoulder, exposing her nude body for Evelyn and Mary to admire as she pranced happily into the living room. The two older women were comfortably seated and eagerly awaiting her. The three of them shared excited grins as Danni walked up to the selection of clothing. She gave the three piles of clothes a quick look as she made her decision as to what she wanted to wear that night. She noted that Mary had given her a choice of two dresses and a skirt/blouse set. One dress was dark blue, the other was black and the skirt was black with a purple blouse. They were all darker colours because Mary knew that Danni sweated quite hard when she danced and preferred to wear darker colours because of that. Danni decided on the black dress. She slipped on the bra that Mary had put with it, happy that it supported her breasts quite well while still allowing the tops of her tits to be exposed. She stepped into the tiny black thong, smiling about the fact that it had a brilliant red heart stitched in the center of it, and slid it up her legs. She looked over to Evelyn and Mary to check that they were still watching her before slipping the dress over her head and then down her body. She put her stockings on last just before her shoes. The watching women appreciated the show as she rolled them up her long, lean legs.

"How do I look?" she asked as she gave them a brief twirl to see how the small black dress rode up her hips as she did that.

"You look as wonderful as you ever do" Mary replied enthusiastically. She loved how the younger woman looked in pretty clothes. The outfits seemed to highlight Danni's best physical assets and made her even more desirable. She liked the look of the younger woman's nude body but felt that clothing on her was like a pretty bow on a present. Evelyn just nodded her approval. Danni smiled her thanks for the compliments back to them.

The doorbell rang and Danni headed to the door. She expected Rose to be at the door to pick her up and that was who it was. Rose greeted Evelyn and Mary before taking Danni's hand to lead her to the car. Samantha waved to them from the driver's seat.

"You look very nice tonight, Danni" Rose gushed. She wanted to slip her hand up under Danni's dress and pinch her round ass but restrained herself. She guided Danni into the back seat and slid in beside her. Samantha put the car in gear and drove off towards the restaurant. They went into The Secluded Grove where their favourite waitress led them to a secluded booth. The special was an orange chicken stir fry and Danni fancied that. She figured her parents would be barbequing steaks the next night and wanted something different from that. Samantha followed her lead on ordering the stir fry even though she knew that she wouldn't eat all of it.

Rose chose to go with a small Chef's salad. They ordered some onion rings as a starter. Of course, Danni consumed most of them with glee as the other two women watched on with pleasure. Samantha ate barely half of her meal and then pushed the remainder over to Danni who'd gobbled down her meal. Danni ate the leftovers quite happily. Danni also cleaned up the remainder of Rose's salad. The waitress was aware of their usual practice and didn't come back to gather the plates too quickly so that she didn't cause Danni any embarrassment. She did come back with the desert menus even though she suspected that they would be ordering a slice of the mud pie like usual. She wanted to give them the option to change if they wished to do so.

They ordered the mud pie with three forks and the waitress brought the dessert back and placed it closest to Danni with a smile. Danni ate most of the gooey concoction while the others had small tastes of it. They paid their bill, leaving a hefty tip for the waitress, and made their way back to the car so that they could drive to The Naughty Nymph.

As they entered the pub, they were pounced upon by Dawn and she led them to the back of the pub where a crowd of women had taken over five tables. The waitress was hauling trays of drinks to the thirsty women and she was grinning happily as the women thrust money into her hands. Dawn pushed through the women, pulling Danni along by her arm to the center of the crowd. There were four vacant chairs there for them and Dawn pushed Danni down onto the leftmost one. Almost all of the women called hello to them and the noise was horrendous for a moment. Danni grinned self-consciously and waved a greeting. Dawn had sat on the inside of Danni but Samantha walked up and pushed her shoulder, indicating that she should move over and let Samantha have that chair beside Danni. Dawn glared up at her, ready to dispute the matter and Samantha actually bunched her fist, prepared to throw a punch. Danni looked at the pair of them and started to get up. She didn't want them fighting over her and was ready to leave. Rose saw what was happening and walked over. She placed her hand gently on Danni's shoulder to stop her from rising and said very loudly "You do realize that Danni is prepared to leave here because of the two of you, don't you? And I will quite happily drive her home if that is what she wants. Are you prepared to ruin everyone's evening because of your petty squabble? Samantha, let Dawn sit by Danni for fifteen minutes and then you can have that chair for fifteen minutes. Okay?" Samantha shifted her angry gaze over to Danni, she saw the concern on Danni's face and softened her stance. She nodded and went over to the farthest chair to sit down. Two of the women from the rear of the group came up and pulled Dawn from the chair and led her over to the washrooms, talking animatedly with her. Rose looked around briefly and then sat on the chair beside Danni. She reached out and took Danni's hand in hers, giving her some comfort. Danni leaned over and whispered her thanks.

The waitress pushed through the women to them and bent over Danni, asking "Are you staying?" When Danni nodded that she was, the waitress asked "What do you want to drink?" Danni thought about it for a moment so Rose asked for a glass of white wine for herself.

"I'll just have a Coke Zero" Danni replied, having decided that she didn't really want any alcohol right then. The waitress nodded and left to take Samantha's order. The woman seated to Danni's right briefly and gently stroked Danni's arm to get her attention and started chatting with her. Danni talked with her for a few minutes before she noted Dawn coming back with her two escorts. She was surprised when Dawn walked past her and stood in front of Samantha's chair.

Dawn stuck her hand out and stated quietly "I would like to apologize. I was wrong. Danni is your girlfriend and I shouldn't interfere between the two of you. I'm sorry for my actions." She kept her eyes downcast in case Samantha didn't accept her apology.

Samantha looked her over briefly as she considered the matter, glanced over towards Danni and Rose, and reached out to grasp Dawn's offered hand. She shook it firmly but lightly and said softly "I was wrong as well. I shouldn't have reacted so strongly. I let my jealousy take control of me. I'm sorry as well."

Dawn smiled and nodded as she asked "Can we agree that we should share her like Rose said, then? Do you wish to be first?"

Samantha barely hesitated before stating "No, I got to have dinner with her. You should take the first shift with her." She gave the other woman a small smile. Dawn smiled and nodded before moving back towards Danni. The waitress bustled up and set down the drinks for Danni and Rose. Rose tried to hand her a twenty to pay for the drinks but the waitress just pushed her hand away.

She grinned and said "The boss says you guys drink for free."

Rose still tried to give her the money, saying "Then keep this as a tip."

The waitress grinned even more as she declined the money once more. "I've already been tipped by five different women to bring you these drinks and expect that to happen all night. Keep your money and use it to buy her a couple of roses or something." She indicated Danni as she said that before moving away once again to gather more drink orders.

Dawn had sat herself in the vacant chair beside Rose while the waitress was in the way. Rose got to her feet to switch chairs with her and Dawn smiled at her gratefully. Rose settled into her chair. A small blonde woman came up to Rose, pushed her arms open and settled her small ass in Rose's lap. Rose looked at her, startled, as the other woman pulled her arms around her as she continued to wiggle her ass, seeking a level of comfort. "Who are you?" she asked but the woman just smiled before giving Rose a quick peck on the cheek.

"I'm whoever you want me to be" she trilled as she leaned back against Rose's large breasts. Rose just shook her head and started chatting with her about other things while smiling about the situation. Danni talked with Dawn for almost ten minutes before someone came up and insisted that she come dancing with three of them. Danni looked over to make sure that Dawn was okay with that and Dawn nodded. She saw that Samantha was also being led up to the dance floor. Danni danced for nearly fifteen minutes with a huge assortment of women; very few of them were able to spend more than fifteen or twenty seconds dancing with her before another took their place. Danni loved it but she began to get somewhat tired so she indicated that she wanted to sit for a while. As she headed back to her seat, the dance floor, which had been very crowded, emptied out a fair amount.

As she settled herself into her seat, Dawn handed her her drink and she gulped down most of it. She was happy to see that the waitress had brought over a second one for her. She knew that she was going to consume both of them fairly quickly; she'd sweated quite a bit while dancing and needed to replenish her fluids. Samantha had gone over to her seat and had also consumed quite a bit of her drinks. Now she was headed slowly over to where Danni was sitting. Dawn had kept an eye on her and since she was now coming over, she got up to let Samantha have the seat like she had promised. Samantha nodded gratefully at her as they passed and Dawn smiled back at her. Samantha descended slowly into the seat as she looked over towards where Rose was sitting with the small blonde woman on her lap. "I think Rose has found a friend" Samantha stated with a laugh.

Danni checked Samantha's face to see if there was any jealousy but didn't find any. She was happy that Samantha wasn't feeling threatened by the other woman and said "That woman does seem to be quite insistent. I don't think that Rose minds all that much, though."

Samantha nodded and said "I think that blonde woman behind them is the girlfriend of the one sitting on Rose's lap. She doesn't seem put out by her partner's actions either. I kinda wonder if they're looking for some group action with Rose and us." She looked over to Danni with a smile.

"Ms. Sturm probably would veto my participation in that until after I pass my tests" Danni mused, expressing a bit of regret. "She's talking of keeping my sex sessions quite short so that I'll have lots of time to study."

Samantha looked at Danni and thought about telling her to ignore Ms. Sturm but she quickly realized that she wouldn't be successful that way. So instead she said "Your schoolwork is important. You want to be able to go to the university of your choice. You'll have lots of time for sex." Danni smiled gratefully at her and they chatted about other things.

After a while, a tall, leggy redhead came up and beckoned for Danni to come dance with her. Danni flashed a smile towards Samantha and got up eagerly to join her; she'd recovered her strength. Other women quickly joined them and Samantha was also guided up onto the dance floor. The tall redhead danced with Danni for almost thirty seconds before it became apparent that she was going to be replaced. The redhead planted a quick kiss onto Danni's lips before they were separated. Danni once more danced with a variety of partners until she tired again.

When they returned to their seats, Samantha gave her a quick peck on the cheek before picking up her drink. "Time to share" she whispered to Danni as she made her way over towards where Rose was seated. Danni smiled at her and her face started to show her confusion as she now saw that Rose had both of the women that Samantha had thought were girlfriends draped all over her. Apparently, Rose was having a very good time, Danni thought happily as she accepted the picture. Dawn waited until Samantha was over beside her before giving up her seat to her; she didn't want to seem too eager to take Samantha's place beside Danni. But then she came over and took the empty seat. Danni was talking with the woman on her right and she started to become aware that the woman seated there had been changing regularly. She turned to greet Dawn and spent a moment or two talking with her before turning back. She noticed that another woman had come up to stand behind the woman seated on her right and was now lightly touching the seated woman's neck. The seated woman smiled at Danni, saying goodbye, and gave the seat up to the other woman. They were signalling each other, sharing the pleasure of being seated beside me, Danni thought with wonder. She smiled at the new woman and talked with her for a few minutes.

The evening passed in a whirl like that. Lots of chatting and dancing. Danni was very happily exhausted when Rose came up to her and said "Well, we have to get you home or you'll get in trouble with your mother, Danni." Danni was quite happy that Rose appeared to be very pleased by the evening; Danni hadn't had the chance to talk to her very much and hadn't even danced once with her even though she'd seen Rose dancing often. Danni made a quick trip to the bathroom before coming back and saying her goodbyes to the women, including the waitress who'd arranged to dance with her. Danni noticed Rose and Samantha talking intently with the two blonde women who'd hung around Rose all night. It amused her to see that Rose appeared to be giving them directions. Maybe the night wasn't over for Samantha and Rose even though it was for her, she thought. She was looking forward to her bed.

Rose and Samantha took her to Evelyn and Mary's place so that she could get cleaned up enough to go home without causing too much trouble. Usually Rose and Samantha waited and took her home but tonight they asked Mary if she could drop Danni off for them since they wanted to get home to clean up for their expected guests. The two blonde women were named Cindy and Micki. Danni wasn't put out by the switch but she did start to think that maybe she needed a car of her own. She understood why Ms. Sturm didn't want her driving herself but it was a bit of a pain sometimes, she thought. Mary was okay with dropping Danni off so that was what happened.

Danni walked into the house. Her mother was waiting up as she normally did. Danni glanced at the clock and saw that she was nearly twenty minutes early for her Friday curfew. She smiled and greeted her mother. "Hi, mom. I'm home. I'm just going to go up and crawl into bed. Good night." Her mom nodded and returned her smile. She was seated reading a book and drinking some green tea. Once Danni was up in her room, she would soon follow her to bed.

CHAPTER EIGHT

Danni woke up early the next morning, feeling quite good. She hopped out of bed and stretched out her muscles a bit to ensure that she hadn't developed any cramps during the night. She pulled her nightgown over her head and slipped into a pair of shorts and a slightly ragged tshirt. This was her normal weekend wear and she enjoyed putting it on. She knew that her family usually slept in on the weekend so she walked as quietly down the stairs as she could. She went to the kitchen and started the coffee maker. While it was processing, she got a small bowl of cereal to tide her over until her family got up. They generally had a large varied breakfast on the weekends and she would be joining them for that later. Once the coffee was done, she poured herself a cup, having finished the cereal earlier, and took it up to her room so that she could do some studying.

About an hour and a half later, Danni became aware that her mother was calling to her, telling her to come down for breakfast; she'd been quite intently reading her history book. She finished the page, put the book down and went downstairs to join her family. Her sisters had already helped themselves and were eating their food. They called greetings to her as she entered the dining room. They were quite excited that she was going to spend her day with them. Danni grinned and greeted them back as she headed over to the coffee maker to fill up her empty cup. Her mother was just finishing putting her own plate together before heading over to join her husband and daughters at the table. Danni greeted her as she went over to put down her full cup and grab her empty plate. Danni came back and heaped her plate with the wonderful variety of breakfast foods that her mother, father and sisters had prepared. She went back to the table and joined the spirited conversation that was going on about some new movies that were coming out.

When they were done eating, Molly begged "Can we play some games before we do the cleanup?"

Everyone looked over to Danni, who laughed and said "I can play some quick games but I do need to do a bit more studying before we really get into playing."

"Well, we'll just pile up the dishes for the moment and deal with them later, then" their mother said. "What would you like to play first, Molly?" she asked her youngest, brightly. Molly loved playing Hearts so they got out a deck of cards and played it. They played three games. Their father very obviously sacrificed himself a few times so that his youngest two daughters wouldn't be punished by the cards earning himself some glares from his wife and two older daughters. Molly won two of the three games and Kate won the other because Danni played her Queen of Hearts to help her out when she could have slipped under the ten of hearts winning the trick. Her mother and father noticed her sacrifice but didn't say anything to the others. They were quite pleased that Danni was willing to allow her sisters their joy so easily.

Danni tried to offer her help in doing the dishes but Gina and Kate volunteered to help so Danni could go study. They wanted her to be done so that they could continue the fun of the day. Danni thanked them and went up to study for just over an hour. When she was done, she came back down. The rest of the family was just finishing playing a board game so Danni got a cup of coffee and sat down to watch the end of the game.

When they were done, Danni's mother told her "We're just having sandwiches and snacks for lunch. Help yourself whenever you're hungry. Dad's gonna grill some steaks for supper. I thought we would have baked potatoes, corn on the cob and salad to go with them. Sound good?" Danni licked her lips exaggeratedly and nodded eagerly causing her mother to laugh. They spent the afternoon playing board games that Danni and her parents carefully lost. The younger girls were quite ecstatic about winning and the family all enjoyed it.

They stopped the fun long enough to prepare and eat supper. After the scrumptious meal, Danni started to gather the dishes. She was prepared to wash and dry them by herself but her younger three sisters all chipped in to help so that they could get back to having fun with her. Their mother was quite proud of all of them as she cuddled with their father. After the dishes were done, their mother suggested that they watch a movie together and they all agreed. Molly and Kate got to choose which movie they watched and they eagerly put it on. Danni settled on one end of the couch and Molly came up to her. She wanted to cuddle up in Danni's lap to watch the movie. She was really too big to do that with, Danni thought, but decided that she would allow it. As they watched the movie, Danni stroked Molly's fine hair. They watched the movie and were happy. They played a couple of more games before their mother insisted that the younger two had to be off to bed. Danni had enjoyed the day quite a lot. She bid them all goodnight as she went back up to do some more studying before she headed off to sleep herself.

CHAPTER NINE

The next morning Ms. Sturm drove Danni over to Samantha and Rose's place; she'd warned the young woman that she wanted her to keep the session short so that she could return back to her studying. She'd asked Danni if she had enjoyed her day with her family and was pleased that Danni had been very enthusiastic in saying that she had. She was quite happy that Danni had a supporting, understanding family, unlike a lot of the women she was involved with, and felt that the young blonde woman was one of the most well-adjusted person that she knew. She knew that psychiatrists would argue that Danni was a sex addict but she felt that Danni just had an extremely high sex drive and wasn't repressed by society into trying to restrain it. She would disagree with the psychiatrists that would label Danni as in need of counselling. She didn't bother to share her feelings with Danni because she didn't want her to have any concern about the matter. They drove over to Samantha and Rose's house without discussing too much.

Danni was a bit surprised when Samantha met her at the door; usually Rose was the one to let her in. Samantha smiled at her and said "Rose is feeling a bit flustered this morning. She wants to ask you to do something and is afraid that you'll say no to it." She then sobered a bit and said quietly "I would appreciate it if you say yes to it. You might find it a bit kinky but she's driving both of us a bit crazy about it. You'll be helping her get over it." Danni frowned in confusion as Samantha talked; she couldn't think what the thing Rose wanted her to do was. She knew that she would try to do anything for either Samantha or Rose so she really didn't see too much of a problem.

Rose was definitely pacing nervously as they entered the living room but she ran eagerly up to Danni and kissed her quite firmly on the mouth. She glanced over to Samantha before she asked Danni "Danni, would you dress up like you were in the video with Samantha? I'd like to fuck you with a dildo when you're dressed like that. I know it's a bit sick but I can't get the image of you looking like that out of my mind. I'm hoping that screwing you like that will soothe my desire. Please say yes." She looked extremely hopefully into Danni's eyes.

Danni thought about the request briefly. Instead of upsetting her or turning her off, she found that it excited her that Rose wanted her looking like that. She knew that most people would be hesitant about the request but she wasn't one to be very

worried about it. "Of course, I will, Rose. I think I'll like it almost as much as you."
She was somewhat surprised to see both Rose and Samantha sigh with relief.

Rose gasped out "Thank you." She began enthusiastically starting to undress
Danni as Danni looked slightly bewildered in Samantha's direction; she hadn't quite
realized the older woman's fervor. But she helped her as much as she could and was
soon completely naked. Samantha helped her into the garter belt and stockings that
she'd worn as Rose started making up her face. Soon Danni looked like she had for
the video. Rose almost growled with pleasure as she looked Danni over. Danni
found that she was becoming quite wet with desire herself. Samantha looked at the
pair of them and rolled her eyes somewhat; she knew that they were both into it at
the moment. She took the heavier leather strap-on belt and started fastening it to
Rose. Danni looked slightly worried that Rose was going to be wearing that one,
normally she wore the lighter one, and wondered how vigorously Rose was going to
fuck her. She was concerned because Rose didn't have the same practice that
Samantha had regarding fucking another woman hard with a dildo; she was usually
the recipient of such action. Danni had some concern that Rose might accidently
hurt her but she steeled her resolve and went up to kiss Rose.

Rose kissed her back enthusiastically and slid her tongue deep into Danni's
mouth. Danni thought briefly, considering if she should do what she was about to do
or not, then decided to go for it. She lightly raked her teeth on the other woman's
tongue. Rose gave a tortured moan and pulled Danni against her as hard as she
could as she wriggled her tongue around in her mouth. Danni gave a small gasp of
surprise but tried to match her intensity. Samantha gave them a look of concern as
she stood there and tried to ensure that they didn't push one another off balance and
end up falling. She tried to guide them over to the couch so that they would no
longer be on their feet. She managed to get them down onto the couch where Rose
pushed Danni onto her back with some strength. Danni grinned uncertainly at
Rose's enthusiasm but just tried to get herself comfortable on the couch. Rose raised
her legs and pushed the tip of the dildo up into Danni's slit. She gave Danni a
slightly predatory smile and pushed the thick dildo up into her. Danni wriggled her
hips to accept the plastic cock and moaned slightly as it spread her open. Rose got
about two thirds of the dildo up into her before encountering resistance. Danni
looked up into Rose's eyes, unsure what the older woman was now going to do; she
felt a small shiver of fear that she might be about to experience some pain.

Even though Rose was tremendously excited, she was still in control of her
actions; she knew that she could cause Danni a great deal of pain by forcing her to
take the dildo before she was sufficiently lubricated. Although a very small part of
her brain was encouraging her to make Danni scream loudly in pain, she knew that
she really didn't want to hurt Danni. So Rose reached down between them to pull
the dildo back out of Danni's cunt a couple of inches. Rose then fondled Danni's clit.

She rubbed it fairly roughly causing Danni to gasp and wriggle her hips. Rose pushed the dildo back up into Danni a little further than before. Danni grunted and pushed her hips back against the penetration as she enjoyed the feeling up inside her. Rose grinned happily at her and began to work Danni's body hard enough to get her to accept all of the dildo with ease. She thrust it in and out of Danni with passion making Danni murmur in pleasure.

Rose worked Danni over harder than she usually did, obviously enjoying her rough treatment of the younger woman. Danni could feel her arousal peak and began to feel the electric feel deep in her hips as her orgasm started to build. Danni could feel her breath catch and she began to pant heavily as her body reacted to the dildo sliding in and out of her. She could feel her mind begin to slip into her usual outlook as she prepared for her climax. Her brain began to shut down as her mind clouded with hormones. Danni loved the feeling as her mind and body concentrated themselves on her arousal. Suddenly, Danni began to buck hard against Rose's thrusts as she climaxed. Rose was tiring from the effort and part of her felt relief as she brought Danni to orgasm. Both of them were sweating quite heavily but Danni was able to get a firm grasp around the woman riding her. Danni arched her back as her body sought some relief from what was happening inside her and she lifted Rose up with her. Rose had to scramble a bit to keep from being bucked off and Samantha rushed over, laughing, to help keep her from falling.

"You have to be very careful with this girl" Samantha chortled happily. "She can sometimes be like a ride at the amusement park." She reached down and massaged Danni's tight neck muscles in an attempt to get the young woman to relax her body once more. Danni moaned her appreciation as she started to enter her post climax stance. Samantha knew that Danni would completely relax her body in a minute or two and tried to make sure that she could support Rose when that happened. Rose was very excited by the sex and was busy fondling her own clit because of her arousal. Danni collapsed and Rose was caught off guard. Samantha supported her so that she could slump down onto Danni without causing hurt to either of them. She encouraged Rose to get up off of Danni, knowing that Rose wanted some immediate relief of her own. She unbuckled the strap-on belt and pulled it down the older woman's legs. Once she had it off of her, Samantha strapped it around her own waist and forced Rose to help her buckle it up. Once it was in place, she pushed Rose's face down into Danni's wet crotch. Rose had been distracted by trying to accommodate her own need and was initially surprised by the move but she responded quickly and began to suck up Danni's sweet juices.

Samantha had expected what happened to occur and had prepared for it. She'd brought over a rather large anal vibrator and now she started coating it with some of Rose's cunt juices. Rose wasn't paying attention to what Samantha was doing as she lost herself in Danni's fragrant pussy. She assumed what she felt against her own pussy lips was the dildo attached to the strap-on belt. She felt quite excited that she was soon going to be riding the same dildo that she'd forced Danni to take. It gave her a pleasurable spurt of arousal. Samantha coated the anal vibrator with as little lubricant as she thought Rose would need; she didn't want the older woman to become wise to what she intended. She knew Rose would enjoy the surprise of what she was going to do to her. She pushed the pointed tip of the vibrator against Rose's asshole and began forcing it up inside her. At the same time, she penetrated Rose's cunt with the dildo. Rose straightened up, lifting her head from Danni's thighs and squealed in surprise and pain. Samantha pushed down on her shoulders as hard as she could to get the older woman back into position. Rose howled slightly but managed to move back into the position Samantha wanted her to be in. She loved the feeling of being unexpectedly violated and quickly responded by trying to assist Samantha in what she was doing to her. With some effort, Samantha managed to get the bulk of the anal vibrator up inside Rose's ass. It was not the first time that Rose had encompassed the toy and she really enjoyed its use. Samantha turned the anal vibrator on to its highest setting. Once that was done, Samantha began riding Rose as hard as she could. Rose moaned her approval up into Danni's wet, blonde pussy as Samantha kept pushing her into it with her hard thrusts. Rose tried to open up her legs so that she wasn't constricting Samantha's efforts to fuck her but Samantha used her lower legs to prevent that. The two of them fought each other for a few minutes before Rose ceased her struggle and accepted her fate. Samantha knew that Rose would find more enjoyment by being forced into the position she was making her adopt. Danni had recovered some of her wits and was watching them with some surprise and amusement.

Danni reached down and wrapped some of Rose's long red hair around her fingers so she could control Rose's head. She pulled Rose's head against her as she pushed her hips forward so that she ran her wet cunt lips all over Rose's face. Rose initially tried to pull away but soon got the message. Danni wanted her to keep licking and cleaning her cunt while Samantha fucked her. Rose energetically slipped her tongue into Danni's sloppy cunt and Danni moaned in appreciation. Samantha grinned at the two of them and tried her hardest to force Rose as far forward as she could manage. Rose loved how hard Samantha was pushing and forcing her but she tried to keep in position. Then she felt herself climax and she lost the battle. Danni was quite surprised when Samantha pushed Rose up her body and Rose accidently caught Danni under her chin with her shoulder. Danni saw stars.

Samantha quickly disengaged herself from Rose and pushed her over to the side, Rose was fairly dazed by her reaction, in order to check on Danni. Danni moaned and felt her sore jaw. She saw Samantha looking concerned at her and tried to indicate that she would be fine. Samantha smiled with relief and started to help Rose to roll over onto her back; Rose was still quite groggy from her climax but with

Danni's help Samantha got her onto her back to a more comfortable position. She also turned the vibrator off and worked it out of Rose's ass; she was quite limp so it wasn't that hard to do. Samantha grabbed Danni's hand and whispered to her "Let's leave her alone so she can regain her composure. We'll go get some ice for your jaw. I'm so sorry about that."

Danni laughed a bit and said "It's all right I know you didn't mean to do that. It just happened. I'll survive." They moved over to a small table and Samantha went to the kitchen to get ice. They sat chatting for about ten minutes with Danni icing her jaw until Rose stirred and came over to join them.

"What happened to you?" she asked Danni, curiously.

Samantha scowled at her and replied "You slammed your shoulder into her jaw when you fell onto her. Don't you remember?"

"No. I'm sorry, Danni, I didn't mean to do that" Rose said contritely. Danni waved her off, indicating that she accepted the apology and knew that it wasn't intentional.

"Well, did you enjoy it as much as you thought you would?" Samantha asked Rose with a huge grin.

Rose rubbed her ass and replied "I liked fucking Danni but you were a little rough on me. I'm gonna have problems sitting for a while." Samantha just stuck her tongue out at Rose, knowing that the older woman was just complaining for show and had really loved what had happened to her. Danni just sat silently watching the pair of them.

"Ummm, we really don't have much time if you want something done to you, Samantha" she said as she looked at the clock.

"That's fine" Samantha replied. "Rose will still be able to use her tongue and I'll make her lick me until she's too sore to do that later. She owes me for agreeing to let her do this to you and I'll collect." She gave Rose a slightly predatory smile that Rose just smiled broadly back at. Danni realized that they were just playing and didn't worry about it.

"Why was Rose so keen on doing that?" she asked.

Rose quickly shook her head at Samantha but Samantha decided that Danni should be informed. "We watch the tape of the two of us each night before we go to bed because Rose gets so turned on by it. She tried to do that with Cindy and Micki, the two blondes that came home with us on Friday. They were willing but she didn't find it satisfying. Therefore she decided that she needed to have the real thing. Namely you." Samantha gave her a huge grin as Rose blushed from embarrassment. Danni wasn't too sure what to make of the whole thing. She was a bit shocked to learn that not only did Samantha and Rose have a copy of that tape but they watched it regularly. She was intrigued that they found it so arousing and somewhat proud about that. She felt some sympathy for Rose because Samantha had exposed her secret but also felt a great deal of attraction to her because of her interest. She wasn't sure what to say so she just remained quiet. Samantha just laughed at the pair of them and said "You better go shower and get ready for Ms. Sturm to arrive." She inspected the bruise forming on Danni's jaw and said "Ms. Sturm is going to want an explanation about how this happened, I think." Danni went off to shower.

When Ms. Sturm arrived, Rose went out to bring her in so they could explain the bruise on Danni's jaw. Ms. Sturm just shook her head at them but didn't bother to do any more than that. She understood that it was an accident. She took Danni home so that she could explain her condition to her mother.

Danni told her mother that she'd accidently walked into an open door. She wasn't sure that her mother believed that but she accepted it. She quickly checked Danni to see if she had a concussion but decided that she didn't. Danni went up to her room and did some studying.

CHAPTER TEN

The next day, Danni took some kidding about her bruise but she didn't really respond too much to it. She'd thought about what Evelyn and Mary had advised and had made her decision. She'd chosen a boy to ask out and she approached him. He was Pierre, a boy that had joined them just last year. He wasn't an athlete nor was he one of the better students but he was a fairly nice person. Because most of the girls found his rather strong French accent off-putting, he didn't have much interaction with the girls. He'd given Danni some help with her schoolwork in the past and she decided that he deserved some consideration. So now she walked up to him, smiled and asked "Hello, Pierre. Have you asked anyone to the Prom?"

Pierre was standing with some of the boys he hung around with and he was shocked when Danni came up to him. He was an inch or so shorter than she was and so he was looking slightly up at her when she spoke. He wondered if she was trying to make fun of him by asking him that question. She had to know that he didn't have a date for the Prom. But he tried to be as respectful as he could be when he replied "Hello, Danni. No, I don't have anyone going with me. I don't think that anyone will. Do you have someone in mind that might?"

Danni liked how he said her name with his accent and gave him a bright smile. "I was thinking that you could take me" she replied.

Pierre gave her a wide-eyed look as he examined her. She was gorgeous even with that bruise on her chin and she was rapidly becoming the most popular girl in school, he thought. Certainly she could go to the Prom with anyone she wanted to. Why was she bothering with him, he wondered. He tried to calculate whether she was playing a joke on him but he didn't feel that she was the type of girl to do that. "Are you serious?" he asked cautiously as he glanced around nervously; they had the attention of everyone around them.

Danni also noticed that everyone was staring at her and Pierre but chose to ignore it; she also ignored the whispered offers to take her to the Prom from the boys that were standing with Pierre. She approached Pierre and pressed her breasts lightly against him as she reached out her hand and stroked his arm. She looked him full in the eyes, smiled and stated "Of course I am serious. Do you need some time to think about it?" She gave him a very innocent smile.

Pierre gave a very heart-felt groan. Of course he wanted to go to the Prom with her, he thought. Why couldn't he just say yes? "I-I-I..." he stuttered as he looked into her bright blue eyes. Then he steeled his nerve and said formally "I would love to go to the Prom with you, Danni. Thank you for asking me."

"Fine" Danni said with a bright, saucy grin as she pushed forward against his chest, flattening her breasts on him before stepping back from him. She was amused to see that he flushed deeply when she pressed against him. "My mom says that you can come over Saturday night at five for supper so that they can meet you. You can help me choose what dress you'd like me to wear." She paused to let that sink in and then asked "Will you check with your parents as to when I can come over and meet with them?"

Pierre was still flustered but managed to nod yes so she smiled and walked back to her stunned girlfriends. She noted that Ronald and his friends were staring at her with open astonishment. She glanced over to catch a very puzzled look from Charisse and she flashed the other girl a small, quick smile. She ignored the furious questions from her friends as she got her books together and headed off to her class. She'd decided that she wouldn't bother to explain herself.

At lunch, Danni walked by the table of her friends and very conspicuously sat at a table by herself. She hadn't bothered to talk to her friends about what she had done that morning and they were all tending to ignore her because they were upset about that. She knew that she wasn't really going to associate too much with her friends once they graduated, especially if they didn't mature, so she wasn't overly concerned about the fact. She just sat and ate her sandwiches as she thought about being in university. So she was a bit lost in a daydream when someone sat down opposite her. She thought it might be Tina or Margaret from her group of friends, instead she looked up into the bright blue eyes of Charisse. She looked a bit startled because Charisse had been sitting with the other cheerleaders when she'd entered. She glanced over to the cheerleader table to see them glaring at the two of them.

Charisse didn't say anything for a couple of minutes as she ate her cookies and examined Danni. Danni didn't know what to say so she just continued to eat as well and looked straight at Charisse's face. Finally Charisse gave a small grunt and pushed her dish of cookies over towards Danni; Danni took one to be polite and ate it delicately. She offered Charisse her cookies and Charisse took one. While she was eating the cookie, Charisse asked a trifle coolly "Why did you go over and ask Pierre to the Prom this morning?"

Danni munched a carrot stick as she contemplated whether or not to answer. Was it fair to talk to Charisse about it when she wouldn't discuss it with her friends, she wondered. She looked at Charisse's overly bright eyes and pinched face and realized that the other girl was quite upset. She decided that maybe the head cheerleader did deserve an answer. "I heard about certain plans that had been made about me that hadn't bothered to consult with me. I didn't agree with those plans so I chose another method. I thought that Pierre needed some help with his reputation so I chose him" Danni replied quite evenly. Charisse frowned at her before reaching out and taking two of Danni's carrot sticks.

She ate both of them while they sat in silence for a moment or so and then asked "I heard that you would be going to the Prom with Ronald. Why did you decide not to wait for him to ask you?"

Danni pushed the remaining carrot sticks forward and replied coolly "I heard what he did to you and I didn't like it nor did I think you deserved to be treated that way. I wasn't going to be a party in rewarding his bad manners."

"So, you've got no interest in Ronald?"

"No, I have no interest him or really any of the boys in school" Danni replied with a shrug. Charisse nodded and sat there thinking. They ate their food in silence for about five minutes when Tina and Margaret both walked over and joined them. The two new girls started talking about a movie they had seen and both Danni and Charisse participated in the discussion. The four of them continued to chat until they had to prepare for afternoon classes.

Danni made her way to the blue car and got in. She smiled a greeting at Ms. Sturm. Ms. Sturm asked her "What did you do in school today, Danni?"

Danni frowned and replied "I'm not sure what you're asking, Ms. Sturm."

Ms. Sturm sighed slightly and said "I heard that you went and asked a boy to the Prom today. Why?"

Danni thought about the question for a while. She didn't think that Ms. Sturm was overly concerned about her social life or school politics but there was really no reason not to tell her. So she explained what she had done and her reason for doing it. She watched Ms. Sturm's face when she'd finished.

Ms. Sturm asked "So you've no long-term interest in this boy?"

"No, I don't" Danni confirmed. "I just thought I would just help him out a bit."

"Are you going to tell him that?"

"Yes, I'm going to talk to him about it on Saturday when he comes over. If he wants to go with someone else, that will be fine with me" Danni replied and flipped her hair a bit.

"He's not going to be foolish enough to do that" Ms. Sturm said dryly. She liked the mature and sensible way that Danni had approached the problem and once more appreciated the young woman's attitude towards life. She drove over to Evelyn and Mary's place.

Danni went up to the door where Evelyn, wearing a bathrobe, let her in; Danni looked at her, puzzled, since Mary usually greeted her. Evelyn grinned and said quietly "You'll see why when you see her. She's in the living room." Danni walked in and Evelyn followed her. Danni gasped as she saw how Mary was made up. She'd obviously seen the video of Danni with Samantha but she hadn't copied how they were made up; she'd just used it for inspiration. Her eye shadow was navy blue and yellow and was beyond the usual application. Her lipstick was a deep purple that exaggerated the size of her lips. She was wearing a tight, navy blue semi-corset that pulled her stomach in and pressed up her heavy breasts and accentuated her plump hips. Danni wondered how she even breathed in that tight piece of clothing. She was wearing a lace and silk see-through robe that had one button that fastened right below her breasts. It had ruffles that helped hide certain areas but also focused attention on her other areas such as her breasts. She was wearing a navy blue garter belt attached to navy blue stockings with pale blue straps. On her feet she was wearing ankle boots with a two inch raise at her toes and a six inch spike heel. Danni knew that she couldn't walk very far in those monsters but they looked great and made Mary's legs look quite long. Danni let her eyes wander all over Mary's body since it was obvious that Mary wanted her to look at her before moving her eyes up to meet hers. Mary was smiling quite happily at the younger blonde woman, knowing that Danni was intrigued and turned on by her outfit.

"You look great" Danni gushed. "Really fucking fantastic."

"We thought you wouldn't mind dressing up in something quite similar" Mary said as she indicated a pile of clothing near her. "We'd love to see you like this as well." Danni nodded eagerly and moved forward, already shedding her clothes. Mary helped her put on the lingerie. Danni didn't need the semi-corset so Mary hadn't included one for her. Where Mary's outfit was navy blue, Danni was wearing powder blue; they both liked the contrast of what they were wearing. Once Danni had the lingerie on, Mary did her face while Evelyn assisted. Danni was also wearing pumps rather than ankle boots. She led Mary over to the mirror so that she could see the pair of them together. Both women grinned about how sexy they looked.

Evelyn said, rather throatily from lust, "If you two peacocks are done admiring yourselves, I think you should come over here and we can pluck some of your feathers." The two women turned and grinned at each other before they moved over to where Evelyn was on the couch. They had to move slowly and carefully to keep from losing their balance.

Once they'd arrived at the couch, Danni asked "How are we going to do this?"

Mary stated "I thought we'd do a threesome. You on your back with Evelyn eating your pussy while you eat mine. Once Evelyn has made you orgasm, we'll turn it into a sixty-nine between the two of us while Evelyn watches. Are you good with that?" Danni nodded and carefully got down onto the couch with Evelyn's help. Those damn high heels made it hard to maneuver, she thought, even though they looked great. Once Danni was in position, Evelyn supported Mary as she swung her leg over Danni's head so that she could place her pussy on her face. Then Evelyn moved down and started running her tongue over Danni's cunt. Danni turned her face up and Mary pressed her own damp cunt down over Danni's mouth. Danni eagerly lapped as hard as she could as Mary squirmed her hips around, grinding her pussy around Danni's face. Danni felt her excitement building; she really liked being in the position she was in. She wrapped her arms around Mary's thighs as tightly as she could to try to pull the older woman closer to her. Mary was initially unbalanced but she laughed and caught her balance against the back of the couch. She was pleased by Danni's exuberance.

The three of them busied themselves for more than five minutes until Danni began to feel the pressure building within her. She whined and twisted her hips as Evelyn pressed her harder, knowing that she was on the brink. Danni bucked her hips but Evelyn grabbed them and pushed her back down firmly as she worked her mouth around Danni's slick slit. Mary was also very excited by Danni's incipient orgasm and she pushed her cunt down onto Danni's mouth harder, restricting the young woman's ability to breathe. Danni had to twist her head somewhat to get air into her lungs but she returned to her task eagerly. Suddenly Danni's mind exploded as she climaxed. She arched her body and Mary and Evelyn had to scramble to keep in place. Evelyn wrapped her left arm around Danni's thighs to support her a bit so that she wouldn't hurt herself.

Then Danni relaxed and fell back to the couch. Mary bent forward fervently to begin lapping Danni's juices; she pressed her own cunt firmer against Danni's wet face. Evelyn sat back to watch them. She had to look away so that she could contain her laughter. Danni's elaborate makeup was now smeared crazily across her face. She resumed watching the pair of them for a few minutes and then she moved up to the couch above Danni's head. She reached in with her right hand and pushed three fingers up into Mary's pussy. She knew from experience exactly where to pressure Mary and began to do so. Mary could feel the penetration and tried to open her hips wider to accommodate it. Danni shifted her attention more to Mary's clit and upper part of her slit to let Evelyn force Mary to climax. She wanted to feel the other woman's warm gush on her face.

Mary started to whine and wiggle as she felt herself losing control; she was going to climax and she really wanted to drown Danni in her juices. Evelyn was putting tremendous pressure on her now and she couldn't concentrate hard enough to suck on Danni's sweet pussy as her own was just about bursting. She tossed her head back and gave a loud lengthy howl as she climaxed. She rubbed her sopping crotch all over Danni's pretty face. Danni felt the warm liquids all over her face as Mary orgasmed; it really turned her on and she also climaxed, although it was a smaller climax than her first one. Evelyn saw what was occurring and she decided that since Mary was otherwise occupied, she would be the one to clean up Danni's second orgasm. She moved around so that she could get to it.

Mary was panting and moaning, tossing her head, as Danni tried to lick up all of her juices. She could barely register the younger woman's tongue on her sensitive parts as her whole body quivered in delight. They continued their actions for about five more minutes before they decided that they needed to rest for a while. Evelyn went off to get some washcloths and warm water. She sponged off the worst of the mess from both of them. Mary had removed her ankle boots as Evelyn left with a groan of relief and then had taken Danni's shoes off her as well. Danni hadn't been feeling the same discomfort that the older woman had but did enjoy being able to wiggle her toes.

The three of them made their way into the kitchen where Evelyn prepared coffee and pulled out snacks for all of them. Danni chatted a bit with Mary as Evelyn was occupied but she waited for the heavyset woman to sit down before she addressed what she'd done with Pierre. She explained what she'd done and why and the women nodded their understanding and agreement.

"So you're gonna tell him right away that this is just for the Prom and that he has no future with you?" Evelyn asked. "Aren't you concerned that he might be offended and change his mind?"

"I think that he will understand that. If he is offended and decides not to go through with it, then he's not the man I think he is. And then I'll be better off knowing it" Danni replied shrewdly.

"You should tell him how he can use his popularity to get a girl who wants to be with him to soften the blow to his ego" Mary said as she sipped on her coffee. She smiled at Danni to show her how proud of her that she was. Danni smiled back and nodded.

"Do you need help paying for your graduation dress?" Evelyn asked Danni. She wanted Danni to look beautiful for her big day. She and Mary hadn't mentioned it yet but they were going to be attending the ceremonies; they weren't going to be part of Danni's party but Ms. Sturm had arranged invitations for them and Samantha and Rose as well. Ms. Sturm had asked them all not to tell Danni about it and they hadn't. Evelyn had protested that Danni might be embarrassed if she didn't know they were showing up but Ms. Sturm had assured her that Danni would know about it before the day.

"No, I'm not going to buy a new dress for the Prom. My mother found out that there's a woman that recycles Prom dresses and we are getting one from there. I think that it's a good idea and it also allows my parents to buy it for me without being put to too much cost. I told my mother that I would return the dress afterwards rather than keep it as well. I'll have my memories and lots of pictures to remind me of it" Danni said very proudly and practically. She liked the idea quite a bit.

"Oh" said Evelyn, a bit disappointed. She still had her high school Prom dress as a reminder.

Mary smiled at Danni and said "That sounds quite nice, Danni. You do what you think is right." Mary understood Danni's way of thinking and approved of what she was doing. She felt that Evelyn was a little too sentimental about her high school past. She knew that Danni was looking beyond high school and more about her future. She then suggested "You should go get a shower. Ms. Sturm will be here shortly to take you home." Danni nodded and left. Ms. Sturm arrived fifteen minutes later and took her home.

Danni had supper with her family and then spent the evening starting the writing of her English essay before going to bed.

CHAPTER ELEVEN

The next day Ms. Sturm took her to Theodore's apartment. Before she got out of the car, Danni gave her a note she'd written to Julie and Ms. Sturm assured her that Julie would get it. She mentioned again that it would be up to Julie if she chose to respond. Danni nodded and walked up to the door where Theodore was waiting for her. He pulled her into him as soon as they got inside and gave her a warm kiss. Danni enjoyed the experience but she was eager for more so after a few minutes she began to push his buttons a bit. She pushed her groin up against his, feeling the hard pressure of his erect cock as she ran her hands down his back.

"Danni, you're gonna make me cum in my pants" he groaned plaintively. "If you don't stop that, you're gonna be very disappointed." He pushed her away from him but still held her hand. He led her down to the bedroom. He had some trouble walking because of his aroused cock. Danni just grinned mischievously at him. Then she looked right in his eyes as she licked her plump lips a couple of times and then touched the tip of her nose with her tongue. Theodore's eyes followed her limber tongue as she did this and then he groaned as he felt his cock straining hard. He urged Danni to move towards the bedroom faster and started pulling her clothes off of her on the way. Danni giggled as he stripped her as fast as he could; she loved that he was so excited by her.

She undid his pants and slipped her right hand into his underwear, searching between his balls for the base of his cock; she put firm pressure on that base until his cock softened. He groaned from her pressure and the fact that he was losing his erection. He understood that she was just making sure that he didn't explode prematurely but still felt some disappointment. "Where on earth did you learn that trick?" he asked her hoarsely.

Danni didn't want to admit that she'd read it in a skin magazine so she said with a shrug "Oh, I just picked it up somewhere. It works, doesn't it?" He nodded and hastily pulled off the remainder of her clothing. He slipped his right hand in between her pussy lips as he used his left to pull her against him once more. Danni could feel his soft cock brush her belly. As she kissed him energetically, she could feel the stirrings as he stiffened once more. She giggled as she felt his cock grow once more in between their bodies. Then she pushed him away slightly and pulled up the bottom of his tshirt. He got the hint and pulled the shirt above his head as

Danni pulled his pants and underwear down his legs. As she was helping him to step out of them, she slipped her mouth over the head of his bobbing cock. He stopped moving immediately, thinking she was going to do more. She spit his cock back out, not wanting to push him into an early orgasm. She wanted that prick inside her, she thought, even as she enjoyed the power of teasing him.

He pulled her back to her feet and walked her backwards to the bed where he pushed her down onto it on her back. Danni grinned and winked at him as he did this; she loved the power of knowing that she was causing his sense of urgency. He lifted her legs so that her calves rested on his shoulders, causing her hips to create a welcome basin for him to rest his groin against. He pushed against her calves so that her toned legs stretched out; she groaned slightly as her muscles stretched pleasurably. She liked his heavy weight upon her; he pressed her hard into the bed. He knew that she was wet from his feel inside her earlier so he positioned his body so that he could enter her. He slid the full way up inside her and knew that she was ready and eager to be fucked. He knew that she would undoubtedly still outlast him before climaxing so he decided that he would take his maximum pleasure of her fantastic body and then take care of her needs later. He thrust in and out of her varying his speed and angle to give himself as much enjoyment as he could stand. She was quite vocal in her encouragement of his actions and he was very appreciative of that. He loved her throaty whining and occasional growling as he rode her; it really helped keep him tremendously aroused. But he couldn't last ten minutes at that pace inside of her warm, wet flesh, so he was soon straining to hold off his climax for as long as he could. Danni had been matching his thrusts into her with her own and now that she sensed him holding off, she refused to allow him to slow down. He looked down into her determined face, her teeth gripping her lips tightly as she locked her ankles behind his back and used her powerful legs to squeeze him hard up against her. He thought about protesting to her to get her to allow him to control the screwing once more but decided that by the time he got her to agree, it would be too late anyways. He could sense the imminent spurt already pushing on his control. So he applied himself once more to fucking her as hard as he could and within thirty seconds had climaxed. Danni hugged him closely to her as she relished the feeling of his warm sperm deep inside her pussy. She kept her ankles locked behind his back so that he couldn't get up from her. She grinned at him as she felt her power surge through her body. Theodore eyed her and then decided to show her that she wasn't totally in control. He slipped his right hand into the area where her right thigh contacted his hip and he applied pressure to the muscle in her inner thigh.

Danni cursed as pain shot through her. That hurt, goddamn it, she thought unhappily. Her legs opened up from the pain and surprise. Theodore let go as soon as she released him. She glared at him and he just smiled at her as he got up to go over to retrieve the toys he wanted so that he could continue on with her. He knew that she was angry at him but she was being somewhat insufferable and needed to be taught a lesson he thought. He got the toys that he wanted and went back to where she was laying. He sat down and displayed the toys; silently inquiring if she wanted to continue or if she was too mad. She let her desire overrule her anger and she nodded at him.

Theodore pushed her back down onto the bed and got the rabbit vibrator ready by sliding the tip of it around her wet crotch to lubricate it. Soon he put it up inside her, making sure that the rabbit ears contacted the lower edge of her clitoris. She groaned in pleasure and gave him a small smile; he was almost forgiven, she thought dreamily. Then he adjusted his body so that he was lying along her left leg with his face close to her cunt. She assumed that he was going to suck on her clit but instead he looped his right arm around her thigh as he used his left to continue to push the vibrator into her. He held a small, powerful vibrator in his right hand and he pushed the rough top of it against the upper part of her clitoris. With the pressure from the top and below on her extremely sensitive clit, Danni received incredible sensations sent to her brain. She squealed and screamed as they began to overwhelm her. That felt incredible she thought as she started to lose her control over her mind. Danni panted from the effort of how her body was treating her and she began to climax. Theodore kept the pressure on her as she started to struggle as she attempted to relieve the stress of what he was doing to her. She moaned out his name and he felt his cock twitch in response; he knew that he couldn't handle trying to take her again for a while but she was arousing him. She climaxed and pushed out some of her juices; Theodore smiled as he saw a glob of his cum slip out of her cunt. Theodore used his finger to scoop up some of their mixed juices and he lifted it to put into her mouth. Danni sucked the liquid off his finger eagerly and smiled widely at him. Theodore smiled back and then applied his effort to licking her pussy clean. Danni settled back to enjoy it.

After a few minutes, Theodore ceased his actions and sat up to look at her; she was lolling easily on the bed, lost slightly in the aftermath of her orgasm. He spent about thirty seconds just admiring her and then he reached out and pulled her up to her feet. She looked at him, a bit confused, and he commanded her "Go get a shower. Ms. Sturm will be along shortly to take you home." He pushed her lightly in the direction of the bathroom. She nodded and moved down towards it.

When she was finished showering, Danni went back into the living room where Theodore was now waiting for her. He'd gathered her clothes so that they were waiting for her and was seated in a chair waiting for her. He'd managed to put on his own pants. Danni walked over to him and sat in his lap, pushing him back as she bent over to kiss him. He let her plaster her warm mouth all over his as he stroked her silky body. He enjoyed the long kiss but knew that she had to get moving so he broke the kiss and urged her to get dressed. She smiled and then did as he told her. While she was putting her clothes back on, he said "Lisa has been asking to have a threesome with the pair of us. You remember Lisa?" He held his open clenched hands out in front of his chest, simulating the woman's huge breasts. Umm, Danni thought happily, I remember that big titted bitch well. Theodore said "I'm gonna invite her for Thursday if Ms. Sturm will approve it." Danni thought happily about it and Ms. Sturm picked her up a couple of minutes later and took her home.

Danni was in a very good mood when she entered the house. The family was preparing supper and she pitched in. Once they'd finished their food, Danni helped to clean up and then was getting ready to go up to work on her English essay. The essay would count for fifteen percent of her final English mark and she wanted to do it right. Danni's mother shooed the younger girls out of the room and said "Danni, your father and I need to talk with you." She gestured to a chair at the table and Danni sat down obediently and looked at her as she waited for her to say what she had to say. Danni wasn't sure what it would be about.

"I know that you have been working hard to keep your marks up" Danni's mother began, somewhat uneasily as she rubbed her arms nervously. "We're proud of you for doing that." She gave Danni a small smile. "But you have to know that we are very limited in what sort of financial help that we can give you for university. I know that you have been applying to lots of universities and are likely to get accepted but we're not going to be able to pay for those universities. I wish that we could do more to help you but I'm afraid that isn't possible."

Danni rushed in and said "Don't worry about that, Mother. I have been getting some help in arranging it so that I can afford to go to university without any money from you and Dad. I know the situation and am trying not to be a burden for you guys. You can save the money for Gina and the others. I'll be alright but I love you for worrying about it." She rushed over to give her mother a big hug.

Danni's mother hugged her hard and then gestured to her to sit back down. "Well, we're relieved to hear that, Danni. Let us know if we can give you any help with anything and make sure you plan to come home to see us if you end up at a university away from here. Go on up and do your homework." Danni got up and went up to do her essay.

CHAPTER TWELVE

On Thursday Danni headed towards Ms. Sturm's Honda, she'd had a fairly good day and was looking forward to an even better afternoon with Lisa and Theodore. Her friends had decided to bury their disappointment in her previous actions and had joined her for lunch. Their conversation hadn't been as comfortable as it had been before but it was a start. She'd also had a fun time with Evelyn and Mary the day before as well. She fairly skipped as she made her circuitous way to Ms. Sturm's car. She opened the door and got into the car.

Ms. Sturm eyed her as she got in and waited until she got herself settled before saying "I've got a solution for you to give to your parents." Danni had confided her conversation with her parents about university to Ms. Sturm and had asked for her help. Danni nodded to indicate that she was listening. "You're gonna tell them that you are going to be a live-in nanny for a rich couple who have an estate over by Richport." Danni frowned as she thought of it. She didn't want to be a nanny, she thought. She liked kids but didn't want to have to take care of them; she wanted to have fun.

"How old are the kids?" Danni asked with some trepidation.

"They're six and three" Ms. Sturm replied, rather sharply. "But what does it matter. You're not actually gonna take care of them. This is just a cover job. It allows you to tell your mother that you are going to spend most of your summer away from them and the house. You'll only be getting one day off. That being Saturday so you can go home and spend that day with them. You go home Saturday morning and leave again on Sunday morning. The rest of the time you'll be considered to be living at the estate. They'll be paying you fairly well so you'll be able to afford to go to school." She paused for a moment as she thought. "We might even be able to extend it into the school year for your mother's peace of mind."

Danni was very confused. "Who will be taking care of the kids then if it's not me? And where will I live?" She let a little bit of a whine creep into her voice.

Ms. Sturm looked angrily at her but let her attitude soften as she started to understand Danni's confusion. She realized that she hadn't explained matters very well to the younger woman. "The kids have a live-in nanny that currently takes care of them. The mother of them is willing to let us say that the nanny is taking the summer off to travel Europe and you will be taking her place. But the nanny isn't going to Europe and you aren't going to take her place. You will be occupied elsewhere. Your parents will believe that you are someplace that you won't be but they won't have to worry about you. You'll be living at a different place that I'll arrange for you. This allows me to book you away for nights so that prospective sponsors can meet you and try you out to see if you fit their plans. I have been getting a very good response from the video you did with Samantha. I will tell you more about that in the future." She paused to let that sink in and then continued in a softer voice "Do you understand now?"

Danni nodded and replied "Yes, Ms. Sturm. Thank you for doing this for me and explaining it to me." Ms. Sturm nodded and drove them over to Theodore's apartment.

Theodore met her at the doorway and guided her in; Danni could tell from his breathing and sweating that he was more excited than usual and wondered what he'd been doing with Lisa while waiting for her. She felt a spike of jealousy but pushed it down; Theodore wasn't hers and he slept with other women. She knew that. She screwed other men in front of him and he never complained; he really enjoyed watching that. These thoughts occupied her mind as she followed him into the living room. Danni glanced over at the couch and the breath caught in her throat. Lisa was sitting nude on the couch with her arms up, hands holding her hair up to the back of her head making her large breasts thrust out prominently and invitingly. Danni admired the huge tits with tremendous appreciation. She finally let her eyes wander down the rest of the gorgeous woman and noted that the other woman's legs were wide open exposing the small blonde landing strip along her shaved cunt. Danni could feel her breathing quicken and licked her lips nervously.

"Come over here Danni and let me undress you" Lisa commanded as she patted the area beside her.

Danni suddenly felt a little shy and retiring. "Maybe I should grab a quick shower first. I've been sweating at school" Danni said meekly. She was concerned with having to compare her own body with the beautiful woman, feeling that she would be coming up short. She was usually happy with her own proportions but now felt that she really needed bigger tits. Theodore looked over at her in surprise. Danni was usually quite forward. Then he thought that he understood. He resisted the urge to go over and support her.

"I don't care how dirty you might be, Danni" Lisa stated, rolling out the words slowly and seductively. "I'm gonna lick every inch of your fantastic body and your sweat and juices will only add to the pleasure I get from doing that. Just a little spice for the meal. Come over here. Please."

Danni felt her confidence come back as it became obvious that this woman wanted her and thought that she was good-looking. She let a smile flood her face and eagerly moved over to sit beside the nude blonde woman. She started to undo the buttons on her blouse but Lisa called out "No. Let me do that." So Danni stopped and moved over to perch beside her. Both of them were ignoring Theodore who moved to a nearby chair to watch. He'd moved his furniture around to give all of them room to do whatever they wanted later and to provide a good viewing area for himself.

Lisa undid the rest of Danni's buttons and helped her off with her blue silken blouse. "Theodore has told me that I get ten minutes with you before he comes over here to fuck you. I hope to get you to cum before that but if I don't, I'll get you nice and wet for him. While he's fucking you, I'm gonna ride your pretty mouth, smearing your elegant, plump lips with my juices as his cock pounds up in your tight, wet cunt. Your squirming while he screws you will hopefully excite me enough to get me to climax all over you" Lisa purred. She'd gotten Danni's bra off and was rubbing her thumb all over Danni's nipple to get it to harden even more than it was. She blocked all of Danni's attempts to fondle her own huge breasts, pushing Danni's arms back down to her sides. Danni was feeling some frustration; she really wanted to handle the other woman's breasts. Lisa slipped down and quickly removed Danni's shoes and socks, rubbing her breasts against the young woman's knees as she did it. Danni resisted the urge to reach out and touch her but showed her unhappiness on her face for being forced to do that. She did like the feel of Lisa's erect nipples rubbing around her knees. Theodore had to smother a lot of laughs as he watched Lisa teasing Danni; he appreciated the fact that Danni would be a firecracker to fuck if Lisa kept frustrating her so much. When Danni glanced over towards him, he shifted his eyes to watch Lisa's firm but plump ass to avoid meeting her eyes.

Danni was very suspicious that Theodore was enjoying her frustration and vowed to make him pay for that fact; she'd take her revenge when he was fucking her later she decided. She also decided that once Lisa let her fondle her huge breasts that she would enjoy it as much as she could, even if she made the woman somewhat sore from her effort. She relished those thoughts even as the rational back portion of her mind told her that she was a good, kind girl and wouldn't hurt another person just to hurt them. They would also have to enjoy that pain being done for her not to feel guilty in the future. Danni gave a small growl of frustration as Lisa grinned up at her as she undid and pulled Danni's skirt down her legs. Danni was now just wearing her brief panties. Since she'd been at school, she wasn't wearing a thong like she'd like to but her panties weren't that much larger; her mother had told her that they were almost indecent for school but had allowed them. Lisa rubbed the soft, silky skin of the inside of Danni's thighs right below her crotch. Danni enjoyed the stroking of her hand and Lisa appreciated the feel of her soft skin. Lisa quickly stroked the fabric above Danni's cunt with her thumb as she massaged the younger woman's muscles. Danni could feel the urge to open her legs up grow as Lisa continued to fondle her. Lisa pulled Danni's panties down and pressed her head against Danni's blonde cunt, pushing her backwards down on the couch.

Danni laughed with joy as she was pushed over. She hadn't been expecting Lisa to do that to her but certainly liked it. Lisa whipped Danni's panties completely off and tossed the wet things over to Theodore so that he could enjoy Danni's aroused scent on them. Lisa pushed Danni's legs up and open so that she could put her head down between Danni's thighs better. She plunged her wet tongue down into the younger woman's fragrant, damp pussy and ran it around her sensitive slit. Danni shivered with pleasure and Lisa dug her tongue in deeper causing Danni to sigh with desire. Lisa pushed her tongue in and out of Danni's cunt and occasionally raked Danni's sensitive flesh with her front teeth causing Danni to cry out. She worked Danni's cunt over as hard as she could for over two minutes. She could tell from the deepening of Danni's breathing and grunts that she was being aroused and was building up her orgasm. Her tongue was too tired to continue so she moved up so that she could kiss Danni's lower belly and pushed the four fingers of her right hand up into Danni's wet cunt. Danni groaned as she stretched out to take Lisa's hand; she closed her eyes and moaned in encouragement as Lisa tried to make her take her full hand. Lisa pushed her hand in and out of Danni as she used her thumb to flick Danni's engorged clitoris. It didn't take long to get Danni to start to buck her hips as her climax took over her body. Lisa smiled as she made the younger woman orgasm with a grunt.

She glanced over to Theodore and he signalled that she still had two minutes so she plunged her face into Danni's messy, smelly cunt. Danni wasn't in full control of her mind, being so aroused, but she loved the feeling of Lisa's tongue on her pussy once more. She decided that she'd forgive the older woman for teasing her so mercilessly.

After letting Lisa know that she had two minutes left, Theodore took off all his clothes so that he'd be ready when it was time for him to move in and join the pair of them. His prick was already standing quite erect from the erotic display that they'd put on and he gave it a few strokes. He loved the feel of his own hand on it. He knew that Danni would be wet and aroused enough to take his cock without any further lubrication or encouragement once he entered her. He thought of how she'd feel around his hard prick and had to quickly cool his thoughts down before he exploded. He grinned and moved over to them. He grabbed Lisa to let her know that her time was up; he made sure to reach around her torso and clutch a couple of large handfuls of her heavy tits. Lisa grunted a bit and stiffened in surprise at the shock of feeling him squeeze her breasts but quickly relaxed to enjoy it. Theodore guided her up so that she could now straddle Danni's face and give him access to Danni's sopping pussy. Lisa tried to sit up as she pushed her aroused cunt down onto Danni's face but Theodore need her to be lower down so that he could more easily enter Danni, so he pushed her down so that she was lying over Danni's face. Theodore pushed the tip of his cock up into Danni's cunt as he rested his head on Lisa's warm, sweaty back. He could smell both women and found their mixed arousal scents to be very intoxicating. Danni had enough wits about her to begin tonguing the damp cunt being pressed against her mouth. Lisa enjoyed the soft stroking from Danni's tongue as Theodore thrust into Danni as hard as he could. He rocked all of them forward somewhat as his groin came in contact with hers. Danni groaned in pleasure as he stretched her out.

Theodore took a small nip of Lisa's back as he rested deep inside Danni's tight pussy. She gave a surprised squeal and twisted slightly; Danni pulled her tighter to her face. Theodore smiled in satisfaction as he started to thrust in and out of Danni. Danni reached out above her head so that she could fondle Lisa's big tits. Lisa gave some thought to pinning Danni's arms down to deny her once more but decided that she wanted to feel the other woman's hand fondling her breasts. Danni loved the warm squishy feeling of Lisa's huge breasts as she worked over her pussy with her tongue. Theodore was rocking Danni's hips quite fiercely and she loved how that made her feel. She was attempting to anticipate his thrusts but couldn't seem to get the timing right; that's when she figured out that he wasn't following a pattern but was varying his thrusts. She wondered why he wasn't allowing her to participate as fully as she usually did. She was concentrating so much on that that she stopped licking Lisa's pussy. Lisa moaned and butted her hips against Danni's face to get her started again. Danni quickly got back to work even though she continued to wonder about Theodore's technique. Theodore knew that Danni wanted to control the sex and he didn't want her to do so; he wanted to make sure that he lasted as long as he could inside her. When she took control, she forced him to orgasm quite quickly. He knew she wouldn't be initially happy with the situation but figured that she would accept it if he could show her that she'd end up being more satisfied by his technique. He was enjoying that his face was rubbing against Lisa's lower back as she straddled Danni's face.

He spent about five minutes with his technique before he settled into his steady rhythm; he knew that he wasn't going to last too long before he climaxed. Both Danni and Lisa were making various noises and groans as they both enjoyed what was happening to them. Theodore loved the sounds that they were making. He was also pleased that Danni recognized the rhythm of his thrusts after about four times and was now meeting them with her own thrusts. He gritted his teeth as his prick threatened to explode to try to keep it in control so that he could continue his thrusts. He grunted and groaned from the effort and Danni wrapped her long legs around his back and squeezed him hard to her. In the tight vice of her strong legs, Theodore surrendered and shot gobs of warm sperm into her; he gave a triumphant scream.

Lisa pushed her round rear end against him trying to move him off of Danni but he was trapped in Danni's legs and couldn't move. "Let him go, let him go" Lisa urged Danni. "I want to suck his cum out of you" she stated urgently. Danni relaxed her legs and Theodore allowed the big breasted woman to push him off of the younger woman. He was too tired to resist too much and was consumed by the aftereffects of his massive orgasm. Lisa quickly got down between Danni's legs and placed her mouth over Danni's slit; she sucked hard on the messy cunt and stuck her tongue up into it. She was rewarded with a nice warm gob of Danni's and Theodore's mixed juices. She savoured the pleasant taste of it, rolling it around her mouth and over her tongue. She sought to suck out another gob. Danni could feel the pressure inside her again because of the erotic nature of the situation and she whined a warning to Lisa that she was about to explode again. Lisa rubbed Danni's hips, encouraging her to go ahead and orgasm; she was prepared for it. Danni gave a shrill whine and climaxed. Lisa's pretty face got covered in messy cum.

Danni decided that she needed to taste the juices so she sat up and pulled Lisa towards her so that she could tongue some of the liquid off of her. Lisa didn't resist, letting the younger woman clean up her face. She was a bit surprised when Theodore joined in but welcomed him eagerly. She enjoyed the feeling of the two soft, questing tongues slithering all over her face. A few minutes later, when they had her mostly clean, she pushed Danni backwards again and reapplied her face to Danni's messy cunt. Danni lay back, closed her eyes and relished the taste in her mouth. What could be better than this, she thought dreamily. Recovering from being fucked hard by a man and having a beautiful woman licking your pussy clean. Theodore cupped Lisa's left breast with his right hand while he fondled Danni's right breast with his left hand. He enjoyed the contrast of how they felt; he thought they were both quite wonderful. He could feel his cock stirring once more and looked at Lisa as she was bent over Danni; he considered mounting her but wasn't too sure that she'd be cooperative or not. He was getting rewarded on Saturday for allowing her to be here with him and Danni. She was going to bring her boyfriend and the two men were going to share her. But he hadn't discussed being able to fuck her that day. He didn't want to destroy his chances with her by taking advantage that she wasn't granting him. He also didn't want to disrupt her. He then gave some thought to riding Danni once more but decided that she was just too insistent for him to be able to handle right then. He slipped up beside Danni's head, turned it and pressed the tip of his cock up against her plump lips. Danni opened her mouth and let him into the incredible warmth inside. Theodore let a groan escape from his mouth as she used her tongue to caress the head of his prick.

Danni sucked Theodore's cock eagerly, she loved the taste of it. She wondered how hard he wanted her to be with him; she didn't think that he wanted her to push him too hard. She was willing to just softly suck on him and decided to do just that.

Lisa glanced up to see what they were doing and decided that she also wanted to have Theodore in her mouth. She scrambled up and put her mouth eagerly beside Danni's. Theodore laughed happily and pulled his prick from Danni's mouth and put it into Lisa's; she used her tongue to bathe the tip of his cock. Theodore spent the next few minutes swapping his cock from warm mouth to warm mouth.

"Which of you is going to give me relief?" he asked with some effort as he continued to hold his orgasm. He was completely stiff.

Lisa looked at Danni and then replied "Danni will make you cum but as soon as you feel your prick spurting I want you to pull it out of her mouth and bathe her face. I'll lick it off of her then." Theodore nodded tightly and then followed her wishes. He moaned as he sent three separate spurts up onto Danni's face. She gave a muffled squeal as some of his cum went up her nose. Lisa moved in and started slurping his cum up. Theodore settled back to watch as he recovered his composure.

A few minutes later he got up and went to get some items to clean them all off. He brought them back and started sponging the two women off. His balls ached pleasantly and the tip of his prick was quite sensitive from what they had done to him. He felt quite blissful. Lisa and Danni were now sharing open mouthed kisses as he wiped them down.

"There, you're clean enough to move around" Theodore stated with satisfaction. "Danni, you should go down and shower. Ms. Sturm will be here shortly for you."

Lisa purred "I'll go down with her and make sure she's nice and clean to go home to her family." She stood up and pulled Danni up to her feet.

"I don't think that's such a great idea" Theodore said softly. "The two of you are liable to take too long to get ready. I don't think you'll be able to keep your mind on just showering."

"Oh, we'll definitely have our minds on things other than just showering" Lisa promised with an immense grin. "But we've got what? Fifteen minutes before Ms. Sturm arrives." Theodore nodded reluctantly. "I promise to have her out in ten so that she can get her clothes on. Come on, Danni." Lisa reached her hand out and when Danni took it, she pulled the younger woman down the hallway.

Lisa cranked the water on and pushed Danni into the shower under the stream. Danni squealed. The water was cold! Lisa laughed and grinned at the upset woman as she adjusted the hot water to a more suitable temperature. "Well, one of us had to test it and I elected you" Lisa said, chortling. She entered the shower and intentionally pushed Danni against the back wall as she let the flow of water stream over her. Danni didn't like being pressed against the wall even though she did really like the feel of Lisa's large breasts against her. She pushed Lisa backwards slightly and was surprised that the woman moved easily. She'd been expecting more resistance but Lisa just remained smiling at her as she splashed water all over Danni. Danni wasn't sure what was going through the other woman's mind and frowned slightly at her. Lisa leaned in and kissed her passionately. Danni responded but Lisa pushed her back slightly and then put soap on her large breasts. She pushed her tits up against Danni's chest and began to slither them all over the front of Danni's torso. It felt and looked incredibly wonderful, Danni thought. She tried to assist but Lisa just pushed her around. Danni lost her temper and gave the other woman a smack on the side of her large left breast. It wasn't a hard hit but more of a warning.

"Oh, you want to get rough, do you?" Lisa purred and gave Danni a smack on her left hip.

Danni looked confused. This wasn't at all what she wanted. She just wanted Lisa to stop pushing her around. "No, I don't want to get into a fight with you. We need to get showered so that we can do what you promised Theodore. Can't we just get to that?" she whined slightly.

"Oh very well, spoilsport" Lisa replied and ran soapy hands all over Danni quickly and efficiently. As she washed down the younger woman she said "I'm going to fuck Theodore and my boyfriend on Saturday. Do you want to come and watch? It should be great fun." She gave Danni a toothy grin.

"I would like to but I'm afraid I can't" Danni replied with regret. "I have a previous engagement." She didn't want to tell the older woman that it was with her family; she felt suddenly shy about that.

"That's too bad" Lisa said as she guided Danni around so the soap washed off her body. Then she had a bright idea. "I've seen video of you so maybe we can film it so that you can watch it. Would you like that?" Danni nodded eagerly, feeling a sudden spike of arousal at the thought. "By the way, you looked fantastic in the video. It made me want to be with you. Your girlfriend was quite yummy as well. Maybe the three of us could get together with my boyfriend or even Theodore. What do you think?"

"Samantha would love to get together with you and me but not your boyfriend, Theodore or any man" Danni replied.

"Oh, she just likes girls then" Lisa said with disappointment. "Too bad. I'm not interested in people who restrict themselves to just one sex. They're too boring. There is a whole world of people out there to have fun with. So why restrict yourself to just one sex?"

Danni was intrigued. "So you prefer being with bi-sexuals?" she asked with interest.

"Of course" Lisa replied as she moved Danni out of the stream of water so she could rinse herself off.

"That means that Theodore and your boyfriend are bi-sexual" Danni stated quietly.

They better be" Lisa snorted with a huge grin. "They're gonna eat each other's cum out of me after they fuck me on Saturday." She guided Danni out of the shower and began to towel her off. Danni was a bit lost as she imagined what that looked like; she found that it aroused her quite a bit. Lisa threw a towel at the distracted girl and commanded "Wipe down my tits, will you." Danni immediately became interested in doing that as Lisa wiped off the rest of her body. After a moment, she said softly "We better get back to Theodore or we'll be in trouble." The two of them walked hand in hand back to the living room where Theodore was waiting for them.

Danni gathered her clothes in preparation for putting them on. She looked around with confusion. She couldn't find her panties anywhere. Lisa brought over a pair of panties in their original package and handed them to her. "Here, wear these" she told the dumbfounded Danni. Danni gave her a confused look until she remembered what Lisa had done to her previously.

"You took my panties again" she accused the older woman.

"Of course, I did" Lisa replied with a very satisfied grin. "They'll make a wonderful memento for this fuck session." Danni gave her head a rueful shake and put on the new pair of panties before getting the rest of her clothes on. Then she just had time to give both of them a quick kiss before going out to meet Ms. Sturm.

Ms. Sturm examined her as she got into the car. "You look like you had fun" she stated as she satisfied herself that Danni had no visible marks on her. She'd been a little worried that Lisa would forget herself and give Danni a love bite.

"Yes, it was tremendous fun" Danni said with a smile. Ms. Sturm nodded and drove Danni home.

CHAPTER THIRTEEN

On Friday afternoon, Danni was walking in a direction away from where Ms. Sturm's car was in order to check to see if she was being followed by one of her friends. She noticed a girl behind her that appeared to be texting on her phone but paying attention to her. Danni scowled and moved a block north. The girl followed and a second one appeared to be approaching the pair of them; she was also texting on her phone. Danni didn't really recognize either of them. She'd seen them around school but didn't recall much else. She hurried to the west to avoid them but a third girl appeared up in front of her. Danni realized that she was being followed and maybe herded to some spot. She decided that she wasn't going to be able to give them all the slip and they were being fairly obvious about what they were doing so she just kept walking towards the west. She was a couple of blocks north and east of Ms. Sturm at the moment so she just strode along, feigning unconcern.

There was a woman leaning against a car about half a block in front of her that stood up and slapped the car three times with her hand. The car pulled out and the woman walked over to the sidewalk. She appeared to be waiting patiently for Danni to come up to her. Danni recognized who she was; she was Jamey, the girl in school who was very openly gay and ran with a group of lesbians who were known to try to help all girls that may be questioning their sexuality. What did she want with her, Danni wondered with some concern. But she walked up and said "Hello, Jamey. Did you want to talk with me? You could have just put a note in my locker. I would have met with you." She gave the short, plump young woman a very tentative smile.

"Most girls don't really want to be associated with me and my group if they haven't decided to declare themselves" Jamey said as she gave Danni a reassuring, friendly smile. "I thought that you might want to meet away from school and any eyes that might comment on your actions. We don't mean you any harm Danni and would like to help you if we can. I've seen some video of you." Jamey let that information hang there as she waited for Danni to respond.

Danni thought about it for a moment or two and then stated boldly "I am not a lesbian, Jamey." Jamey smiled at her and quirked an eyebrow to say that she had seen video that proved differently but didn't say anything. "Yes, I do like eating women's pussies and having them do the same to me. But I am bi-sexual. I like men as much as I like women." Danni stopped to find out what Jamey's response would be.

Jamey waved her hand dismissively, indicating that the clarification didn't matter. "We want to help anyone who may have questions about their sexuality or personality, Danni. There was a lot of discussion among our group as to whether or not you need help. Most of us believe that you don't. But we'd rather not be proven wrong. Therefore we'd rather let you know that we are here and willing to help you if you need it rather than risk you feeling all alone in this matter." She paused for a moment but Danni just watched her and didn't say anything. "I think that you have people that you can talk with if you have any doubts." She gave Danni another grin and Danni was reminded that Jamey's mother was involved with one of the groups that Ms. Sturm was involved with. She wondered how much Jamey knew about her and Ms. Sturm.

"I thank you and your group for their offer of help. If I feel that I need help, I'll take advantage of your kind offer" Danni said respectfully. She really did feel that Jamey and her friends did their best to help people and she liked that about them. She just didn't feel that she fell in the category of needing help.

Jamey nodded and pulled a brochure out of her backpack. She offered it to Danni while saying "This is a listing of people who are professionals who can help you no matter what you may need. There are coding words with all of them so that they can be paid for their work. It will cost you nothing if you need to contact them. Various organizations have contributed to the funds that pay these people." She also offered Danni a business card and stated "This is my phone number as well as Zoe's. If either of us is too busy to answer, it will be forwarded to another of our group. Whoever you contact amongst us will help you in any way that you need. Feel free to phone us even if you just need someone to talk to. We really do want to help." Danni remembered that Zoe was Jamey's girlfriend and was probably the one driving the car that dropped her off. Danni nodded and put them into her backpack as Jamey started to head away. "Goodbye, Danni, you looked beautiful in the video" she stated as she walked off. Danni watched her head toward the car parked further up the block and looked around. She didn't see any of Jamey's friends around but she kept an eye out for them as she walked up and then headed back towards Ms. Sturm's car. She didn't see anyone watching her.

"You're late" Ms. Sturm said with some concern as Danni got into the car.

Danni settled herself, grimaced slightly and said "Jamey and her friends waylaid me."

"What did they want?" Ms. Sturm interrupted, letting a cool tone permeate her voice.

"They just wanted to offer me their help if I needed it" Danni reassured her. "Jamey has seen the video of me and Samantha. She offered me a brochure and told me that if I had any questions about my sexuality that I could contact those people for free."

"Do you have any concerns?" Ms. Sturm asked with a touch of worry.

"No" Danni replied honestly. "Do I love getting fucked and eaten? Yes. Do I care if it is a man or woman doing it? No. I only care if I like the person I'm with and I seem to like lots of people." Danni gave Ms. Sturm a smile.

"Yes, as far as I can see, you only have one issue with sex" Ms. Sturm said.

"What is that?" Danni asked with surprise. She didn't think that she had any issues as far as sex was concerned. Sure she needed some more training and experience to do some things but that wasn't really an issue, was it?

Ms. Sturm faced her and looked her right in the eyes before stating "You're insatiable." Danni looked at her with a touch of disbelief. "That's not necessarily a bad thing" Ms. Sturm continued with a bright smile causing Danni to smile and laugh. Then she drove them to Evelyn and Mary's place.

Danni walked up to the door and rang the bell; Mary answered the door wearing a long silken robe. She ushered Danni in with a large smile and Danni grinned back. "We thought we would try something different this afternoon" Mary stated. "You may think it a little weird but we'd like you to give it a try." Mary led her into the living room and stripped off her robe. Evelyn was sitting naked on the couch. Danni noticed that Mary was wearing a somewhat different leather harness, not the usual one she used for strap-on sex with Danni. Danni couldn't figure out exactly what the new harness would help Mary accomplish; she gave the older woman a quizzical look. Mary smiled at her and picked up another harness while saying "Evelyn will help you undress and then we'll put this on you." The harness she held also looked different to Danni.

But she went over to Evelyn and let the older woman undress her; she only moved to allow the older woman easier access to her clothing, knowing that both Evelyn and Mary liked to take her clothes off. She only grinned as Evelyn removed all her clothes and gave her upper inner thigh a friendly grope. Mary came over and the two women fastened the heavy leather harness to her hips and thighs while Danni watched them; she still couldn't figure out the reason for it.

When they had it attached to her, Mary said "You're going to lay on Evelyn and fuck her with this dildo. At the same time, I'm going to fuck you with this dildo. I'm going to be attached to your harness with straps so when I pull out of you, I'm gonna pull you backwards and out of Evelyn as well. When I push forward, I'm gonna penetrate you and force you into penetrating Evelyn. With a little practice, we should get the timing right so that both you and Evelyn are getting fucked hard enough to enjoy it."

Danni looked at her dubiously and asked meekly "So you're gonna stick that dildo on you up my ass?" She wasn't sure she wanted to experience anal sex and definitely didn't want it in this situation.

"No, the dildo will go into your cunt. There'll be enough room. The harness is designed that way. Part of the reason for the straps around your thighs" Mary reassured her. "Get down and I'll get the straps between us adjusted. We need to get them tight enough that I can still keep the tip of the dildo buried in your cunt when I pull out of you and tight enough that I can help you out of Evelyn without too much strain but loose enough that I have some dildo to push up into your cunt. We'll do it fairly slow at first so we can get the rhythm down." Evelyn lay on her back and Danni crawled on top of her. Evelyn helped Danni get the rather large black dildo started into her cunt. When that was done, Mary moved in behind Danni and pushed the pink dildo up into her about half way. Danni felt its familiar shape and was pleased by the sensation. Then Mary attached the straps on her harness to the heavy metal attachment points on Danni's harness.

When that was all done, Mary said "Now, move forward into Evelyn as I penetrate you. I'm gonna push fairly hard against you to get you to take this dildo. You must try to push back against me as you also move forward into Evelyn." Mary had put a gel on the two dildos so that they would have some lubrication on them. She moved her hips forward strongly to get Danni to take the rest of the dildo. Danni had been moving forward slowly into Evelyn when Mary basically slammed into her, pushing her off balance so that she collapsed onto Evelyn.

"I thought we were gonna take it slow" she complained to Mary as she got sandwiched between the two older women. Evelyn basically had the breath knocked out of her as the two other women landed on her and was pushing them back off her so that she could catch her breath.

"Sorry, that was my fault" Mary confessed. "I wanted to get you to take the full length of the dildo and didn't realize that I'd force you off balance." She stopped to consider the matter for a moment and then continued "Maybe I should just fuck you for a few minutes and get the dildo sliding easily in and out of your cunt and then we can position you so that you can fuck Evelyn. How about that? Evelyn, can you just brace her shoulders for a few minutes?"

Danni grunted out "Fine, let's do that." Evelyn just nodded her acceptance as she recovered her breath. Mary positioned Danni so the younger girl could accept the dildo up inside her easily and she began working her hips forward and backward. Danni started to match her pace, enjoying the feel of the toy up inside her. She whined in frustration when Mary stopped and blocked her from continuing as she started putting Danni back into position above Evelyn.

"Okay, let's work together now. Forward" Mary commanded. She tried to move just slightly faster than Danni did so that she could slowly push the dildo up inside the younger woman. She did however help push the dildo on Danni the final two inches into Evelyn. She waited for about ten seconds and then began to back up, pulling on Danni's hips with her hands to help her extract herself from Evelyn. Then she held Danni in place as she pulled the dildo out of Danni as far as the restraining straps would allow. Then she guided the whole process forward once more. The two women moved slowly through the actions until they began to find the proper pace. Then they began to move with more confidence and surety. Danni started to enjoy the feeling of being in the middle.

Mary started to tire from the effort of not only her own actions but also helping Danni in her movements. "I don't think we're gonna be very successful today, Danni" she panted in the younger woman's ear. "So let's stop and Evelyn will eat your pussy until you cum while I take a rest." She pushed Danni forward and unhooked the straps to free her from being attached to her before pulling the pink dildo out of her. She then unhooked the harness on Danni before urging her up onto Evelyn's face. She felt exhausted and sweaty as well as slightly disappointed with the escapade. She sat back and watched as Evelyn enjoyed Danni's wet cunt.

After a few minutes Danni started to show the signs of her impending climax and Mary moved up beside the two of them and began massaging the back of Danni's neck with her right hand. Her left hand went for Danni's left breast and she squeezed and fondled that. Danni was groaning and making small almost squeaking noises as she enjoyed what the other two women were doing for her. She could feel her intensity build up in her pussy and began moaning, indicating that she was close to her orgasm. She gave a deep grunt, held her breath as her hips shook and then pressed herself hard into Evelyn's wet face. She relished the lapping of Evelyn's tongue on her wet slit. Mary removed her hand from Danni's neck and dug three of her fingers into Danni's sodden pussy. She transferred them up to her mouth so that she could enjoy Danni's sweet juices. Danni initially stiffened in surprise as Mary's fingers violated her but she quickly relaxed to let her have her way. She felt relaxed and satisfied as she always did after good sex.

Mary let Evelyn have a few minutes to enjoy cleaning up Danni before she said "You better go have a shower and then come back here to dress if you want to be ready for Samantha and Rose to pick you up. I'm sorry that our little experiment didn't work out as well as I thought it would." She gave Danni a light tap on her bare behind.

Danni straightened up and kissed both of the other women. "I think with some practice we might get those harnesses to work so don't give up on it entirely" she said as she headed towards the shower. Danni washed herself off thoroughly, giving brief thought to yesterday's shower with Lisa fondly. Then she toweled off and combed her wet hair. She used the blow dryer to finish it off and headed back to the living room. She heard Mary's grunts of pleasure as she neared the room and walked in quietly to see what was happening.

Mary decided that she needed some relief so she was now kneeling in front of Evelyn on the couch. Evelyn was pushing a thick dildo in and out of her quite fiercely, giving Mary intense pleasure. Danni noticed that there were three piles of clothes up in front of them so they could watch her dress and went over to examine them. She chose a dark burgundy dress that came down a few inches below her crotch but had a fringe that extended coverage down to an inch or so above her knee. She thought the fringes would look fantastic as she wiggled her hips as she danced. She noticed that Mary had chosen a small scarlet red thong and scarlet lace bra to go with the dress. She wasn't sure that the combination worked but put it on to check it out. She found that she liked the way the brilliant red bra peeped out of the top of the dress as she moved around. She glanced over to where the two women were on the couch and found that they were finished and were watching her. She grinned at them as she adjusted her silk stockings and slipped her feet into a pair of red shoes that were low enough to allow her to dance but had enough heel to make her wiggle as she walked. She twirled slightly to show them and they smiled and nodded at her. Then she put on her light makeup; she had a tendency to sweat her makeup off dancing so she didn't use too much. She didn't want to look like some rabid raccoon or anything.

Just as she was finishing, the doorbell rang. She hurried over and kissed the two women goodbye before heading to the door. It was Samantha, as she thought it would be, and she greeted her. Samantha grabbed her hand and pulled her down the driveway after Danni closed the door. They piled into the backseat of the car and Rose drove to the restaurant.

After a delicious and pleasant meal, they went over to The Naughty Nymph. There was a bit of a crowd around the door and Danni despaired at the thought that they might not get in but Dawn burst out of the crowd and beckoned them in. Danni thought that the waiting women might object as they made their way through them but the women just smiled and nodded at them. Danni was relieved when she saw Dawn's girlfriend Jill waiting for them inside the door along with Dawn. Jill hadn't been present the previous week when Dawn had her incident with Samantha and Danni hoped that her presence would stop another event like that. She was somewhat bemused when Dawn grabbed Samantha's right hand and started to pull her through the pub. Jill took Samantha's left hand so the the two women were now guiding Samantha over to the five empty chairs. Danni was used to being the one being pulled everywhere and felt a small pang of jealousy and regret. Rose just laughed and took Danni's hand to lead her over.

Dawn and Jill led Samantha through the crowd towards the crowd of women waiting for them; there were five empty chairs in front of the group. Dawn and Jill took the ones to the right, seating Samantha between them. They continued to hold her hands as they sat down. They were also chattering energetically with her. Danni went to sit down on the chair in the middle near the three of them but the woman sitting at the edge jumped up and guided her over to the chair near her. The woman grinned at her and stroked her arm as she introduced herself and started talking with Danni. Rose felt a bit neglected but she sat down and looked around; it appeared to be quite crowded in the pub and she was surprised that the women had been able to keep the chairs open for them. She glanced over at Danni and noticed that the woman seated to her right was now trying to pull the young blonde woman up onto the dance floor. Danni initially resisted but soon let herself be persuaded. Two other women quickly followed them up to dance. Rose looked around for the waitress and her lap was quickly filled by Cindy who kissed her throat wetly. Micki quickly filled Danni's empty chair and reached over to grasp Rose's thigh just under the edge of her dress as way of greeting. Rose was quite elated by the welcome of the pair of them. The waitress made her way over with a tray of drinks and dropped off what they had been drinking the week before for them. "If you want something different, let me know" she informed Rose. Rose tried once more to pay for the drinks but the waitress shook her head. "Same conditions as last week. You drink for free and I'm still collecting lots of tips from this mob." She waved her hand to indicate the group of women who laughed with her. Micki saluted her with her rum punch.

Danni danced with a variety of women for over ten minutes. Micki and Cindy led Rose up to dance with her. Danni gave them a bright, wide smile as she bumped hips with and older, plump brunette woman that was currently dancing with her. She was happy that they were paying that much attention to Rose and that Rose was enjoying their company so greatly; she was pleased the older woman found people to attend her at the pub. Danni recognized that the group of women tended to see her and Samantha more as the prizes than Rose. Danni did wonder if the group of women had designated Micki and Cindy to keep Rose busy and happy; it didn't really matter to her but she hoped that everyone involved enjoyed themselves. The heavier woman bumped her a little too hard and she stumbled slightly away but a tall, blonde woman grabbed her to steady her. The woman gave her a quick peck on her neck as she helped Danni regain her balance and then pushed her gently back towards her partner who was quite contrite about what she had done. Danni just laughed with delight and gave the brunette a brief hug. A few minutes later, Danni determined that she was tired and needed a break. She told her new partner that she needed to sit down for a while and was led back towards the group. She chortled slightly as she saw Dawn and Jill leading Samantha up to the dance floor.

Her dance partner led her to her seat and then disappeared back into the group of women. The woman sitting to her right handed Danni her drink and waited for her to drink about three-quarters of it before she started stroking Danni's arm and talking with her. Danni enjoyed the conversation. The waitress was over about a minute later with a new drink for Danni who finished the dregs of the one she was holding before putting it on the tray. "Are you fine with the Coke Zero or do you want something else next time, Danni?" the waitress asked. Danni indicated that she was fine with the Coke Zero and took a refreshing sip of the new drink. The waitress grinned and nodded before grabbing the five dollar tip that the woman beside Danni held out to her. She moved off to get further drink orders from the women. Danni thanked the woman for her gesture and the woman just smiled brightly at her.

The woman seated beside her chatting to her changed three times in the next ten minutes and then Danni was dragged back up to the dance floor. Danni danced enthusiastically before taking another break. When she was seated this time, Micki was sitting by Rose; the blonde woman smiled at Danni and greeted her by name before returning her attention to Rose. Samantha came over to sit and talk to Danni. She paused to consider where she was going to sit but Micki immediately jumped up so that Samantha could have her seat. Micki went to meld back into the crowd but Rose grabbed her hand to hold her near her so Micki stood behind Rose's chair. Jill noticed that and moved over so that Micki could have the seat on Rose's left hand side. Danni was somewhat amazed at how the women all tried to share the attention of the three of them.

"Pretty crowded in here tonight, isn't it?" Samantha asked as she took Danni's left hand in both of hers. She didn't wait for Danni to do more than nod and then stated "I want to be the first to dance with you the next time you are ready. Then Dawn and Jill will take their turns. You okay with that?" Danni nodded eagerly once more, saving her breath, knowing that she was going to need it later. It appeared that she would be doing quite a bit of dancing that night and it excited her.

They all danced for over three hours and Danni was feeling slightly exhausted from how many times she'd been taken up to the floor. She was pretty sure that she'd danced at least once with everyone in the large group and the pretty waitress had gotten in two dances with her. Rose came over to tell her that it was time to go and Danni could sense the exhilaration that the older redhead was feeling. It was pretty obvious to Danni that Cindy and Micki would be visiting her and Samantha and Danni felt happiness for them. Rose and Samantha took her to Evelyn and Mary's place so that she could get cleaned up and changed to go home. Danni expected them to ask Mary to drive her home once more but they stayed and took Danni home themselves. "Cindy and Micki want some time to get ready before joining us" Rose explained. "They won't be coming over until later so we have time to take you home ourselves." Danni thanked them for the ride and the evening and they told her it was their pleasure.

Danni entered the house where her mother was waiting up for her to come home. She was ten minutes ahead of her curfew so her mother just smiled a greeting at her. Danni blew her a kiss and headed up to her room. She was still feeling a little keyed up from the night so she grabbed her books and did just over an hour of studying before retiring for the night.

CHAPTER FOURTEEN

Danni got up the next morning and put in about an hour of study before joining her family for breakfast. Since Pierre was coming over about three to spend the afternoon with her before eating supper with her family, she'd promised her sisters that she would spend most of the morning playing some games with them. She did that and enjoyed their happiness that she was participating with them. When she was done that, she hit the books for about another hour before she started to get ready for Pierre's arrival. She had a shower and washed and moisturized her body in preparation. She checked to make sure she didn't need shaved or trimmed anywhere before she put on a very nice pink panty and bra set that Rose had given her the evening before. It was more conservative that most of the items that she kept over at Evelyn and Mary's place but was the sexiest underwear that she had at the house. She wondered what her mother would say about them once she'd noticed. She hoped that her mother wouldn't make too big a deal about them. She knew that she wasn't interested in Pierre but felt that he still deserved for her too look very good for him. That was why she'd asked Rose to bring the underwear for her. She put on a tight pale blue tank top that allowed her breasts and bra to peep out of it quite nicely. Then she put on a darker blue pair of short shorts that exposed her long, lean legs. She put on the lace-up sandals with the highest heel that she had. She looked at herself in her full-length mirror and thought that she looked quite sexy and desirable but still conservative enough that her mother wouldn't make too much of a fuss.

She went downstairs at about five to three. Her mother glanced at her as she entered the kitchen and then did a double take to stand with her hands on her hips as she examined Danni. Danni looked her right in the eyes and set her face in an immobile expression. She was prepared to object to any lecture her mother might make. Her mother recognized Danni's attitude and realized that if she made any fuss that she and Danni would end up in a screaming match. She didn't really want to do that to her eldest daughter right before the boy who was going to take her to the Prom arrived. She also realized that her daughter was grown up and deserved to be allowed to show how sexy she was. She couldn't be protected forever. So she sighed and said "I would have preferred you to wear something less revealing, Danni, but if that is what you want to wear, I'm not going to object. It does show you off quite a bit. I'm sure that Pierre will love seeing you like that." She gave Danni a small, tentative smile. Danni grinned back at her gratefully and didn't say anything. She went into the living room and positioned herself so that she could spring up and answer the door when Pierre arrived. She wanted to take him out for a walk before he met her parents so she could set the record straight about what was going on. She hadn't wanted to do it at school.

When she answered the door, Pierre smiled at her as he met her eyes. Then he was drawn by the irresistible urge to examine her so his eyes crawled down over her exposed chest. He gave a stifled gasp as his eyes greedily crawled over the tops of her nicely formed tits. She pushed it out a bit so that he could see her pink bra more and he gave a low groan. Then she watched with amusement as his eyes crept down her waist and hips to inspect her legs. She stood up on her tiptoes to expose her leg muscles slightly better and she saw him wince with desire. She didn't mind that he was looking her over so intently; she liked the attention. After a minute, she broke the silence and said, slightly huskily, "Let's go for a walk. I want to get some things straight with you before we go any further." She stepped forward and pulled the open door closed behind her before pulling his right arm into her and pressing her breasts against the back of it. She guided him down the walkway so that they could walk around the block. Once they were out the gate and on their way, Danni stated bluntly "I'm not going to be your girlfriend, Pierre. Once the Prom is over, I'm not going to see you again. I have different plans and you aren't in them. Also, I'm not going to suck your cock or let you fuck me just for taking me to the Prom." She paused as she heard him groan audibly as she said this. He was imagining what it would be like to watch her kneel in front of him as she sucked on his stiff cock. Danni examined his flushed face curiously wondering if the groan was one of dismay and then she realized what he must be picturing. She gave him a broad mischievous grin as she let him have his fantasy. She didn't mind him thinking of her that way. She knew that she wasn't going to fulfill his desire.

When he'd managed to regain control over himself and banish the fantasy image of her, they resumed walking and he said "I know that you aren't looking to be my girlfriend but I am truly grateful that you are doing this for me. It's something that I'll remember for the rest of my life. Thank you. And I don't expect any more from you than getting to accompany you to the Prom. I promise to be a gentleman and behave myself. Are you gonna want a favour from me for this?"

"No, no" Danni assured him with a smile. "You just have to arrange the usual things to take a girl to the Prom. You know. A car and flowers are nice. Don't spend too much money." Then she looked at him with a more somber look and asked gently "Is there a girl that you would like to get to know better? Someone who might be available to be your girlfriend? I might be able to help you with that by making her jealous of me being with you."

They walked along in silence for a moment and then Pierre confessed slowly "Well, there is this girl that I like. I'm not sure she likes me or not though. You know her. Rosa."

Danni screwed up her face as she tried to picture the girl. No one came to mind and then she remembered. Rosa was a short brunette girl with a slightly plain olive coloured face. She'd been hoping that Pierre hadn't set his sights too high on someone that he wouldn't be able to get even with her help but she thought that Rosa was someone who was below the level that Pierre would be able to attract on his own. "Short brunette about this tall" Danni said holding her hand up just above her own chin. Pierre nodded somewhat eagerly and Danni frowned at him. She wondered if he had a confidence problem when it came to women and considered if she should bolster his self-assurance or not. She asked "Does she have a boyfriend?"

Pierre shook his head and replied "I don't think so. I think she'll be going to the Prom with a bunch of the other girls."

Danni nodded and said "Okay, I'll play up to you for the next couple of weeks to see if we can get her to want to take you away from me. Don't get too hot and flustered about it though when I do it. Try to keep your cool. I'll kiss you and press against you. You can fondle me back but don't try to go too far or you'll get the sharp point of my elbow. Okay?" Pierre nodded his understanding and noticed that they were almost back at Danni's house again.

He turned to face her and said "Thank you for doing this for me, Danni. I do appreciate it." She nodded and stepped into him giving him a brief kiss on the lips before moving back from him again and leading him towards the house.

As they approached the house, Danni could see Molly peering out the front window watching for them and when she ducked back from the window, Danni knew that Molly would be shouting to her family that they had returned from their walk. So she wasn't surprised that her mother had lined up the whole family to greet Pierre as they entered. All of her family greeted Pierre warmly and Danni's mother offered them a drink and a seat on the couch. Pierre requested some ginger ale. "You wouldn't prefer a glass of wine or even a beer?" Charlene Archer asked him with a small frown. She was pouring three glasses of white wine. She handed one to Danni and Pierre could see the surprise on Danni's face. He was pretty certain that Danni didn't drink with her parents often.

"Well, if everyone else is having wine, then I'd be glad to join you" he said, trying to project confidence that he really didn't feel.

"Well" Charlene said with a smile. "Not everyone is having wine and if you would prefer not to, we can get you some ginger ale." Pierre assured her that he would love to have some wine with them so she poured him a glass and handed it to him. Danni had sipped slightly at her wine, feeling slightly awkward about drinking it in front of her parents. Her mother hadn't even asked her if she wanted some but had just handed it to her, signalling to Danni that she knew that her daughter drank alcohol. Charlene held up her wine glass in a toast and said "Here's to a lovely Prom. May you have lots of fun." They drank to her toast. Danni's younger sisters were watching them all quite intently; they were intrigued by the adult ceremony and were very proud of their older sister.

Pierre and Danni sat with her parents and chatted easily with them for over a half hour. Pierre's parents had been invited but his mother worked on Saturdays so she couldn't come and his father was too self-conscious of his lack of English to come without her. She had arranged to be off on the Saturday of the Prom though. Pierre and Danni would be having dinner with his parents on Thursday. Charlene had coaxed Pierre to tell her of his plans for after high school and she was quite impressed with them. She suspected that Pierre wouldn't be remaining Danni's boyfriend since she'd never mentioned him previously but decided to treat him as though he might be. It was easier that way, she thought.

Danni got up and stated "I think that maybe it's time for me to show everyone my choice of Prom dresses. What do you think?" Pierre nodded enthusiastically and saw that Danni's younger sisters were also excited about seeing her in the dresses. Charlene nodded her agreement and Danni's father just smiled at her. Danni went up and put on her least favourite of the three. It was pale blue, high necked with puffy sleeves and extended down to her lower calf. She felt it made her hips look too boxy. She wore it down to get their opinion.

"That doesn't look too bad" Charlene stated as Danni walked in. Danni glanced around at the rest of the group. Pierre showed a noncommittal expression to her but her younger sisters all scowled, displaying that they didn't think too much of the dress.

"What do you think, Daddy?" she asked as she turned to her father.

"I think you would make anything look beautiful" he replied unhelpfully. She gave him a brief scowl before doing a small turn to let them all see all sides of the dress. Then she went up and put on the red dress. This one plunged nicely in the front and had small straps that exposed her shoulders. It draped not too badly over her hips but also came down to her lower calves. She didn't really like the shade of red that it was either but it was better than the first one in her opinion.

When she walked into the living room this time, her mother frowned; Danni was aware that Charlene didn't like the exposure of her daughter's cleavage in this dress. Pierre showed more interest in this dress than the first one but Danni wasn't sure if that was just because of the exposure of her tits or not. Gina gave her a wolf whistle and the younger two giggled in happiness; they liked the dress and thought it showed Danni off very well. Danni turned to her father and he just smiled at her, trying to remain aloof of the situation. Hmmph, she thought, no help there.

Charlene came over and adjusted the dress slightly as she considered how well it fit Danni.

"It'll need a little adjustment" she stated. "But so will all of them. Let's see the last one and then we can discuss which one you should wear." Danni went up and put on the last one. This dress was black; it had black lace on the top and bottom of it. Her shoulders would be covered with lace but it had quite a wonderful hole that exposed the gap in her breasts. The lace ended at the point of her shoulders so her arms were completely bare. It also left her upper back mostly bare. The material of the dress ended just below her knees and the lace down there covered her legs down to mid-calf, which she liked. It fit quite snugly on her hips, accentuating her figure but still allowed her to move around enough that she felt she could dance.

When she entered the room this time, Pierre examined her with a contemplative look on his face; he wasn't sure if he liked her better in this new dress or the red one. Danni's sisters smiled their approval of the dress at her, liking most of the features of it but they'd liked how the red dress exposed the tops of her breasts which this one didn't. Charlene came up and checked to see that the lace wouldn't be a problem for her. She was concerned that it might be too scratchy for Danni to wear for any length of time but it seemed pliable enough. She pulled at the material at Danni's hips to see how much room it gave her. She turned Danni towards her husband and asked "Now that you've seen all three dresses, which one do you think looks best on her?"

"She looks good in them all" her father hedged. "But if I had to choose, I would say that I like this black one the best."

Charlene turned Danni towards Pierre and asked "Pierre?"

"It would be a choice between the red one and this one" Pierre replied. "Both of them look very good on her. I kinda like the red one more though." Charlene hmmphed at their opinions while Danni grinned at Pierre; she thought that he just liked the red one because it exposed her tits so much. Charlene didn't bother to check with her younger daughters because she knew that they liked this black dress. Danni had worn all of the dresses for her mother and sisters earlier in the week when they'd been making their elimination selection of them. Charlene favoured this black one even though she felt it was too tight on Danni's hips.

"What do you think, honey?" she asked her oldest daughter.

"I think I like this one the best" Danni replied. She looked down at herself and said "The lace will allow me to remain cool but still cover up most of my skin so I won't get too many frowns. It fits quite nicely but allows me to move around. I think that I can easily dance in it and I like the colour more."

Her mother nodded and then looked over at Pierre. "It seems we all like the black one more. Do you have any objections to her wearing this one?" Danni frowned at her mother; she didn't like that her mother seemed to be allowing Pierre the final say on her dress. She was the one who'd have to wear it.

Pierre thought for a moment and then realized what he had to do. He said "You looked absolutely gorgeous in both the red and black dresses, Danni. But if you feel more comfortable in the black one, then I think that you should wear it. But you have the final say in the matter." He smiled at Danni and she forgave him for liking her more in the red dress.

"I'll wear the black one" she told her mother. Her mother nodded and went off to see how dinner was going. Danni went back up to her room and changed back into the clothes she'd been wearing. Pierre chatted with Danni's fathers and younger sisters.

They had a wonderful dinner of roast beef, mashed potatoes, gravy and peas because that is what Pierre had told Danni he wanted to eat when she'd asked him earlier in the week. The family was quite happy with the meal and were grateful that he hadn't asked for something more elaborate. Pierre enjoyed both the food and company. He went home just after eight having played a number of games with Danni and her family. He'd really enjoyed the whole evening and Danni had given him a kiss goodbye. He loved the feeling of her in his arms even though he knew they had no future.

CHAPTER FIFTEEN

Sunday morning Danni made her way to joining Ms. Sturm so that she could be taken over to Samantha and Rose's place for her Sunday sex session with them. She was in a good mood and skipped the final thirty feet to the car. Ms.Sturm eyed her with a smile on her face as she noted Danni's happy mood. After she'd sat down, Danni asked Ms. Sturm "May I kiss you, Ms. Sturm?"

"Why?" Ms. Sturm asked as she let her puzzlement show. She hadn't done anything out of the ordinary lately as far as she was concerned.

"Because I am happy and want to share it. And because you have been doing so much for me that I want to thank you for" Danni replied with a tremendously saucy grin.

Ms. Sturm eyed Danni carefully. It really wasn't a sufficient reason in her books, she thought as she considered the matter. But if she didn't let Danni get some of her exuberant feelings out of her system, Danni might do something more reckless, she thought. It really didn't do any harm to let the young woman have her way sometimes, she reasoned as she pushed the thought that she wanted to feel those beautiful plump lips on hers. "Very well, Danni. That is not a sufficient reason but since you have been very good lately, I will allow it." Danni immediately grabbed the sides of Ms. Sturm's face and planted her moist mouth on the older woman's mouth. Danni held the kiss for almost two minutes until Ms. Sturm broke it. Wow, that young woman could kiss when she wanted to, Ms. Sturm thought as her body felt a wave of warmth pass through it from her increase in desire. She moved back from Danni and caught the younger woman watching her with a sly mischievous smile on her face. She knew exactly what she was doing, Ms. Sturm thought. She smiled at Danni and told her "That was extremely pleasant. You're a good kisser. But you still need a good reason to ask to kiss me. So remember that. I have some bad news for you." She paused to let Danni think about that, watching as a flash of dismay crossed her face. "I have decided that until your Prom that your sexual sessions will be fast and quick so as to give you only the relief that you need. I want you to spend as much time as possible on your studies and then your Prom preparations. I have informed Samantha, Rose, Evelyn, Mary and Theodore of this so they will take the appropriate steps. It starts today. Samantha and Rose only get you for an hour today and then I will pick you up and take you to the library to study for two hours before taking you home." She paused once more to assess Danni's attitude. She was pleased that the young woman was nodding in agreement and understanding even though she was showing signs of disappointment.

"I have that dinner with Pierre's parents on Thursday. I need to go to that. Is Theodore going to fuck me first?" Danni asked hesitantly as she looked slightly woeful. "I really need to get fucked before that."

Ms. Sturm nodded and replied "You'll get fucked by Theodore on Thursday but he'll be quick about it and you'll go to the dinner. Also, you'll still get to have your Friday night dates. You need to have some fun. As long as you work hard the rest of the time, you can keep that. Okay?" Danni nodded eagerly in agreement. Ms. Sturm started the car and drove over to Samantha and Rose's place.

Rose met her at the door and ushered her in. "Ms. Sturm told you that we don't have much time?" she asked Danni as she guided the young woman down the hallway. Danni nodded and Rose began helping Danni off with her clothes as they walked down the hallway. Surely we have more time than that, Danni thought, as she had to grab her jeans as they fell down her hips. Rose knew that she could have waited for Danni to get to the living room before trying to strip her but she wanted to tease the younger woman a bit. She chortled as Danni frantically tried to keep her pants up as she walked. Samantha already had the leather strap-on belt around her waist and was applying a good coating of lubrication to Danni's favourite pink dildo when she turned to watch the pair of them walk in. She could see Danni's irritation and frustration as she came in and recognized that Rose had been harassing the younger woman. Rose was displaying an intense air of satisfaction about her.

"Come over here and we'll get the rest of your clothes off" Samantha said with welcome in her voice. "Even though Rose has appeared to have made a very good start at stripping you." Danni went over and Samantha quickly had her clothes off and was stroking her slippery fingers in and out of Danni's cunt. Some of the lubricant she'd been applying to the dildo transferred to Danni's pussy and Danni began supplying some juices herself. Samantha knew that she didn't have enough time to get Danni fully aroused so she just wanted Danni wet enough so that she could accept the plastic toy without too much discomfort. It didn't take too long to get her that way; Rose's harassment of her had actually allowed Danni to get into a more receptive mood sooner. Both Samantha and Rose were well aware of how to push Danni's buttons; the young woman liked to be pushed around sexually. Although Danni had a strong personal character, sexually she was an almost complete submissive. Samantha loved that because she knew that she was well on the way to becoming a dom.

Samantha pushed Danni down onto her back and spread her legs so that she could push the tip of the dildo up into Danni's cunt. She rocked the tip of the plastic cock in and out of Danni's slit to get her a bit more prepared for the penetration.

Danni smiled up at her and moaned her approval. Then Samantha pushed as hard as she could to force the dildo up into Danni. Danni groaned and wriggled as the dildo slid up into her. She loved the feeling of being impaled by the plastic toy. She was wet enough that the dildo entered her almost completely. Samantha didn't allow her to enjoy her penetration but started pulling it back out of her almost immediately. Danni whined her frustration at the brunette. Samantha gave Danni's right hip a light slap with her left hand and snarled "We don't have time for that, Danni." Samantha pushed the dildo up into Danni's cunt once more and almost bottomed it out in Danni this time. She didn't allow Danni to enjoy the full feeling she wanted but once more pulled it back out. Danni grabbed her upper lip in her teeth so as not to moan in frustration once more. Samantha grinned at her and started to set a fast pace of thrusts to get Danni aroused enough to climax.

Samantha fucked Danni with the dildo furiously for over five minutes. She felt herself tiring and could feel a sheen of perspiration all over her body from her exertion. Danni had her eyes closed and was moaning as she continued to meet Samantha's furious thrusts. She was enjoying the action and could feel her body building up its orgasm. She grew concerned when it became apparent that Samantha was tiring and her pace was slowing. She looked up in concern because she wasn't going to achieve her climax if Samantha couldn't keep up the pace.

Rose pulled Samantha off of Danni and took her place. It only took her a few seconds to fit the thick dildo she wore up into Danni's wet, sloppy pussy. She fucked Danni as fast as she could and Danni howled in happiness as she was quickly pushed over the edge where she knew she was going to orgasm. She wrapped her legs tightly around the older woman's waist as she pressed her hips as firmly against the plastic cock as she climaxed. Rose understood what was happening to Danni and rested her weight on the younger woman as Danni bucked and thrashed around. She liked the feeling of Danni's strong legs holding her in place as the younger woman smashed her body against hers. As Danni began to settle down to enjoy the aftermath of her climax, Samantha moved up and pushed the dildo she wore up into Danni's mouth. Danni resisted but Samantha forced her to take the plastic cock into her mouth. Danni sucked on it listlessly because her mind was still exploding with endorphins. Samantha gave some thought about pushing the dildo farther down Danni's throat but decided that the younger woman was too out of it to react well. So she pulled the dildo out of Danni's mouth and offered it to Rose. Rose slurped eagerly on the toy for a moment or so. Rose loved the taste on Danni on the dildo.

Then Samantha moved over to help Rose disentangle herself from Danni's grasp. They had some trouble because the semi-conscious young woman didn't want to let Rose go. Samantha leaned over and said softly "Danni, you need to give us access so we can eat your pussy." Danni immediately relaxed her hold and Rose moved back from her. Rose looked over to Samantha to see if she wanted to be the first one to lick Danni's sopping pussy but Samantha gestured for Rose to enjoy herself so Rose applied her mouth to the wet cunt. Danni murmured her thanks as Rose tongued her. Rose spent a few minutes working on Danni before giving way so that Samantha could take her turn. Samantha tweaked Danni's clitoris firmly and the young blonde wriggled and pushed her hips up to entice further mistreatment from Samantha. Samantha grinned and started to abuse Danni's sensitive areas even further. She contemplated whether or not she should try to push Danni to climax a second time right away and decided that it would take too long for her to recover. Samantha and Rose wanted to fuck her again before Ms. Sturm came to collect her and Danni wouldn't be able to respond if she didn't regain her composure quickly. So she restrained herself, gave Danni's wet cunt a final suck and then left her alone to go over and join Rose.

The two of them sat drinking wine as they watched Danni recover; they didn't say too much to one another but just sat there in a companionable silence. After a bit more than five minutes or so, Danni sat up and stretched before getting up and joining them. When Danni sat down, Rose pushed a plate of cookies over towards Danni. There were a dozen cookies on the plate and she'd bought them from the bakery especially for Danni, knowing the younger woman would need to recover her energy. She'd also placed a cool, fresh bottle of water near them. She offered Danni a glass of wine but Danni declined and grabbed the water. She thirstily drank more than half of it before she tackled the cookies. Neither Rose nor Samantha tried to talk with her as she satisfied her appetite and thirst. When Danni drank the dregs of the first bottle of water, Rose pulled out another one for her from the ice bucket at the edge of the table. Danni nodded her thanks to Rose and gave both of them a bright though messy smile.

Seeing that Danni was now receptive to being talked to, Samantha asked "Did you enjoy being taken like that? You looked like you did." Danni just nodded and crunched another cookie. "We would like to make you cum again. This time over Rose's face. Are you game?"

Danni grinned and replied "You know that I'm always game for sex. Give me a couple of minutes and we can get started once more." Samantha nodded and the three of them chatted for a couple of minutes, mostly about the previous Friday night.

Then the two older women led Danni back to the couch where Rose lay down on her back and Samantha helped Danni get in position above her. Rose began to vigorously slurp at Danni's pussy above her as Samantha got in behind Danni. Samantha pushed the dildo up into Danni again. Danni forced her hips backwards so that the dildo pressed deeply inside her slick, stretched cunt. Danni gave her hips a wiggle to seat it more comfortably and Rose grabbed hold of her hips to stop her from moving around too much. Danni laughed but held her hips more steady so that

Rose could continue to lick her cunt. Samantha began a more relaxed pace of thrusting knowing that Rose would be able to get Danni hot enough to orgasm with her warm, wet mouth. Her intention was just to help keep Danni aroused enough for Rose to be able to push her over the edge. The two women worked on Danni slowly but steadily for nearly ten minutes until Danni started grunting and twisting as the pressure built on her. Samantha could feel the strain of the effort begin to affect her and gave a small sigh of relief. She wondered if Rose was still strong enough to get Danni to climax. She stopped so that she could look between Danni's legs at the older woman. It appeared that Rose was doing just fine to her so she increased her thrusts into Danni's pussy.

Danni started to moan and shiver as her body took over; she tried to keep her hips from bucking since Rose was right below her but she still moved them a bit pushing her cunt all over Rose's face. Rose enjoyed the slimy feeling of the young blonde's pussy sliding all over her but sought to hold Danni in place so she would orgasm right onto her. Samantha knew that Danni was beyond her threshold so she backed away, pulling the plastic cock out of her so she could climax unobstructed. She shifted to the side, pressing the toy into Danni's hip as she tweaked the younger woman's nipples firmly to get her even more excited. Danni weakly tried to bat Samantha's hands away from her tits but her orgasm was occupying all of her concentration. Samantha ignored Danni's protests as she continued to fondle the blonde; she knew Danni was loving what was happening to her. Danni stiffened, clenching her teeth to muffle her screams as she thrust her hips down against Rose's face. She forced out almost a cup of liquids onto the redhead's face making her sputter a bit as she lapped it up.

Samantha wrestled Danni off of Rose and forced her down onto her back on the couch above the redhead. Rose had lots of Danni's cum to enjoy, Samantha thought, as she slipped her own face down between Danni's thighs to enjoy her sweet juices. Rose sat up to watch the pair of them as she cleaned up her face with her fingers, sucking vigorously on them. She was pleased to see that Danni was somewhat dazed and lost; she loved the young blonde's look when she was relishing her orgasm, it really turned her on. She moved up to stroke Samantha's lower back as Samantha buried her face in Danni's sopping cunt. Then she moved her right hand up under the brunette to grab and squeeze Samantha's large right tit. She crushed the firm flesh as hard as she could, eliciting a moan from Samantha as she enjoyed the feeling. The three women continued their actions for about five more minutes before Samantha decided that she was finished and pushed Rose away from her as she got up from Danni.

She looked down to see reason starting to return to Danni's eyes and smiled widely at her. She really loved seeing Danni like this, she thought. Rose went to go get materials so that they could all get cleaned up. When she returned, she ran a cloth over Samantha's face and upper chest while the bowl with warm water, Rose had removed the worst of her own mess. Samantha pulled Danni to her feet and helped her over to the table before handing her a bottle of water. Danni drank it down greedily before sighing with pleasure. Her body felt both relaxed and satisfied but a trifle boneless. Rose came over and knelt beside her, wrapping her arms around her waist and pressing her face into Danni's side. "Thank you, Danni" she said softly. Samantha grinned at the pair of them, savouring the relationship she had with the two of them.

Then she looked at the clock and realized that Ms. Sturm would be arriving in about two minutes to collect Danni and Danni wasn't going to be ready. "Danni, you need to go jump in the shower right now. Ms. Sturm will be here right away. Go, go!" she insisted as she hauled Danni to her feet and pushed her towards the bathroom. Danni tottered off to shower.

When she came out of the bathroom, drying her long hair with a towel but not bothering to cover up her body, Ms. Sturm was seated with Rose and Samantha drinking a cup of coffee as she waited. Danni looked her over carefully to see if she was upset but she couldn't tell. She continued to look guiltily at the three of them as they chatted while she gathered and put on her clothing. It was only when Rose and Samantha stood up that she saw the stripe marks on their asses; Ms. Sturm had exacted her price from them because Danni wasn't fully ready when she arrived. Danni was feeling slightly appalled because of their marks but they didn't seem to mind them. They grinned and kissed Danni goodbye as Ms. Sturm led her out to the car.

"It was my fault as well" Danni told her as she arranged her body in the passenger seat. "I should be punished as well." She faced Ms. Sturm bravely even though she wasn't looking forward to being whipped.

"Nonsense" Ms. Sturm snorted. "It is their responsibility to have you ready. You're too out of it when they are done with you to take accountability; they are not. I will punish you however I think you need to be punished when I think you deserve it, not before. Now, we are going to the library so that you can put in two hours of study and then I will take you home." Ms. Sturm started the car and drove off.

CHAPTER SIXTEEN

The days passed quickly with Danni working hard and getting her sexual relief from her various partners. On Thursday, she was headed towards Theodore's place for a quick fuck before going to have supper with Pierre and his parents. She was quite happy about what had been happening to her recently and was looking forward to the night's dinner. But first she was going to get fucked hard, she thought excitedly. Ms. Sturm had greeted her with tolerance, knowing that the young woman was incredibly thrilled by all of the things happening in her life right now. While she drove, she questioned Danni on how she was doing with her schoolwork and Danni answered truthfully that she was working as hard as she could. Danni had asked about the progress in finding her a sponsor for university and Ms. Sturm had deflected her from the subject. Ms. Sturm was very pleased by the response and had credited the fantastic video of Danni and Samantha for the interest but she didn't want Danni to be thinking about that right now.

When they reached Theodore's apartment building, Danni rushed up to his door and jumped into his arms when he answered. Theodore could tell that Danni was feeling passionate and was ready to be fucked hard, even though he'd done that to her on Tuesday. He closed the door and began to work her clothing off of her as she continued to kiss him fervently. He knew that he had to be careful not to damage or stain her clothing because she would be wearing it to supper later. She was making it slightly hard to accomplish that because she was moving around so much. She was also grinding her lovely body against him and he was getting more excited himself. Finally he said to her "Danni, calm down and let me get you stripped or we won't be able to fuck. I'll just sit here and watch you squirm with desire while I enjoy your discomfort." He gave her a mock look of severity. She backed away from him and looked at him with confusion before jumping against him to give him a quick kiss. She moved back away from him and stood still so that he could get her clothes off of her. She grinned a welcome to him as he carefully took all of her clothes off of her. Her panties were soaking with her desire already and he hoped that she'd brought along a fresh pair to wear to supper.

He took her hand and led her down to the bedroom. He took her over to the bed and put her down on it on her back before sitting beside her and running his hand up her silky inner thigh. He worked three fingers into her nicely lubricated pussy and started thrusting them in and out of her. He used his other hand to flick on the rabbit vibrator that he'd put on the bed and began to massage the top of her clitoris with it. Danni shivered in enjoyment as she looked him in the eyes, licked her plump lips and gave a long, low moan of pleasure. Damn, Theodore thought as his cock twitched intently, she certainly knows how to push my buttons. He knew that he had to get her on the brink of her orgasm before mounting her if he wanted her to climax before he did. He wondered if he could last long enough to do that since she was enticing him so much. He started to think about sports to keep his mind occupied while he worked her over. Danni was amused and let some merriment slip out of her mouth as she noticed that Theodore wasn't looking at her as he fondled her. She knew that he was doing that to keep from getting too aroused by her and she savoured the power he gave to her. She squirmed around and used her hands to guide his hand to a better spot in her cunt. She began panting from her desire as he stroked the most sensitive area of her. She took the vibrator from him, flicked it up to maximum and applied it to the tip of her clitoris. She bucked and shrieked as her arousal grew. She was quite close to her climax.

"Fuck me, fuck me now" she cried out to him. Theodore climbed up on the bed over top of her and lifted her legs up so that her ankles rested on his shoulders. He moved down a bit and wrested her into position so that the tip of his hard cock penetrated her. He pushed his cock into her warm willing flesh and she moaned her approval. He grunted with pleasure as he penetrated her. She wiggled around a bit to get his weight into a slightly more comfortable position as she whimpered her delight in her situation. Theodore paused until she was finished and then began pulling his cock out of her before slamming it back into her as hard as he could manage. He smashed down hard on the backs of her stretched thigh muscles and she straightened her legs a bit to bring her crotch up against his, taking his prick as deep inside her as she could. Both of them gave grunts of pleasure and then he repeated the process. He kept his mind occupied on other matters so he wouldn't succumb to his arousal as he fucked her as hard as he could manage. Danni started to feel her hips becoming liquid and knew that she was going to climax quite soon. She couldn't think of any words to utter since her mind was whirling as her desire overtook her control so she just panted and whined to let him know her condition. Theodore smiled almost cruelly with pleasure as he realized that she was losing her control; he was on the brink himself. Danni shrieked and tried hard to straighten up her legs, pushing Theodore back from her. Theodore shouted in alarm as he felt himself sliding out of her and within seconds of climaxing himself. He quickly pushed her legs to either side of him, robbing her of her leverage to push him away and stuck his cock back up into her cunt. Danni was barely aware of what he was doing because her mind was exploding. In two quick hard thrusts, Theodore climaxed deep up inside her and then collapsed on top of her. He was quite pleased with his performance and a trifle smug that she seemed to be so happy as well. He gave a number of groans as he lay on top of her and thought about what a great fuck she was.

After more than five minutes of resting, trying to get his shattered mind back under control as well as his tired body, Theodore looked down at Danni's sweaty face to gauge her condition. Her eyes were clearing and she was grinning back up at him. She was content. But Theodore knew that Ms. Sturm wanted Danni to do some studying before proceeding to supper, so he got up off of her as she wrinkled her face in disappointment. "Ms. Sturm told me to fuck you hard and fast and then call her to pick you up. She insinuated that she'd geld me if I kept you too long so go down and take a shower as I call her." Danni nodded reluctantly and then went to clean up. She knew what Ms. Sturm wanted her to do as well.

Since he knew that Danni was occupied for a couple of hours before coming over for supper, although he certainly didn't know what she was doing, Pierre decided that it would be a good idea to go arrange for a car and driver for them. He walked into the rental agency where a boy that he recognized as being from their school was arguing with a pretty young woman at the counter. "That's outrageous" the boy stormed.

The woman sneered slightly at him and stated in a slightly bored voice "Take it or leave it. I don't care. That's one of our busier nights and all our cars will be out if you take one or don't." The boy left the office cursing as Pierre watched him stalk by. Pierre walked up and the woman gave him a look of disinterest.

"My name is Pierre Cartoum" Pierre stated, slightly nervously. He was surprised when the woman stiffened slightly and then seemed to be looking at something below the counter. "I would like to rent a car and driver to take me and my girlfriend to the Prom on July Second." He felt a flash of pride as he called Danni his girlfriend.

"What's your address?" the woman asked him in a neutral tone. Pierre gave her the information and she nodded. "What is your girlfriend's name and address?" Pierre relayed Danni's information and the woman looked up at him with a quite friendly smile. The information he had given her was the information she'd put on the card below the counter a few days earlier. Pierre wondered why she needed that information but didn't see any harm in giving it to her. "Jerry, come up here and take over" she commanded to a man behind her before smiling in a rather friendly fashion to Pierre. "Come back here and we can discuss this better" she offered. She led Pierre down to a desk towards the back and a fair distance from the front counter. "Would you like a cup of coffee or some water?" she asked brightly as she sat him down. He declined so she sat down opposite him and said "We're running a Prom Special. We'll supply you with a car, driver, a boutonniere for you, a corsage for your date and a bottle of champagne for the pair of you to share. Can I interest you in this? It is very reasonable." She gave him a pleasant smile.

Pierre gave the offer some consideration. He was planning to get flowers and champagne anyway, he thought, so why not take advantage of their offer if it was reasonable enough. He expected the car and driver to cost $125 to $150, flowers to be around $50 and champagne to be $30 so an amount near $200 would be good. "How much would that be?" he asked cautiously.

"Thirty-five dollars" the woman replied with an open smile.

Pierre goggled at the amount, sure that he'd misheard her. "Do you mean one hundred and thirty-five?" he asked, gaping at her.

"No" she replied seriously. "I meant thirty-five dollars." She watched his face as he contemplated this. That was a fantastic bargain, he thought. Why would they offer this to him? He wondered if she was having fun with him but couldn't figure out why she would do that. What did she gain by offering this and not delivering, he wondered. Even if he risked thirty-five dollars and he was forced to borrow his uncle's car to drive Danni to the Prom, he thought it was worth the risk.

"Payable in advance?" he asked.

"No, we'll bill you after the Prom" she stated as she handed him a paper that detailed what she'd promised him and gave him a contact number. "Phone me if there are any problems and I will sort them out for you." Pierre nodded, stunned and then walked out of the office. The woman waved goodbye to him, smiling at him.

Pierre considered talking to Danni about the incident but then decided not to worry her with it. He was also busy trying to calm his mother. She was very excited that he was having a girl over and was tremendously anxious to meet Danni. She was skeptical of his description of Danni because in her opinion, pretty, popular girls didn't ask boys out, they were the ones being asked out. She'd decreed that they would all speak English with Danni since she was the guest in their house. Pierre knew that his mother wasn't fluent in English and had a fairly prominent French accent and that his father was even worse. He knew his father wasn't looking forward to having to puzzle out conversations that were in English. He tried to assure his mother that Danni was fluent in French and had very little accent. She would find it much easier to talk to his parents in that language than her parents would be in talking to her in English. He also knew that Danni certainly wouldn't mind doing that. But his mother wouldn't hear of it, she was determined to be the best host possible. Also, she was concerned that Danni had asked for tourtiere, a rather common French Canadian meat pie, rather than something more extravagant. She wondered if the girl might be snubbing them in some way.

So, Pierre was busy trying to calm his agitated mother when Danni rang the bell to announce her arrival. Pierre hurried to the door to let her in. She was standing at the door, looking quite lovely in her navy blue dress and low heels; she was smiling pleasantly at him as he ushered her in.

His parents were just inside the door and his mother greeted her with "Hello, Danni. Welcome to our home. We hope you are well and are pleased to meet you." She spoke in her heavily accented English.

Danni had been looking around the house and was impressed with the decorations that Pierre's mother had put up. "Hello, Mrs. Cartoum. You have a very lovely home. I am pleased to meet you and your husband and look forward to having a lovely conversation with the both of you. I hope you don't mind if we speak in your impressive language instead of English. I really need the practice of speaking with someone who's grown up speaking French. I really don't get the chance to do that." She said all of that in her almost flawless French before she paused and smiled at Pierre's mother. Then she continued "Unless you feel you need to practice your English on me even though I am sure that you have that opportunity every day." Pierre's father brightened considerably, sure that his wife would have to give in to speaking French since their guest was asking to do so and she was so fluent. He wouldn't have to feel left out of most conversations.

Pierre's mother frowned and looked questioningly at her son to see if he'd tipped Danni into asking that. He shrugged and looked back at her innocently; he hadn't asked Danni to do that but wasn't surprised that Danni had reacted like that. "We don't want to make you feel uncomfortable, Danni. You are our guest. If you want to speak French then we will do that" Pierre's mother said in French. Danni nodded and smiled prettily at her. Mrs. Cartoum realized that her son was never going to hold onto this vivacious beauty but he might as well enjoy her as much as he could.

Danni spent a very pleasant evening with Pierre and his parents and she really enjoyed the meal. Ms. Sturm had taken her to a sandwich place and bought her a corn beef sandwich after her session with Theodore so she wouldn't appear like a starving person at Pierre's home. But she'd still surprised Pierre's mother with her appetite. Mrs. Cartoum had assumed that since Danni was so slim that she carefully watched everything she ate. She'd served vegetables and dip as an appetizer and was somewhat amazed at how fast Danni consumed them. When she cut the meat pie, she'd offered Danni the first slice and had indicated a fairly small wedge. Danni had frowned and gently indicated that she wanted a more normal slice. Mrs. Cartoum cut and served the slice but didn't really expect Danni to eat it all. Danni also took a healthy helping of roast potatoes and asparagus. She consumed everything on her plate. Mrs. Cartoum had prepared a wonderful cherry custard pie for desert and when she went to cut it, she offered Danni a small piece once more. Danni had shook her head so she offered a more normal piece that she would offer her son or husband and Danni nodded enthusiastically. She'd taken a smaller slice of the tourtiere and the dessert herself. Danni ate her pie so quickly and happily that Mrs.

Cartoum offered her a second piece. Danni barely paused before accepting thankfully. Mrs. Cartoum found that she liked the younger woman quite a bit.

Pierre drove Danni home and she gave him a kiss on the cheek before she went into her house. He drove home feeling quite pleased about how the evening had went. He knew that his parents were impressed by Danni and how she handled herself. His father had been able to chat with her quite extensively and was pleased about that. He liked how he felt at the moment.

Danni went in and greeted her parents before she went up to do some studying. She told her parents that she had enjoyed her evening and she had. When she went to sleep, she did so feeling quite content with her life.

CHAPTER SEVENTEEN

The next two weeks passed very quickly for Danni; she was occupied with studying for her finals and writing them. Ms. Sturm assured that Danni got enough sex to keep her healthy and happy but ensured that all of her partners didn't take up too much of her time. Danni had appreciated that and had studied as hard as she could. She was fairly confident that she had done well on her tests and was now picking up her marks. Ms. Sturm had arranged to pick up Danni after she got the transcript of her marks. She was going to take Danni to The Secluded Grove for an early lunch so they could discuss her marks and what her plans were going to be for university. Ms. Sturm wanted to ensure that Danni was fully committed to the plan Ms. Sturm had for her before they began it. She was fairly sure that Danni was still on track but wanted to give her the opportunity to back out now if she wanted to do so.

Danni picked up her marks and took a look at them; she was a bit disappointed with her chemistry mark but otherwise felt that she had done very well. She knew that she wasn't in line with obtaining the top scholarships but she had done well. She made her way along to Ms. Sturm's blue Honda and got in the vehicle. Ms. Sturm watched Danni climb in; she already knew what Danni's marks were but was curious to see how the young woman perceived them. Danni looked over and saw Ms. Sturm watching her; she suspected that Ms. Sturm already knew her marks. She gave the older woman a smile and stated "I think I did fairly well." She waited to see what Ms. Sturm felt. Ms. Sturm nodded without saying anything and then drove them to the restaurant so they could talk. Danni took the hint and remained silent during the trip.

When they arrived, Danni was surprised to see that the restaurant was closed; she'd assumed that Ms. Sturm would've known something like that. She waited for Ms. Sturm to take them elsewhere but Ms. Sturm put the car in park and started to get out. "The restaurant is closed, Ms. Sturm" Danni pointed out quietly.

"Not for us, it isn't" Ms. Sturm stated and walked up to the doorway. The waitress immediately opened up the door for the pair of them and smiled broadly at them. She led them to a table where they could see out the windows onto the street but anyone outside wouldn't be able to make them out. She waited for their drink order. "Coffee for me. What do you want Danni?"

"I'll take coffee as well" Danni replied and smiled at the waitress. She saw that there were two glasses of ice water at the table for them.

While the waitress was off getting their coffee, Danni sipped on the ice water. She noted there was a large crystal pitcher of water on the table so that they could top up their own glasses. "We are having lasagna for lunch, Danni" Ms. Sturm stated. "I requested a double sized salad for you as an appetizer and some onion rings as well. I know the owner of this restaurant and so she allowed me access to it so that we could talk in private. I also know the chef and waitress." While Ms. Sturm was talking, the waitress came back with a carafe of coffee and a pitcher of cream. She looked to Ms. Sturm to see if she should bring out the appetizers and Ms. Sturm nodded her approval. "Your marks are quite good, Danni" Ms. Sturm began. "If you wanted to, you could afford to pay your way into a junior college with the scholarships you would be offered and with a little other financial help. I could arrange that for you if you wanted it." Ms. Sturm paused to wait for Danni's reaction.

Danni frowned intensely, feeling very bewildered. "That's not what I want at all, Ms. Sturm" she protested. "I want to go to a university and be able to enjoy my time there. I don't want to have to just scrape by. You said that you could help me do that. Are you now telling me that you can't?" Danni was confused because it was obvious to her that Ms. Sturm could get almost anything done. Look what she did in arranging for this restaurant, she thought.

Ms. Sturm had just calmly sipped at her coffee and watched Danni as she talked. The waitress interrupted them to bring them their salads and onion rings. She placed the onion rings right in front of Danni, knowing that the young woman would be the one to consume them. She smiled at Danni before she recognized the tension at the table. When she did, she excused herself quickly to allow them their privacy. She was perturbed that Danni was upset because she thought that this meal was a celebratory one for the young woman, whom she liked very much. Once the waitress left, Ms. Sturm told Danni "Eat your onion rings while they are hot. I will speak for a bit and you'll just listen. Okay?" When Danni nodded, Ms. Sturm proceeded, gesturing for Danni to eat the onion rings. "I can do all that I told you that I could do. I am offering you a chance to get out of it if that is your desire. Your reaction tells me that you are willing to go ahead with what we discussed. Is that true?" Danni nodded as she chewed on a hot onion ring. Ms. Sturm smiled and said "Okay then. You have told your mother about your nanny job?" Danni nodded again as she grabbed another onion ring.

"Okay then. For the summer, starting next week, we are going to let your possible sponsors meet you and try you out. I have placed some very rigid restrictions in regard to these meetings and I will detail them to you in a moment. I'll lay out the broad outlines first for you to understand. Please keep any of your questions until I have finished because I will probably answer them. Do you understand?" Danni nodded mutely once more; she'd eaten more than half of the onion rings already. Ms. Sturm smiled at the young blonde woman. "Your sponsor for the day will get you at noon. When we arrive at the room that they have rented, you will strip off your clothes and they will examine you to make sure that you don't have any marks on you. I will remain while they do that and will take your clothes away with me. Your sponsor will provide you with any lingerie or other clothing that they desire you to wear while you are with them. They are not permitted to mark you in any way. You will not be disciplined at all; this includes any nipple clamps. I know that some of your friends use them on you but they have been told not to do that anymore. There will also not be any anal sex. Later in the summer, I will demonstrate whether or not you can handle disciplining and bondage. I will also arrange for someone to give you your first anal sex experience." Danni frowned and started to say something but Ms. Sturm gave her a stern look and held up her hand. Danni remembered that she was supposed to wait with her questions.

"I will pick you up again the next morning at eight. I will examine you to determine whether you have any marks on you and then you will dress and we will leave." She smiled and said "Simple enough, right?" Danni nodded and tried to speak once more. Ms. Sturm shook her head and said "Now for some more specific details. You are to be shown a gift, preferably earrings, once you have been accepted. If you perform well, you will get that gift when you are turned back over to me. They are expected to provide you with lingerie and clothing so that you will not remain naked for the whole day. If they do not, you will let me know. You will keep all items given to you. We will supply all of the approved sex toys that can be used on you. You will carry a suitcase of them. If they have something that they truly desire to use on you, I will have to approve it beforehand." Ms. Sturm paused momentarily to take bites of her salad. Danni ate her salad hungrily as she listened. "You may ask your questions now" Ms. Sturm commanded.

"Why can't you just do the B & D demonstration for everyone? As well as the anal?" Danni asked with a frown as she thought about whether or not she really wanted to experience either of those. She felt that she wasn't being given a choice in the matter but what did it matter how many people watched her doing that, she thought.

Ms. Sturm noted Danni's reluctance but replied "There would be too many people to be able to watch easily. Next question."

Danni scowled as she thought about the answer. Too many people, she wondered, how many could there be? Eight, maybe ten because there couldn't be more than five or six sponsors, she thought. Ms. Sturm felt that she couldn't fit that many in a room with them, Danni wondered. But she asked "How will the people know my sizes? Rose has said that almost every manufacturer is slightly different in size. I don't want to wear ill-fitting lingerie or dresses all day."

"The sponsors have been told that they must attend Rose's boutique to buy your lingerie since she has your measurements and colour preferences. I thought Rose deserved to get the business and she is quite thrilled about it. Your dresses and other outer clothes are to come from Progressive Lady since they also know how to fit you."

Danni was impressed. "So after I've spent a day with these sponsors, you'll decide which one gets me. There will be what? Five, six?" The waitress had noticed that they were done with their appetizers so she brought over the plates of lasagna and collected the dirty dishes. Danni noticed that her helping of lasagna was much larger than Ms. Sturm's. The waitress quickly moved off once more to give them their privacy to continue talking.

Ms. Sturm had been watching Danni somewhat critically while the waitress was attending them and once she was safely at a distance asked "Why would I choose your sponsor, Danni? You're the one who's going to be talking and interacting with them."

Danni had taken a mouthful of lasagna and she almost spit the delicious food out when Ms. Sturm asked her that question. But Ms. Sturm would be the one to know how much they could afford and what they should be asking for, Danni thought. How could she determine that? She might know who she liked but that wasn't the important thing was it, she pondered. "I'm not going to know what they can afford" Danni whined, once her mouth was empty once more. "You're the one who has to make the choice for me. I can't do it."

Ms. Sturm frowned at her and stated "You seem to be under a misapprehension about our relationship, Danni. I'm not your mother nor am I your owner. I am here to help you. Just like a consultant might do. You are the one who makes the decision. I just give you information to assist you in making that decision." Danni looked at her bewildered because she hadn't had the impression that their relationship was like that at all. Ms. Sturm was always commanding her with what to do. "Besides they will all be leaving a half million dollar cash deposit with me before taking charge of you. Anyone who can afford to do that can definitely supply all of your needs. Unless you decide that you require a lot more than you should, that is."

Danni's eyes widened at the mention of the deposit and she agreed with Ms. Sturm that anyone who could do that could pay her way easily. "Okay" she said as she scooped up another forkful of lasagna. "So how many people have chosen to do that?" She couldn't imagine that the number would be that high; her estimate of six seemed quite unreasonable now. She was still somewhat perturbed that Ms. Sturm was laying the final choice on her; she felt unprepared to make that decision. She chewed her food as she looked at the other woman.

"Twenty-six so far" Ms. Sturm replied with a small smile. "Your video with Samantha was extremely effective. Close your mouth, Danni, that is very unattractive."

Danni's mouth had gaped wide open when Ms. Sturm told her the number and she now closed it hastily. The number was inconceivable in her mind. How could that many people be interested in her? How could there be that many people willing to offer that much money for her? The questions whirled in Danni's confused mind. "That many men want me?" Danni asked.

"Oh, it's not just men. There are some single women, couples and two families that want you. I told you that you looked extremely sexy in that video. Now eat your food before it gets cold or Dorothy and Joyce will be extremely disappointed." Ms. Sturm turned her attention to her plate of food. Danni quickly followed suit although her mind continued to spin about the information that she had just been given.

Danni ate the rest of her meal in almost silence; she was busy thinking about what her summer was going to look like. She determined that the number of possible sponsors interested in her both scared and excited her. She was sure that she couldn't live up to their expectations of her, she thought despondently. But on the other hand, she was tremendously and smugly pleased that they were that interested in her. She finished her delicious meal and looked up to smile at Ms. Sturm. She was looking forward to what her summer held for her but she had some further questions. "With that many sponsors, how are we going to proceed? Do I get any time off for myself or am I going to be kept busy? What happens with my friends that have been fucking me? Where do I live?" The waitress came over and collected the dirty dishes. Ms. Sturm gave her an approving nod when she flashed her a questioning look.

"I've decided that it would be best to let you go home Saturday morning to visit your family for the day so you'll sleep at home that night. On Sunday, you'll go over to visit Samantha and Rose and spend the night with them. I feel that they have earned that from you. Then from Monday to Friday you'll spend those nights with five different sponsors. That will cover the first month or so. Then you'll winnow the field down. We'll do the two demonstrations and let the people you have chosen to try you out for a second time. If you can make your selection after that, you'll go on vacation until university starts. If not, you'll do a third round with the sponsors still eligible. Then you'll have to make a decision. I'm afraid Evelyn, Mary and Theodore will see very little of you. You can discuss with all of your possible sponsors what your expectations are of them and what they desire of you. Some may allow you to have contact with your friends while others may insist that you fuck no one but them. Make sure you find out. If you're not getting sexual satisfaction, you won't be happy and if you're getting used too much by too many people, I'll be unhappy." She snorted slightly and said snidely "But you'll probably love it." Danni gave her a mock glare. The waitress brought in a double helping of the mud pie and placed it right in front of Danni. The chef had put them on a large dinner plate and had written ConGRADulations alongside them in chocolate. Danni grinned as she appreciated the sentiment as well as anticipating the wonderful taste of the dessert. The waitress also put a wrapped package about an inch wide, eight inches long and a half inch high down beside the plate.

"What is this?" Danni asked curiously as she dug her fork into the dessert. She lifted the gooey, sweet forkful to her mouth and moaned in pleasure as she savoured it.

Ms. Sturm smiled at Danni's noises of pleasure and said quietly "It's a present for your graduation. Open it and see what it is."

Danni unwrapped the present eagerly and opened up the jeweler's box to find a gold chain with a gold pendant of a female archer. She loved how pretty it looked and enjoyed the meaning of the pendant. "It's beautiful" she gasped. "Thank you."

"Your other friends will also have gifts for you today so get used to thanking people" Ms. Sturm told her, slightly superior in tone.

"May I hug and kiss you in appreciation for your generosity?" Danni asked as she shivered in joy and excitement.

Ms. Sturm gave her a slightly disdainful glance, focusing on her messy mouth and stated "Not until you're finished your dessert, I think. Go ahead and finish it and then rinse your mouth with some water and I will consider it." Then she looked over at the waitress who was watching with a happy expression on her face. "Perhaps Joyce will accommodate you if you feel you need someone to kiss." The waitress eagerly approached and Danni hugged and kissed her for a few minutes as they both enjoyed the contact. Finally Ms. Sturm commanded "Enough. Eat your mud pies. We need to get you over to Evelyn and Mary's place." Danni obediently demolished the remains of the dessert. Then she wiped down her face and mouth and rinsed out her mouth before giving Ms. Sturm a suggestive smile without saying anything but just raising her eyebrows. Ms. Sturm sighed and watched Danni for a half minute before granting her the wish she was trying to convey. "Fine, you may come over here and kiss me. Then we have to leave" Ms. Sturm said, trying to express her mock unwillingness. Danni rushed over and the two women kissed enthusiastically for over two minutes before Ms. Sturm broke them apart. They gathered their stuff and headed for the car.

After they were seated, Ms. Sturm didn't start the car right away but addressed Danni. "I have some bad news to tell you. I waited until now so that I didn't affect your celebration dinner. This will be your final visit with Evelyn and Mary. They've known about this for some time but agreed to keep it secret from you so as not to put any pressure on you. So expect some tears this afternoon." Danni nodded somberly as she felt tears forming in her eyes. She knew that she would miss the two women greatly. Ms. Sturm watched Danni for a brief time and then continued "Tomorrow you will be tied up with your Prom. On Sunday, I will be taking you over to Theodore's place rather than Samantha and Rose's. You will be seeing him for the final time then. Lisa and her boyfriend will be there. I've also convinced Anna and George to collect what they owe from you then." Ms. Sturm paused as she watched Danni take in that information and then said "Theodore has also extended invitations to eight or nine men." Danni's eyebrows shot up as she calculated the number of people. Were they all expecting to fuck her, she wondered with some dismay. She couldn't handle that many. Ms. Sturm grinned slightly at Danni's shock and stated "The plan is for you, Lisa and Anna to play a bit with each other to get you in the mood. Then Lisa's boyfriend will fuck you as everyone watches. Then you get to watch Lisa being fucked by one of Theodore's friends. Then George gets to have you. Lisa gets fucked again and the pair of you take care of the men until you decide you are too tired to proceed." Danni got quite wet thinking about what would occur. Ms. Sturm didn't give her too much time to ponder it but said "On Monday, you're going to practice your pussy eating at Samantha and Rose's place. They've lined up a number of women from the club for you to sample. On Tuesday, they're going to give you a lesbian gangbang. You get to have a quiet day on Wednesday before meeting with men sponsor prospects on Thursday and Friday. So you're going to have a very busy week." Then she started the car and drove them to Evelyn and Mary's place. Danni's mind whirled as she considered what was planned for her; she could feel her arousal growing.

Mary met her at the doorway wearing a robe. Danni could tell that she was trying not to be too despondent; she was desperately trying to put on a brave face but it disappeared when Danni threw herself into the older woman's arms. The two of them cried for a bit before Mary guided Danni into the living room where Evelyn was. Evelyn had heard them sobbing and she'd shed some tears as well but she didn't want to repeat the crying session so she steeled her resolve. "Come over here, Danni. I don't want us to waste time crying about something that we can not change. We all knew that this day was going to come when we started this and I would rather that we remember our good times together fondly. So, no more crying by anyone. Okay?" Both Danni and Mary nodded and Mary put on a brave face. Then she stripped off her robe and showed Danni the pretty lingerie that she was wearing. She was wearing the peach baby doll outfit that she'd worn before with stockings and heels. Danni also noticed then that Evelyn was wearing a leather corset/bustier with stockings and heels.

"You look quite fetching" she told the older fat woman who snorted at the compliment. Evelyn was very aware that Danni would look much better in the same outfit.

Evelyn started stripping Danni's clothes from her while Mary came up and began stroking and fondling the younger blonde. "We're gonna spend the afternoon eating your pussy, Danni. It will be our last chance to do so and we want to make the most of it. If you need a break to recover a bit, please let us know. Otherwise we're gonna tag team you all afternoon. Is that okay with you?" Mary asked as she squeezed Danni's bare left breast. Danni nodded happily as Evelyn pulled her panties down her legs and got her to step out of them. She was pleased that they wanted to eat her cunt all afternoon. Mary helped her get down on her back and lifted her hips to put a large pillow underneath them so she would be comfortable.

Evelyn placed her head between Danni's thighs and started licking Danni's damp cunt; Danni was already fairly aroused. Mary sat by her head and fondled Danni's breasts. Danni indicated that she wanted the older blonde to straddle her face so she could lick at Mary's pussy. Mary didn't need too much persuading and quickly got into position. Danni knew that she'd end up cumming before she pushed Mary hard enough to make her orgasm so she really didn't even try to do that. Instead she just softly licked and sucked on the other woman's pussy, enjoying the soft feel of the sensitive skin in her mouth and Mary's aroused smell. Evelyn worked Danni's cunt over hard enough to make her begin to squirm around as her orgasm built. Danni had a quick wet orgasm less than a minute later. It wasn't the mind-blowing climax that she usually liked because she was a bit down because of the situation but it was still quite pleasant. Danni sighed happily into Mary's crotch. Mary decided that she had to do something to get Danni out of her down mood so she grabbed hold of Danni's long blonde hair and vigorously rubbed her damp cunt against her pretty face. Danni was surprised by Mary's actions but soon burst out with laughter. She reached up and tweaked Mary's nipples hard with her fingers. Mary laughed at her forwardness and clamped Danni's head firmly in her thighs and wiggled her hips, smearing her pussy all over the younger woman's face. Evelyn voiced a bit of protest as Danni's body squirmed around but didn't lift her face from between Danni's thighs.

The three women spent a good deal of time playing with each other. Each woman ate Danni out twice before she begged for a break. Danni didn't orgasm when Mary licked her the second time but she was quite happy with the encounter. They took a break for coffee and Evelyn fed Danni a piece of cake and some cookies that Danni relished immensely. Evelyn handed Danni a wrapped box; when she opened the jeweler's box inside, she found a pair of gold earrings with a female archer as the pendant. She thanked the pair of women for their gift. She felt immensely touched by their affection of her. After a half hour, they got back to matters. Danni got eaten once more by each woman before she determined she couldn't do any more. The three women spent some time cuddling and talking. Danni promised to remain in touch with the women and to keep them up to date with her life. She regarded the two older women as pseudo aunts. Then it was time for her to get ready for her date and she headed to the shower.

When Danni headed back to the living room to dress, she saw that Evelyn and Mary were seated on the couch waiting so they could watch her dress. It was obvious to Danni that they had been crying and commiserating with each other and were feeling down. She decided that she would try to improve their moods by putting on a bit of a show in dressing. She pranced around a bit before slipping her foot into her right stocking and then spent a lot of time rolling it up her leg and adjusting it. She was pleased when both women grinned at her, aware of what she was trying to do and appreciating her effort on their behalf. It took Danni a fair amount of time to slide into her clothing which consisted of a dark blue dress with some cut outs over her hips, some pale blue silk stockings and blue pumps. The dress was short enough to show off most of her legs but wouldn't ride too high to expose her when she danced. Danni went over to kiss the pair of them goodbye and to thank them for her gift.

Samantha rang the bell and Danni went to answer. The brunette looked at Danni and stated "If you need a few minutes more to say goodbye to Evelyn and Mary, Rose and I understand. We can wait in the car for you to be finished." Danni thanked her for her understanding but assured her that they were done and that she was ready. Samantha nodded and took her hand to lead her down to the car. They drove off to the restaurant.

When they were seated in the restaurant, Rose complimented Danni on her new necklace and earrings. Danni thanked her for her interest knowing that Rose and Samantha understood who had given them to her. The three of them enjoyed a wonderful meal with Danni having a steak. Both Samantha and Rose noticed that the waitress tended to touch Danni lightly every time she came by but didn't make an issue of it. They knew that Danni tended to attract admirers very easily. Before the dessert was brought for Danni, they presented her with their gift. Danni was having a large banana split. She opened up the jeweler's box to find a gold charm bracelet with three charms already attached. There was an archer for her, two linked hearts to represent Samantha and a rose to indicate Rose. Danni teared up in looking at the wonderful present. "You guys must have discussed with one another what you were getting me" she said as she snivelled slightly with emotion.

"We did" Rose confirmed. "Ms. Sturm suggested the theme of the archer for you." She gave Danni a smile even though tears glinted in her eyes.

Soon they were on their way to The Naughty Nymph to dance the night away. Once again, Dawn and Jill escorted them in, taking Samantha by the hands once more and leading her over to the group. Danni didn't feel the jolt of jealousy this time; she just felt pleasure that the group was very responsive to all three of them. Danni had removed her jewelry and left it in the trunk of the car so she didn't have to worry about it. She never even got to put her ass on her chair before a woman was begging her to dance with her. Danni grinned and let herself be persuaded; she waved bye to Rose, noticing that Cindy and Micki were rapidly approaching Rose. She smiled as she was pulled up onto the dance floor by her eager brunette partner, knowing that Rose would be entertained while she was gone. Danni danced energetically with a wide variety of partners for the next twenty minutes before she begged for a respite. The crowded dance floor almost completely emptied out when she headed back to her seat. There was a nice cool, refreshing Coke Zero waiting for her and she sucked most of it down as she waved her hand about, trying to cool her face down.

Danni spent a wonderful evening with the group of women; a number of whom told her that they would be interacting with her on Monday when she would be practicing her pussy eating. She saw that Rose and Samantha also appeared to be having a great deal of fun as well. When it became time for them to leave, most of the women came up to wish Danni well on her graduation exercises and slip her a small package. Danni was bewildered as to what they were giving her and didn't have time to open each of them at that time. Rose had brought out a bag to put the small gifts in, suggesting that she knew what was going to happen.

When they were in the car and headed to Rose and Samantha's place for Danni to clean up to go home, Danni asked "What's in those packages, Rose?"

Rose grinned and replied "Each of them chose a charm for your bracelet to remind you of them. It's going to be too many for you to mount on it and wear it comfortably but you can switch them around as much as you want." Danni liked the idea of that and settled back happily. Samantha gave her a warm kiss and she enthusiastically responded. The two of them necked for quite a while.

When Danni got home she went right up to her room to go to bed so she could rest up for her busy next day. Her mother had told her that her days of curfew ended with her graduation from high school but she wasn't much later than what that curfew time had been. Her mother had still waited up for her to arrive home and they'd exchanged greetings.

CHAPTER EIGHTEEN

Pierre and his mother were fussing with his tie, trying to get it to look perfect when Pierre's cell phone rang. He answered it and a lovely, musical female voice informed him that his car and driver had arrived for him and that she was waiting for him at the door. He hadn't expected a female driver but decided that it didn't make a difference. He gathered up his things, kissed his mother goodbye until later and answered the door. When he opened the door, his jaw dropped with what he saw. The woman waiting for him was a tall blonde, probably taller than Danni, wearing an extremely revealing pink outfit. The short leather skirt seemed like it was molded over her round ass and her legs seemed to go on forever. She was wearing a very brief red silk shirt with a short linen jacket over it. Her brief shirt didn't do anything to cover her upper chest but rather framed her quite massive chest and the linen jacket had no chance of fitting over top of it. The jacket just served to frame her wonderful cleavage and ended at the bottom of her ribcage to expose her fabulous bare belly. It also had tails at the back that ended half way down her beautiful ass. A small pink chauffer's cap sat on her high piled long blonde hair. She was wearing pink silk stockings with red suspenders holding them up. On her feet and lower legs were a pair of lace-up, open-faced, pink leather boots with heels of at least six inches. This goddess smiled brightly at him in welcome. Pierre stood there stunned into immobility for more than two minutes as the woman just waited for him to regain control over himself. She was used to this reaction from men.

When he finally managed to tear his eyes away from her, close his mouth and get his brain off of his fantasies with her, he glanced out to look at the car she'd brought. He didn't notice the car right away because there was another woman waiting by it that was wearing the same outfit as this gorgeous woman in front of him. There were two of them, he thought in wonder. When he could tear his eyes away from her, he looked at the vehicle they'd arrived in; it was a long black limousine with sharp pink highlights. It was definitely an attention getter. The woman in front of him had gently moved him forward out of the doorway and closed the front door to his house. She offered her arm to lead him up the sidewalk to the car. As they approached the car, he realized that the waiting woman wasn't only dressed like the woman on his arm, she was the twin of that woman. Twins, he thought in wonder; gorgeous, sexy twins displaying their fine assets to the world. It was a dream come true, he thought and gave a small groan of desire. The woman guiding him gave a musical little giggle and pressed her large breast against the back of his arm.

Pierre found his wits and then his voice. "There must be some mistake" he said sorrowfully, knowing that his thirty-five dollars wouldn't even cover the tip that these fantastic twins would be expecting. "I'm afraid you must have the wrong booking. I can't afford you."

"You are Pierre Cartoum. You're at the address we were told to go to and we are on our way to pick up Ms. Danni Archer, aren't we?" the woman pressing herself against him asked. He agreed and she said simply "Then we're at the right address." Pierre thought about calling the service but then decided that he'd argue what their bill was after the fact and just enjoy the evening.

Molly was watching out the window, eagerly waiting for Pierre's arrival, when the car drove up and the twins got out to escort Pierre to the door to pick up Danni. She was quite excited about what was going to happen and enjoying her older sister's day. "Jesus Christ!" she shrieked as she took in what she was seeing.

Her mother spun immediately towards her; she'd been fussing with Danni's hair, trying to get it just perfect. Danni was perfectly fine with how it looked and knew that her mother was just showing her nerves by fussing with it. She was content to let her mother work out her nervousness on her hair, knowing it would keep her occupied. She also turned to look at her youngest sister in shock. "Molly, we don't use that type of language in this family, young lady" Charlene admonished her. Then she went over to look at what had caused Molly's outburst and caught sight of the gorgeous twins walking Pierre down the sidewalk. "Jesus Christ" she uttered in shock. Molly glared at her mother, thinking that if she wasn't allowed to swear that her mother shouldn't also. Danni couldn't help but giggle at the pair of them but she also made her way over to look.

"Oh, my. I wonder how much money that pair cost him" she said breathlessly. She hoped that he wasn't spending all of his money on her because he wasn't going to get any return for it. She hurried over to open the door for them and managed to get the door open before they arrived at it. She invited them in, knowing that her mother wanted to get pictures of her and Pierre before they left for the Prom. She also wondered, slightly archly, if her mother would want pictures of this incredible pair of women. The rest of her family had arrived and was openly gawking at the twins who were posing and showing off eagerly. They certainly didn't mind being looked at and were used to being the center of attention. They also held onto Pierre for a while rather than releasing him. Danni spent a moment examining them and comparing herself to them; she was slightly dismayed to feel that they beat her in almost every category. Then she calculated that most of their height advantage over her was because of the height of their heels and hair. She decided that she would ignore the size of their chests.

The twins smiled widely at her and chorused "Hello, Danni. Pierre is here to pick you up so that we can take you to your Prom." They released Pierre and gave him a slight push toward her. Danni recognized that they were trying to show her that they weren't interested in competing with her for attention; this was mostly her show.

Charlene had got her camera and posed Danni and Pierre so that she could take pictures of them. She took a number of snaps of the pair of them and then got her younger daughters to pose with them. Then she got Gina to take some pictures of her and Danni's father with them. She had trouble in getting her husband and daughter's attention away from the gorgeous twins whenever she wanted them. When she was done, she gave the twins a brief glance wondering if she could ask them to pose. The twins took care of matters by stepping forward and posing beside Danni and Pierre so she could photograph them. They also were willing to pose with the younger girls and Danni's parents; smiling widely as they were admired. One of Charlene's favourite pictures was one of the twins seated on chairs, one holding Molly on her lap while the other one had Kate and Grace stood happily between them. Everyone in the picture appeared so happy, she thought in wonder. In one picture that she took of her husband with the twins, the women had put his hands cupping their breasts as they snuggled in against his body.

Then they insisted that Danni and Pierre had to leave. Danni thought that they were insisting too early; there was time for them to travel to the arena where the dinner and then ceremonies would be held. One twin stated "But we have to drive you up and down the main street to show you off before we take you to the arena. You don't want to miss seeing all of those envious stares, do you?" Pierre eagerly agreed with them; Danni didn't really care what other people thought about her, she was quite happy in her own skin and willing to let other people live their lives if they left her to her own. But she was happy to go along with them all.

The twins marched them slowly up to the car so that the neighbours had lots of time to gather and watch. Danni noticed that most of her neighbours were gathering to smile and wave at her; her family came out of the house to observe as well. When they got to the car, one twin moved around to the driver's seat while the other one helped them enter the spacious back area before sliding in and seating herself on the leather covered jump seat by the door. She let her short skirt ride up her thighs as she adjusted her position. She slyly observed both Danni and Pierre looking at her exposed inner thighs; she didn't mind it at all. She reached over and gave each of them a box. Danni opened hers and was slightly confused. She'd expected it to be a corsage but it looked more like a boutonniere. The twin laughed and indicated that Danni should put it on Pierre; she'd given them the opposite's flowers so that they could put them on each other. Danni grinned and put it on Pierre, pulling him close to her so that she could accomplish that. Pierre enjoyed leaning in so close to Danni and smelling her wonderful perfume. Danni noticed his attention but didn't really mind it.

When Pierre opened up her corsage, Danni was amazed by how pretty it looked; it was obviously a very expensive arrangement. "How much did you spend on this?" she gasped in astonishment.

Pierre looked at her with an uncomfortable expression on his face and blurted out "They said they were running a special. I took it because of that but I certainly didn't expect this. They said they would bill me thirty-five dollars." He glanced around uncertainly.

Danni scowled as she too looked around; there was no way that thirty-five dollars would cover any of this, she thought. She saw the twin looking intently at her and suddenly she understood. She mouthed "Ms. Sturm?" to the twin who nodded and mouthed back "And others." Danni nodded in understanding that this was being paid for by her friends.

Pierre caught some of their movement out of the corner of his eye but didn't see what they mouthed to one another. "What do you think this is going to cost me?" he asked Danni worriedly.

"I think you're gonna be billed thirty-five dollars" she replied assuredly. She estimated that the twins and limo would cost over three thousand, the flowers probably over five hundred and the champagne that the twin was now holding about two hundred dollars. "You better put that corsage on me and then we can enjoy the champagne" she told him. Pierre fastened the flowers to her with somewhat fumbling fingers but she patiently waited for him to accomplish that. The twin handed them all glasses of champagne and they drank a silent toast.

They started down Main Street and the twin urged them to stand up through the sun roof so that they could wave at all the people walking down it. She joined them, making sure that she only pressed against Pierre. She'd been told that Danni would enjoy her presence but that she mustn't out her so she carefully avoided Danni. Danni felt that the twin was interested in her but that she was avoiding contact for a reason so she didn't push matters. She enjoyed the wind rushing around them as they hooted and hollered from the sun roof.

After more than a dozen trips down the street, the driver pulled the car over into a parking lot. She got out of her seat and joined them in the back. The twin that had been with them pulled a small bag of makeup out of a cubby hole and the driver began to repair the wind damage on her sister. When she was done and her sister was back to looking her best, the driver examined and repaired Danni's makeup for her. The other twin combed and restyled Pierre's hair for him. Now that they were all back to looking their best, they drove up to the arena where the ceremonies would be taking place.

The twin inside with them held them in place until her sister came around to open the door and then she stepped out to join her. The twins stood there making sure that everyone at the entrance to the arena noticed them before allowing Pierre and Danni to get out; they knew how to make an arrival. They slowly walked the couple up to the entrance making sure that everyone's eyes were upon them. At the entrance each girl pressed herself against Pierre and gave him a warm, wet kiss. Danni knew what they were doing and approved of it; she didn't feel any jealousy at all. She grinned as Pierre enjoyed himself. She was a bit surprised when the first twin pressed a card with their information into her hand when she was done with Pierre and he was occupied by her sister. Danni took a quick look at the card and written upon it was the word 'Anytime!' She knew that the twins were interested in her and felt a sharp spike of arousal at the thought. When the twins were finished with Pierre and were leaving, it became obvious that Pierre had also enjoyed their attention. Danni could see that Pierre's prick was standing at full attention and he wouldn't be able to move for a while.

She smiled and stepped close enough to him to cover the fact. She began talking to him about their marks in school to take his mind off his arousal. She became a bit concerned when it didn't look like he was subsiding at all and she peered at his face with concern. Pierre found that Danni's voice, even though she was talking about mundane things, was keeping him aroused because he desired her so much. "I think you should just stop talking and let me recover" he begged her. Danni frowned at him in confusion initially but then understood and gave him a warm smile. "Oh, don't do that" he moaned quietly to her. She quirked her face in amusement and focused on their surroundings to give him time to deflate. She was feeling quite pleased that he found her arousing even though she really had no interest in him. It fed her ego.

A few minutes later, he was able to suggest that they go inside so she took his arm and let him lead her in; she was careful not to look him in the face and set him off once again. Pierre found that he could slowly relax as they walked into the arena and he could focus his mind on other things. One part of his mind rued what had happened to him but he knew that he would hold the memory of kissing those beautiful twins forever. He quickly had to shift his thinking to prevent a reoccurrence. He was pleased to see most of his friends looking envious at him; he knew part of it was because of Danni being on his arm and the rest was because of the twins. He led Danni over to where a group of graduates were waiting to be instructed how to proceed across the stage and accept their diplomas.

Mrs. Cartoum was waiting quite nervously by table number nineteen, which was the table Danni and Pierre would be sharing with their guests. Each graduate was allowed to invite seven people to dinner but Pierre only had four people he wanted to invite so he let Danni have the other three so she could invite her sisters. Mrs. Cartoum, her husband, her sister and her husband were Pierre's guests; they all spoke little English and were concerned that they were going to be left out and ignored by the proceedings. She looked around anxiously and noticed a beautiful blonde woman that looked like what she thought Danni would look like in five or so years heading towards them. The woman looked like Danni's sister but Danni had said that she was the eldest. Mrs. Cartoum assumed this must be one of Danni's aunts but she was leading over three girls that were the image of her and Danni. Charlene hurried up and apologized for them being late; she introduced herself as Danni's mother. Pierre's family was shocked that she spoke in the same almost flawless French that Danni had used. Mr. Cartoum was happy that there might be someone else available to interpret as well as Danni and Pierre. Charlene introduced her husband and he spoke to them in halting, hesitant French; they greeted his attempt with approval and nods. Then Charlene introduced Gina and she spoke in extremely fluent French with them. Kate displayed that she could also converse in French and even Molly managed to express herself well enough in the language to be able to speak with them. As Molly was talking with them, two more pretty blondes came up; these were obviously Charlene's sisters and Danni's aunts. They had their husbands with them. When Charlene introduced her middle sister, Gina, she spoke to them in the same French that Charlene and Danni spoke in. Her husband could only greet them in broken French but he tried. Charlene's younger sister, Kate, also spoke as well as her sisters and niece and her husband was able to converse on about the same level as Molly. Pierre's family was amazed that they would be able to converse in French with so many people. They wouldn't be the ones sitting at the table feeling left out of the conversation.

They sat down and started chatting amiably; Mrs. Cartoum was thrilled to listen to Danni's younger sisters talking to her about their activities in French. She really missed interacting with children in her native language. A blonde woman arrived and Charlene and her sisters and daughters greeted her fondly; Mrs. Cartoum realized that this was Danni's grandmother, even though she didn't look old enough to be that. When the woman was introduced, she spoke impeccable French as well.

Pierre was worried that his parents would be feeling left out of matters so he tried to hurry Danni over to their table when they were released from their rehearsal. When he got close enough to see them, he was amazed that his mother was laughing uproariously at something Molly was telling her. His father was chatting animatedly with his uncle and two pretty blonde women who looked like Danni. His aunt was talking with Danni's mother and older sister Gina. They were all having quite a wonderful time and it showed. Pierre wondered how they were managing to do that with their limited English but then he realized they were talking in French once he got close enough to hear. He was surprised that Danni had so many French speakers in her family. When he glanced back at her, she smiled happily at him; she'd known that his family would be able to converse with hers. Pierre slowed down so that he wasn't rushing as much and wouldn't be out of breath once he arrived since there was really no need for him to hurry anymore.

He greeted his guests and was introduced to Danni's invitees and then introduced Danni to his aunt and uncle before letting her greet his parents. Pierre's father teared up slightly and said solemnly "Thank you for making this so easy for us. We appreciate your kindness." Danni nodded and gave him a quick kiss which left him smiling. Pierre felt a great deal of desire for her and knew it wasn't just because she was pretty; she was a truly wonderful person. They sat down and had a fantastic dinner even though the food was only mediocre. Their table tended to be the loudest of all of them and they drew glances more than once from surrounding tables.

After the meal, Danni and Pierre had to report to the back of the stage for the graduation ceremonies while all the guests were invited to go out and take in some air while the arena was rearranged. The ceremonies would begin about a half hour later. Danni's and Pierre's groups went out together to continue what they had been talking about. When it was time to return, they went in together and chose a block of seats so that they could continue to be by each other. Mrs. Cartoum was ecstatic about how well Danni's family treated them; she wasn't used to being able to have such fun with people who weren't native French speakers.

Danni was scheduled to be the fifth graduate to cross the stage and get her diploma since they were doing it in alphabetic order. She waited nervously for her cue and when it was given, she strode across the stage. She looked out and gave her family a discreet wave, having been told not to do that. As she glanced around the assembled people, she noticed a great number of people she knew. There was Ms. Sturm, Samantha, Rose, Evelyn and Mary as well as some women from The Naughty Nymph. She was surprised to see all of them and realized that Ms. Sturm must have arranged for them to be able to get tickets. She felt a small surge of pride that they were so interested in being here to see her get her honour. She knew that she couldn't wave at all of them so she just concentrated in getting to the Principal to get her diploma.

After the ceremonies, there was a brief pause while the chairs were put away and the band set up on the stage for the dance to follow. Danni was relieved that none of her friends approached her so she didn't have to explain how she knew them to her or Pierre's family. She did catch them smiling broadly at her though and felt warm inside. Her younger sisters were going to be allowed to attend the first hour of the dance before her mother was going to take them away and they were very excited about it. Gina had been invited to Danni's Prom by one of her classmates but their mother had decided that she was too young for that; Charlene knew that she would have to allow Gina to be an escort for next year's group though. Danni wasn't embarrassed that her family wanted to share her festivities and in fact was quite proud that they found time to be involved with her life. Pierre had promised to dance with each of her sisters. The usual practice was for each of the graduates to start leaving the dance after about two hours so they could go off to the bush party. Buses were arranged so no one would be driving because they would all be drinking. Danni had no interest in going out to the bush party and would be going home to celebrate with her family. Pierre had decided that he would go out to the party.

Danni danced with a variety of her classmates because Pierre was also quite popular; he not only danced with all of the women in their party but also with a large number of girls who'd come without proper escorts. Danni was happy to see those girls showing interest in him since she had no plans for him after that night. She wished him well. She did turn down some of her classmates and a number of fathers as well but she liked dancing so she was often up on the dance floor.

When it came time to leave, Danni let Pierre drive her home since her family had left about an hour earlier. When he stopped in front of her place, she put her arms around him and kissed him firmly; he'd been a perfect gentleman and she was happy with his effort. Pierre hadn't been expecting such a fierce kiss and didn't know what to do; he didn't feel comfortable enough with putting his arms around her and pulling her against him but he didn't want to dissuade her too much. He really enjoyed the feeling of her lush body against him. She then pushed herself away from him, gave him a bright smile and opened up her door. "Have a wonderful life" she said as she climbed out.

"Thank you, Danni. I'll never forget you" he called after her as she headed up to her door. She turned and waved at him before going inside. She had a good time talking with her aunts, uncles, grandmother and rest of her family for a few hours before heading up to bed. She knew she had a very busy day the next day. She had to move her stuff over to Samantha and Mary's place with Theodore's help and then there was the sex party that was also planned. She fell asleep with a big smile on her face.

Thank you for reading this book.

Please rate this book. I would like to remind you that all independent authors rely on you as the reader to help them to spread the word about their works and you can help them continue to publish by letting your friends know about them or rating them on the different websites. If you would like to send a comment or two to the author, please email lizrshaw@nili.ca. You can also check me out on Goodreads and any feedback is gratefully accepted.

You may also be interested in the following works by me:

Danni Archer: The Making of a Mistress The Beginning
Danni Archer: The Making of a Mistress Continuation of Learning
Baroness Molly: Bi-Sexual Dominatrix And Other Erotic Stories Volume 1
Baroness Molly: Bi-Sexual Dominatrix And Other Erotic Stories Volume 2